Nerdy Girl Nation

A
Nerdy *Girl* Novel

Lindsey Gray

Nerdy Girl Nation
A Nerdy Girl Novel

Cover Design by T.M. Franklin
Photos courtesy of Dollar Photo Club: Maksimshirkov and Incomible
Formatted by Lindsey Gray

IBSN-13: 978-0692550700
IBSN-10: 0692550704

For Sydney and Gavin
You make my world a better place to live in.
I love you.

	Dedication	
	Prologue	Pg 1
1	Chapter One	Pg 3
2	Chapter Two	Pg 9
3	Chapter Three	Pg 13
4	Chapter Four	Pg 21
5	Chapter Five	Pg 27
6	Chapter Six	Pg 41
7	Chapter Seven	Pg 52
8	Chapter Eight	Pg 60
9	Chapter Nine	Pg 67
10	Chapter Ten	Pg 74
11	Chapter Eleven	Pg 85
12	Chapter Twelve	Pg 90
13	Chapter Thirteen	Pg 95
14	Chapter Fourteen	Pg 107
15	Chapter Fifteen	Pg 117
16	Chapter Sixteen	Pg 128
17	Chapter Seventeen	Pg 134
18	Chapter Eighteen	Pg 140
19	Chapter Nineteen	Pg 150
20	Chapter Twenty	Pg 157
21	Chapter Twenty-one	Pg 166
22	Chapter Twenty-two	Pg 171

23	Chapter Twenty-three	Pg 180
24	Chapter Twenty-four	Pg 184
25	Chapter Twenty-five	Pg 193
26	Chapter Twenty-six	Pg 199
27	Chapter Twenty-seven	Pg 206
28	Chapter Twenty-eight	Pg 210
29	Chapter Twenty-nine	Pg 217
30	Chapter Thirty	Pg 221
31	Chapter Thirty-one	Pg 226
32	Chapter Thirty-two	Pg 238
33	Chapter Thirty-three	Pg 243
34	Chapter Thirty-four	Pg 247
35	Chapter Thirty-five	Pg 255
36	Chapter Thirty-six	Pg 259
37	Chapter Thirty-seven	Pg 272
38	Chapter Thirty-eight	Pg 279
39	Chapter Thirty-nine	Pg 287
40	Chapter Forty	Pg 297
	Character Map	Pg 303
	Acknowledgments	Pg 306
	About the Author	Pg 307

Prologue

"You can do this," she chanted while wave upon wave of nausea crashed through her body.

Emma MacLean recognized the feeling of her stomach rolling with upset. Most of her major life conflicts caused nausea with the strength of gale force winds.

Please, God, don't let me mess this up. No repeats of the fifth-grade Maria DeFazio vomiting episode.

She tried to keep herself calm as she listened to the words of her dear friend echo throughout the arena. Long deep breaths with her eyes closed didn't stop the memory of how she suffered over the years.

To say Emma's peers disapproved of her would be an understatement. They teased and bullied all throughout her middle and high school years. All because she puked on Maria DeFazio during the fifth-grade spelling bee. Well, it all started right there. One act of humiliation for Maria was worth seven years of torment in Maria's book. When Emma received an invitation to her ten-year high school reunion, she tore the invite up without a second thought. Those who picked on and tormented her for a majority of her youth now banged her door down for favors. Never did they imagine Emma would be the most likely to become a reality television star.

Now, she stood on the precipice of the next chapter of her life. She needed to flip her switch, pull on the reigns, and show the world she *is* the boss.

"You can do this." Her confidence began to rebuild.

A hush fell over the crowd with one elongated guitar note.

Times up. It's time for the new Emma MacLean to take charge.

"Good luck, Miss MacLean."

"Thanks," she whispered to a security guard before climbing the last few stairs. "You can do this," she muttered to herself one last time before stepping up to the point of no return.

1

Three weeks earlier . . .

"You're fired."

Emma MacLean stared at the woman who uttered those words in complete confusion.

"I'm what?" She pushed her glasses up the bridge of her nose while trying to shrug off the fog surrounding her. *The* call sometime earlier in the day left her shaken and disoriented.

"Fired! I am tired of picking up your slack. You missed the conference call about the London merger. We are at a critical juncture in these negotiations. You blew a vital meeting off. For what? To sit here and enjoy your two fanboys stroking your ego? You're pathetic."

Ouch.

The woman in front of her vibrated with anger. The

daughter of her boss was a force to reckon with when upset. Waves of fury billowed off her like fire in a furnace on the verge of explosion.

Emma slipped her glasses off and took a deep breath. She shifted back into a professional mode. "Irene, I don't want to sound like a bitch, but—"

Irene huffed and folded her arms under her ample breasts.

"You don't have the authority to fire me. I have an employment contract with Hunt Consolidated. Also, I talked to Gregory Burnett yesterday. Today's meeting was for marketing and Reggie was supposed to be in on the call. Was he there?"

"Yes, but—"

"But what, Irene? You have been pissed ever since this deal started. I am the VP of Operations. London is *my* deal. Your father knows about every single step I've taken with these negotiations. If he wants me gone from Hunt, he's going to need to tell me to my face."

"I don't care who you think you are, but I am *the* member of senior management in charge while my father is unavailable. If you want to contest your contract, we'll see you in court. Clean out your desk. Security will wait with your assistant and escort you out." With a twist of her statuesque form, Irene Hunt turned and stormed out of Emma's office.

Emma turned her head toward the crew who caught the whole ordeal on film. Her days as the nerdy Vice President of Hunt Consolidated were over.

"We just got a ratings boost," the cameraman whispered to the sound guy.

The crew captured snippets of her daily life since

Terrance began filming his reality television show, *Hunt for Life*. Launched into the limelight as soon as the first episode aired, her entire world transformed. Not the typical female form, her five foot nine frame curved where most celebrities slimmed into straight lines. Her hair, an odd shade of black, made her crystal blue eyes stand out from her face. Emma had many flaws outside of her perceived appearance she'd spent years in therapy attempting to overcome. But, her major malfunction according to the tormentors from her teenage years was being a complete nerd from head to toe.

Fame brought invitations to parties and galas all over the world. With more than a little help from a personal stylist, hairdresser, and makeup artist, she transformed into a more exquisite version of herself. Thankfully, she only attended those events she was contractually obligated to. She displayed an inherent shy nature but had a head for business unlike anyone else at Hunt Consolidated. The number one reason she got the coveted job of Vice President of Operations five years earlier.

"I don't have time for this." She wiped a single tear from her cheek.

With a shaky hand, she reached for her cell phone and dialed Terrance's number. Four rings later his voicemail message came on. She clenched and unclenched her fist while waiting for the beep.

"It's Emma. I don't know if you've talked with Irene yet, but she fired me this afternoon. Something she thinks I did with the London deal. I'm not sure what is going on today." Another tear slipped down her cheek. "I found out my mother died this morning. As soon as I can get a flight, I'm going home." She swallowed hard to keep herself from sobbing. "This whole thing is such a mess. I am going to take care of my family for the next couple of weeks. My desk will be cleaned out within the next hour. Please give me a call when you get this so we can figure things out." She pressed the end button and fell back in her chair.

"They want us to come with you," the cameraman, Al, announced as he moved in for a close-up.

"Who?"

"The producers. They want us to go with you. Troy is on his way here," the sound guy, Ben, said while adjusting the levels of his equipment.

"Fine. If he gets here before I clean out my desk, I'll talk to him, but I need to make arrangements to get home."

Al nodded and continued to film as Emma sifted through the physical form of the last five years of her professional life.

"What's going on?" Sharon, Emma's assistant, asked when she caught Emma packing.

"Who the hell knows?" Emma wiped away another tear. No matter how many deep breaths she took, the flow of saltiness continued. "Reggie was in on the conference call with London, right?"

"Yes. I talked to him about twenty minutes ago. He said the meeting went well." Sharon grabbed Emma's hand to stop her from placing a picture frame in a box. "What did Irene do now?"

"She's amped up her bitch mode to DEFCON one."

"That bad?"

Emma nodded, and Sharon let go of her hand. "She fired me." Sharon gasped. "I don't know if it will stick. She has no authority to fire a member of upper management, plus I have a contract. I suppose it will get sorted out when Terrance gets back. I'm not sure what this will mean for you in the meantime."

"Don't worry about me. What are you going to do?"

"I'm going back east for a while." Emma stacked the last of her private papers in the box. "Keep an eye on Irene and the whole London deal for me. I know the woman hates me since I saved her ass with the Kenya mess, but this is a little extreme."

"I will." Sharon came around the desk and gave her a tight squeeze. "Call me when you can."

"Sure."

Sharon walked toward the door when it opened and smacked against the wall.

"The company jet can take you wherever you need to go." Troy Banks, the executive producer of *Hunt for Life* explained. He approached her desk and laid her contract out in front of her.

Emma eyed him while Sharon shut the door behind her. She read through the first couple of pages of her *Hunt for Life* contact. If the fine print was correct, her contract stated she would be filmed through the rest of the scheduled season, whether she worked for Hunt Consolidated or not.

"Please, Troy. I'm going home to bury my mother, not on vacation in Cancun."

He took her hands in his. "Al and Ben will be the only ones with you. I will be the first to view the footage and will give you final approval on what we air. No one has ever gotten a deal like this."

She nodded while she gazed down at her hands. Troy

had always been kind to her. He was the reason some of her most embarrassing moments never aired in the final episodes.

"All right, but I want everything in writing to go over with my lawyer. Email me and I'll fax a signed copy back."

"Fantastic," Troy sighed as he pulled her in for a hug. "I'll call our pilot. Where do you need to go?"

"Marblehead, Massachusetts."

2

A car waited for Emma, Ben, and Al when they arrived at Logan International Airport in Boston the next morning. The driver, Phil, would be at their disposal for the duration of their stay. Phil helped load their luggage and gear into the black SUV, and they began the short drive to Emma's hometown.

Six weeks since her last visit, Emma expected the same welcome calm entering Marblehead always brought her. Now that Elaine MacLean was gone, the sensation fled with her.

Dozens of cars littered the street in front of the MacLean home. She called ahead to warn her older brother, Harry; the cameras would be coming with her and to inform everyone to act naturally.

Emma's feet hit the ground, and her eleven-year-old

niece appeared in front of her. She took Charlotte into her arms and held tight.

"Aunt Em, I can't believe you're finally here!"

"I'm here."

Charlotte took Emma's hand and led her into the house with Ben and Al trailing behind. They entered through the back kitchen door to find the room full of food. It seemed as if almost all of the twenty thousand residents of their town donated a dish for the grieving family. Apparently, when the Mayor of a small town passes away, food appears on the family's doorstep as if by magic.

"Hey, Sis," Harry called as he sifted through the casserole dishes and desserts.

"Hey." Emma left Charlotte's side to hug her big brother. "How are you?"

"Hanging in there." He drew back from her as he detected the cameras.

"Ignore them as best as you can."

Harry nodded. "Annie is out front with the rest of the town."

"What about the baby? Where's Sam?" Her six-month-old nephew got her through her last visit to Marblehead for her thirtieth birthday in March. She needed her baby fix. Some baby love would hit the spot.

"Nan is feeding him his bottle on the couch."

A sweet pang struck her chest at the thought of her eighty-year-old grandmother, Moira, feeding the infant.

"And Dad?"

Harry had gazed at her for a long moment before he reeled in a harsh breath.

"The boat?" she asked.

Harry nodded. "He's out there most of the time.

Annie and I started making the arrangements, but we need him with us. Do you think you could talk to him?"

"Sure."

After an hour of reintroductions and some strange stares at Al and Ben, they climbed back into the SUV, and Phil drove them to the marina.

Her father's boat wasn't hard to spot. It resided in the same slip off and on for years. She ambled across the wooden boards until she stood in front of the boat where she spent most of her childhood.

"Permission to come aboard, Captain?"

Her father stopped sweeping the deck to take in the sight of his daughter. The corners of his mouth lifted up, and he tossed his broom aside.

"Permission granted," he stated while he offered his hand to help her aboard.

As soon as her feet hit the deck, he brought her into his arms. One of the things she missed the most about home, the feel of her father's arms around her making her believe everything would be all right.

"How are you?"

"Not good, Princess." He led her to the bow and leaned his forearms on the railing. "I feel so lost without her."

The same thought plagued Emma as well. Her mother was not only a hero to the community, but the glue that held their family together.

"She would want us to celebrate her life and go on with ours."

"Getting through this is going to be hard without you here."

"I'll be around for a while. I kind of got fired yesterday."

He looked at her, at the camera, then back to her.

"I'm still under contract with the show until the end of the season, so we will see what happens."

"There is always an opening with my company. We don't do the kind of business Hunt does, but you always seemed to like the work."

A simple life helping Dad manage his charter business?

Calm waters spritzed with a few rough seas were a piece of cake compared to her life at Hunt.

"Sounds wonderful to me, Dad."

3

After the long day, Al and Ben settled into the nearby Marblehead Bed and Breakfast.

Alone at last.

Emma snuggled under the covers of her old bed in her childhood bedroom and tried to get some sleep.

With no luck after an hour, she decided to do a little reading to ease her mind. On her bookshelf, between Shel Silverstein and Kurt Vonnegut sat her favorite novel, *The Hobbit*.

Emma removed the book and flipped through the worn pages. She remembered the day her mother took her beloved geometry book away and placed the Tolkien novel in her hands instead. A little girl with a head for numbers needed a release, according to her wise mother. Thus, her love for fantasy bloomed. Her mother opened a Pandora's

Box that would never close with one simple gift. The book expanded Emma's world and helped her create new ones in the recesses of her mind.

Two chapters in, her eyes began to water, and exhaustion took hold. A memory of her mother's voice whispering to sleep tight and dream of sweet tomorrows hung in the air. The picture of her mother's smile comforted her while she drifted off.

What seemed like only moments later, Emma's phone beeped with a text message. Her first thought, Terrance. Perhaps something about the meeting scheduled for the next week, then the notion struck her: she wasn't sure if she worked for him anymore. She put on her glasses, picked up the phone, and checked the text. An unknown number informed her to check the *Gossip Greeting* website.

She clicked the Internet browser on her phone and found the top story.

AMERICA'S FAVORITE HUNTRESS GETS FIRED!

The news spread faster than she thought. The network tried to keep the big dramas out of the press until the specific episode aired. Since the episodes they were filming at the moment wouldn't air for at least six months, the last few days wouldn't be a surprise to their viewers..

One more click and she started the video under the headline.

The familiar face of Garrett Green came on the screen.

"Can it be true? Our hearts are breaking with the news of our favorite nerdy girl being fired. Rumors are flying fast and furious about a blow up between Emma MacLean and Irene Hunt. These are two of the women featured on the reality show *Hunt for Life*, following the escapades of billionaire Terrance Hunt.

"Mr. Hunt is said to be vacationing and unavailable for an official comment, but an inside source from the show reports Irene burst into Emma's office and fired her. Miss MacLean was later escorted out by security with cameras still following her. We're keeping our fingers crossed Emma stays on the show.

"Further investigation led us to a network-owned jet flying Emma and a small crew to Logan International. Viewers might remember Emma's hometown of Marblehead is right outside of Boston. After we had figured out she returned home, we discovered some rather sad news. Emma's mother and Marblehead's mayor, Elaine MacLean, died in a tragic car accident yesterday morning. Our thoughts are with Emma and her family at this difficult time.

"While we haven't reached out to Emma, we hope she will come to us when the time is right. If you're watching this Emma, we love you and hope to see you soon."

Emma couldn't read the article or any of the comments. She discerned Garrett probably sent her the text. They formed a friendship when his Internet gossip show became her personal cheerleader during season one. The sudden fame overwhelmed her at first, and Garrett rallied the Nerdy Girl Nation to support her.

She pulled up Garrett's contact information and sent him a text telling him she would call him after the funeral, not to worry.

"Terrance, you idiot!" Aaron Russell laughed when he finished watching Garrett Green's report. "The girl is gold." He flipped his laptop shut and reached for his tumbler of scotch. Out of his chair and over to his office window, Aaron admired the Boston skyline.

After he had drained the glass dry, the fog of an idea settled over his mind.

While Terrance amassed billions, Aaron's accounts totaled over eleven figures. He turned a failed wrestling circuit into an international sensation, garnered himself millions of dollars and household recognition. He would admit Terrance's seed money helped, but Aaron paid him back ten times over. The time for Aaron to take a little from his old pal arrived. The International Wrestling Association needed Emma MacLean to take them to the next level.

Aaron had been fortunate to form an amazing relationship with Emma since they met through Terrance four years earlier. Few people knew of their friendship since most of their time together took place off camera. If not for the twenty-year age difference, he might have considered a more intimate relationship with her. For now, he would put out the proverbial olive branch and offer Emma the chance of a lifetime, a career with the IWA.

The pulsating jets of his tiny shower worked wonders on Rob's sore muscles. After another day at the IWA training facility, where he mentored some of the newer wrestlers, he became mindful of his age.

Should I be feeling like this at only thirty?

Rob shook his head at the thought and splashed more

water on the shower wall. In one sense, he hit his peak at thirty. In the best shape of his life, Rob "Bobby" Breyer weighed two hundred and twenty pounds with less than ten percent body fat. Stretched over his six foot four frame with messy dark brown hair and clear blue eyes, women wanted him and men strived to be him.

All of his friends outside the business married and started families years ago. The guys would complain about feeding and sleep schedules or soccer practice conflicting with a birthday party. Things he wanted to complain about. He needed to stop living vicariously through his friends. Not everybody wanted to be the cool uncle. Rob wanted to be a dad, but so far, no woman made him crave to take the leap with her.

Emptiness continued to hold him in a tight grasp. No woman curbed the loneliness in the morning after moments. Alcohol had been his mistress for a time, but the lady spun his life out of control. Every day of the last nine years was spent fighting off the cravings. Meetings at least once a week and a sponsor on speed dial certainly helped.

One final rinse and he hopped out of the shower. He walked into the bedroom in only a towel and turned on the TV to the opening credits of *Hunt for Life*.

Emma MacLean's face came across his forty-seven-inch screen. Rob's blood began to pump faster, and his heart rate picked up speed. He threw on some boxers before he sat to focus on the first moments of the episode.

After few minutes, they showed Emma's inner sanctum, her apartment. During the first season, she attended meetings and business functions. As her fan base started to grow, so did her airtime. By the time the second season aired, Emma socialized with Terrance and his wife on vacations and dinners at the most exclusive restaurants.

Rob cherished a more intimate glimpse into Emma's life. They showed her making a gourmet dinner for a few co-workers to enjoy at her dining room table.

A raw, unyielding pleasure filled him when he heard her laugh before she took a sip of wine. The sight of her licking remnants of wine from her lips turned him into the eighteen-year-old he'd been when he first set eyes on her.

Twelve years.

Hard to believe twelve years passed since he'd knocked her over and ruined her shirt at an IWA event in Boston. Rob apologized numerous times, embarrassed beyond belief. He took her and her brother backstage to get her a new shirt and to meet some of the wrestlers. Emma and her brother posed for pictures with his father, Big Bobby Breyer, who held the heavyweight champion title at the time. The awe on her face throughout the night leveled all his defenses. The moment presented itself and he went in for a kiss when she withdrew. He heard her say "boyfriend" and the smile fell from her lips.

Fate tempted him again only a few months later when he found himself as a participant in the high school wrestling nationals. He won the finalist spot from Maryland and Emma's boyfriend, Derek McInerney, represented Massachusetts. Rob reconnected with Emma and befriended Derek over the few day span of the tournament. Derek and Rob advanced to the final match to face each other, and Rob pulled out with a hard win. The win meant nothing compared to how Emma hugged and kissed Derek after the loss. Rob would've gladly taken the loss if he had Emma to console him.

He discerned a few facts about Emma's life over the last few years. Single and living in LA. *Gossip Greeting* boasted how Emma never missed an IWA broadcast.

The idea struck him so quick; the air whooshed from his lungs. Emma and his boss, Aaron Russell, knew each other. Some even called them friends. An invite from Aaron to the event in LA at the end of June wouldn't be odd. He made a mental note to talk with Aaron during their next meeting.

Rob turned his attention back to the end of the episode with Emma and Terrance celebrating the culmination of a big deal. He turned off the TV, climbed under the blankets, and prepared himself for another dream starring Emma MacLean.

Not long after he fell asleep, Rob's phone beeped with a text message. He rubbed his eyes and read the message. His best friend and fellow wrestler, Chance, texted to tell him to check out the *Gossip Greeting* website.

He scrolled through the article with a lump in his throat and viewed the video.

Emma's mother was gone. He massaged the ache taking over his bare chest.

What can I do? Is there anything I can say?

His mind flipped through the protocols of what to do when an acquaintance experiences this type of loss? Cards and flowers? Yes, but what kind of flowers?

He glanced at the clock. It was late, but he knew she'd be up.

She picked up after the second ring. "Hello, Sweetie. Why are you calling so late?"

"Hi, Mom. I just needed to ask you a few questions."

"Sure. What's on your mind?"

"Um." Where did he start? How could he explain? "Well, I just found out someone I met several years ago lost her mother recently."

"Oh, how awful."

"Yeah. I never met her mother, but I wanted to send something to the family. I'm not sure what, though."

"Tricia Phillips got something last month when her sister passed away." Rob heard the rustling of papers on his mother's end of the line. "Here it is. Do you have a pen?"

Rob wrote down the information his mother gave him and thanked her before saying goodnight.

With his laptop booted up, he found the website his mother suggested and placed an order with overnight shipping.

Even though the clock on his phone read after midnight, Rob grabbed a few sheets of paper and a pen to write a letter to Emma and her family.

4

"What's for breakfast?" Emma asked her sister-in-law, Annie, while she sat down at the kitchen table with her laptop.

"Take your pick. Mrs. Blakely's Potato Chip Tuna Casserole or Mrs. Savoy's Chocolate Lava Bundt Cake?"

Emma smiled and licked her lips at the sight of the cake. "Cake, definitely."

Annie cut her a big slice and handed the cake to her on a plate with a fork. "Searching for another job so soon?"

"No," Emma answered while she scrolled through her emails. "The executive producer is supposed to email me a codicil to my contract about filming while I'm here. He's going to give me final approval before anything airs."

"Unusual," Annie remarked and sat down across

21

from Emma with her piece of cake.

"Troy's wonderful. You should see my blooper reel. I'd be mortified if some stuff ever aired." She shivered at the thought. The fact she often forgot to turn off her personal microphone threw the crew into hysterics at times. "Here it is." She pulled up the email and downloaded the attachment.

"So is there anything going on there?" Annie took a bite of her cake.

"No," she replied firmly.

"Is there anybody?" Annie reached across the table and grabbed Emma's hand.

Emma shook her head, slipped her hand out from underneath Annie's, and scanned her screen.

"I thought they kept the personal stuff off the show. Your love life is off limits."

"What love life?" Emma scoffed.

"You dated the writer guy, Patrick, for what, a year before you told any of us, and I'm one of your best friends. Within a few months, poof. Bye-bye, Patrick."

"Yeah, because I found out the magazine he worked for wanted him to dig up dirt on Terrance for a story. Guys only seem to sniff around to get close to Terrance. All the fame or interest people see in me is because of him." Emma re-read a few lines her morning-addled brain didn't comprehend.

"What is the Nerdy Girl Nation, huh? Those kids admire you. You're a role model. Charlotte is so proud of you. She has at least five Nerdy Girl Nation tee shirts she wears to school. She even asked to get glasses like yours even though her eyesight is perfect."

Emma pushed her glasses up the bridge of her nose

out of habit. She didn't realize how much Charlotte wanted to emulate her until that moment.

After Garrett Green declared Emma's followers as the Nerdy Girl Nation, she decided much more needed to be done with the name. She started a charity specializing in education about bullying to schools, parents, and educators. The charity's headquarters was in one of the several teen outreach centers in LA. Not spending time with the kids would be one of the most painful things about leaving her life on the west coast behind.

"I love how I'm able to help those people, but if not for Terrance, there wouldn't be a Nerdy Girl Nation."

"You're not going to abandon them, are you?"

Emma closed her laptop and placed her attention on their conversation. "No. As long as they want me, I'm eager to lead the charge. But life won't be too interesting the rest of the season. Helping my dad run the charter business won't be very exciting. "

"You're going to work for Mick?" Annie seemed shocked.

"I said I would for a while. I still haven't heard from Terrance, but I don't want to live in LA anymore. I moved out there for him. I want to be *here* with you guys. Besides, I need to bond with my nephew. Is he awake yet?"

"Yes," Annie sighed. "He hasn't slept well here the past two nights we've stayed here. He misses his crib at home. Harry's giving him his bottle and a bath."

Emma cut into the cake with her fork while all the things to be done before the funeral ran through her mind.

"Nell seems to be MIA. Where is she?"

Annie's identical twin sister and Emma's other best friend, Nell De Lacy, evaded the MacLean household.

Odd since she usually appeared the second Emma arrived home.

"She's not doing too well." Annie's eyes glistened with unshed tears. Emma took Annie's hand in hers. "She saw the accident and got to your mother first. The medics told her she did all she could."

"But Nell doesn't believe them." Emma closed her eyes and imagined what her friend saw when she came upon the accident. Elaine MacLean wasn't only Annie's mother-in-law, but a surrogate mother to Nell and their younger brother, Seamus, as well. "Please tell her to come over. She shouldn't be alone."

"I'll tell her, but she's as obstinate you are." Annie rolled her eyes.

Nell's tender soul suffered as much as Emma's over the years, yet they never gave up hope they could be happy with who they are someday. So much alike, sometimes people would believe the two sisters instead of friends. They both were shy and introverted growing up. If not for Annie, the two would've been happy to spend every weekend watching episodes of *Doctor Who* and pouring over the latest science journal articles.

With a glance at the clock on the microwave, Emma saw the time. "Al and Ben will be here soon. How about I get dressed then get in some baby time. You can fill me in on what I've missed these last few weeks while Sam and I play."

"I will even allow you to post a picture of you, Sam, and Harry. Let your fans see how you're doing."

"The whole thing hasn't hit me yet I don't think. I've spent so much time controlling my emotions. I'm half expecting her to walk through the door with her beat-up leather bag and give us both a hug."

"I understand. Now finish your cake before the camera gets here. I don't think Mrs. Savoy wants her secret recipe to get out."

Emma took a big bite of her cake and moaned.

The sun's rays warmed every inch of Terrance's skin as he snoozed in the hammock outside his vacation home on the small island of Tinos in the Greek Isles. No cameras, no phones, only sunshine and fresh air for two more days.

The slight sway of the hammock caused him to open his eyes. His wife of thirty-one years stood above him. He smiled with delight.

At fifty-five, Lydia Hunt didn't appear a day over thirty-five and all without the aid of any cosmetic surgery. His libido stirred as much at the moment as it did when they first married. He took her hand and tried to bring her down for a kiss when he noted her worried expression.

"What's the matter?"

"I've gotten word from Troy. We need to cut our trip short." She pulled on his hand and got him out of the hammock.

Terrance wrapped his arms around his wife's waist and waited for her to drop the bad news.

"Irene took advantage of your absence and fired Emma."

"What? She can't do that." Terrance let go of Lydia and fell into a nearby chair. "They never got along, but why the hell would she fire her?"

"Something about a missed conference call with London."

Terrance dug through his memory. He remembered

the scheduled call, a mere formality of the deal. Nothing so important to require Emma's presence. "I don't understand."

"Terrance?" Lydia took his hands in hers. "Troy sent the footage, but . . . Emma found out her mother died after a car accident. The cameraman told Troy he believed she was in shock after she received the call."

"Elaine? Oh my, God. I need to call Emma. And Mick." He clasped his hand over his mouth at the thought of Emma's father. "Did Irene hear about this?"

"Not at the time, but she told Troy it didn't matter. You gave Irene carte blanche while we're away."

"Not to fire a Vice President of the company." Terrance sensed his daughter didn't get along with Emma, but Emma shrugged off Irene's attitude and did the job. He never believed Irene to be so cruel.

"I'll get your phone," Lydia said as she caressed his cheek. "You make your calls and I'll start packing."

He nodded and wondered what the hell to say.

5

Emma laid Sam down for a nap after a few hours of serious playtime. The picture she posted of her snuggling with her nephew and Harry got an overwhelming response. The Nerdy Girl Nation rallied behind her one hundred percent and would be there for her when she needed them.

After she read some of the comments, she took a moment to check her phone. Disappointment held her heart as she noted no calls were from Terrance. Another number stood out, though.

"Aaron Russell?"

Al perked up and went in for a close-up at the sound of the name.

Emma listened to the voicemail Aaron left. Her mouth dropped, and eyes went wide. Without another thought, she tapped the screen of her cell phone to turn on the speaker and call him back.

"Emma, darling. Thank you for calling me back. How are you?"

"Still in shock, Aaron. Thanks so much for calling." She enjoyed a marvelous relationship with Aaron. He reminded her of home and everything she loved about the east coast, not to mention how much fun they often had when they went out together. Aaron was a helpless flirt. He made her feel so much younger than her thirty years.

"The reports are true?"

"I've only seen the report on *Gossip Greeting*, but Garrett was pretty accurate."

She heard Aaron sigh on the other end of the line. "I was praying the reports were false. I am so sorry for your loss."

"Thank you. I'm trying to concentrate on my family right now."

"I'm glad you're with them. You will send my regards to Mick for me?"

"Of course," Emma responded. Aaron remembering her father after only meeting him once at one of the IWA events they'd attended in Boston was touching.

"This might be the worst possible time to bring this up, but do remember the last time you visited me in Boston?"

"I do." Aaron took Emma to the new IWA training facility. She got to meet a few of the wrestlers and their trainers. A short segment even aired during the last season of the show.

"Together, we can do tremendous things." Emma gasped in shock. "Admit you want you to work with me.

The IWA is ingrained in your DNA. There is no better place for you."

"Are you offering me a job?"

Aaron laughed. "Of course I am. We have a large vacancy."

She swallowed hard. Two weeks earlier, Aaron fired his general manager on a live IWA broadcast. Her heart quickened at the thought of stepping into the role.

"Yes."

"Don't be coy, Emma. We *all* know about your IWA obsession. I've even talked with a certain former wrestler about your sessions at his gym in LA."

She blushed, Al capturing every second. "Are you offering me a position as a wrestler or as management?"

"I want you to be my new GM of Televised Events and Executive Vice President in charge of Talent and Creative. If you're willing to go in the ring, I could certainly see that happening in the future. There is a lot of travel involved, but your main office is here in Boston. You would be closer to your family and be around more often than in the last few years. I'm confident you can do this. Some people collect football or baseball stats; you collect wrestling ones."

"I can't believe this." Emma's head spun at the offer. Could she, in fact, combine her business savvy with her all-time favorite obsession? Not to mention all her crushes on the wrestlers. Her blush deepened even more at the thought of coming face to face with some men she considered the sexiest men alive.

"Believe, darling. I can email you a tentative schedule for the next few months and a full job description with salary details today. Wait until after the funeral to decide.

29

There is a live event in Boston the first Monday in June, so your decision can wait until the end of this month."

"I'll call you later in the week." She bit down on her thumbnail, not believing what she'd said.

"Wonderful and please don't hesitate to call if you need anything. I'm in Boston for the rest of the week, so if you want to get away for a cup of coffee, give me a call."

"Thanks." They ended the call, and she set her phone on the coffee table.

She took a few seconds to let everything sink in. Emma turned to find Harry leaning against the archway to the living room with a huge smile on his face.

"You think I should take the job?"

"As your lawyer, I would advise you to read through all your contracts with Terrance and the network before making any decisions. As your brother, I say hell yes!" He pulled her up from her chair and into his arms. They twirled around in circles like when they were younger. He set her down after a round of laughter. "Can you believe this?"

"No. I never saw myself working for anyone else. Except for Irene and the long hours, working at Hunt is a dream job." She shrugged her shoulders with a smile.

"What's going on?" Her father, Mick, entered the living room and gave Harry a pat on the back.

"Em got offered a job working for Aaron Russell."

Emma gave Harry the stink eye. She wanted to tell her father herself.

"With the IWA? Wonderful news, Princess."

She shook her head. "No, Dad. I told you I would help you."

"Emma, don't you worry about me. Things might be

tough, but with my personal angel guiding me, I'll be fine." He smiled with tears in his eyes.

"I'll think about the offer."

When the doorbell rang the morning of her mother's funeral, the sound surprised Emma. The local police kept the media away from the house and stopped all deliveries. With cameras rolling, she answered the door to find an officer and a teenage delivery guy with a large box.

"Your brother inspected the package and said he could come up," the officer stated with a head nod to the teen.

"Thanks," Emma replied and took the offered board to sign for the package.

"It's from Mr. Breyer, Miss MacLean. He told me to make sure to deliver the package into your hands." The teen exchanged the board for the package.

A flush of excitement flowed through her at the sound of his name. The thought of Rob Breyer taking the time to send a personal condolence touched her.

"Thank you. I will make sure to let him know you did as instructed." Emma smiled back at the teen.

The officer rolled his eyes and hauled the teen off the porch.

Emma took the package to the kitchen table to open. Al and Ben were only feet away catching every moment.

The box contained another box. A *Seeds of Life* logo adorned the top. This box contained an oak tree planting kit. The instructions detailed how to plant the seeds in a smaller container first. After the tree grew so much, she could plant it in a special spot in memory of her loved one.

Emma let a few tears slip before she spied the

envelope with her name scrawled across the front. She sat down to find a personal note from Rob.

Emma,

There is not much I can say at a moment like this that you haven't heard a hundred times over. I hope in some way this tree will help remind you and your family of the wonderful life you shared with your mother. I was never fortunate enough to meet your mother, but after meeting you and Harry, I know she had to be a spectacular woman.

I guess hearing from me might seem completely out of the blue. I've thought of you often over the years and enjoy catching a glimpse of your life on television. When we met, we didn't get the opprotunity to be more than acquaintances. We might not even have a chance to be more now. If you ever want to talk or get together, I'm living in Boston when I'm not traveling. I would love the chance to get to know you again.

Rob

There was also a card with his phone number and email address enclosed with the letter. She remembered what a connection she shared with him the two times they met before. In love with her high school sweetheart, she didn't understand how she could feel so strong for someone she just met. Could it be possible their brief encounter impacted his life as much as hers? If she took the job Aaron offered, their lives would intersect a third time.

Third time's the charm.

The funeral of Elaine MacLean took place in a packed church. Several people stood in the back, including Terrance and Lydia Hunt.

The town of Marblehead said goodbye to their beloved leader and a family laid to rest the woman who made them one. Terrance pulled out his handkerchief to dab the tears away from his eyes while his wife held his hand tight in hers.

As the priest finished his final words, Terrance, Lydia, and their camera crew were able to slip out a side door. They waited at the family house for the MacLean's to return from the cemetery.

When the family vacated their limo, Terrance, Lydia, and their crew got out of their SUV and approached.

"Terrance?" Emma walked over to him with a trill of shock in her voice.

"Hello, Emma." He took her in his arms and gave her a tight, but he hoped, comforting hug.

Lydia pulled Emma from her husband's arms and into her own. "I'm sorry we didn't get here sooner."

Emma pulled back as her father came to stand behind her. "I'm surprised to see you here."

"Mick." Terrance held out his hand, and Mick extended his to shake Terrance's.

"I think you might want to discuss a few things with my daughter. Why don't you come in and use the office? The funeral dinner starts in about an hour, so there's time for you to talk." Mick kissed Emma on the cheek before he led them all toward the house.

Emma sat in her mother's desk chair and waited for Terrance to speak from his perch on the couch. Al and

Ben situated themselves in the corner of the room to capture every second.

"I'm not sure where to begin," Terrance stated with an unusual uncertainty to his voice.

"I don't either." She crossed her legs and smoothed down her knee-length black dress.

"You are not only an employee to me. You're like another daughter to Lydia and me. Irene was in the wrong. There was no reason for you to be in on the conference call, and all the other reasons she presented me with were utter bullshit."

Emma let out a soft laugh. "You think?"

He scratched behind his ear, a nervous tick Emma recognized over the years. "I want you to stay on. You are an important member of the team and irreplaceable to me."

Emma shook her head, and a few tears ran down her cheeks. She did some serious thinking while she was at home. Harry scoured all her contracts down to the last detail. There were less than six weeks left of filming on *Hunt for Life*. She would fulfill her commitment to the show without working for Terrance. The time to move on arrived.

"Talk to me, Emma. You're lost in your head again."

"I hate leaving things like this." She held her hand up to stop his imminent protest. "Let me finish." He nodded with a tight-lipped smile. "Irene has never been fond of me. Some *things* happened between us, things you aren't aware of. When she fired me, I wasn't sure what to think. I love you and Lydia and will always cherish the time I worked for you, but I think now is the time for me to move on."

"You can't. We have a contract."

Emma furrowed her brow. "Are you telling me I'm not fired?"

"Of course you're not fired. You've done more in your position in the last five years than your predecessor did in twenty. You can take as much time off as you'd like. I know how much Mick and Harry must need you now."

Emma shook her head in disbelief. She had made her decision to take Aaron Russell's offer. Life at Hunt was her past.

"If I'm not fired, then I resign."

"Emma, that is just not possible. Legally speaking, you have certain obligations."

Some nerve. Emma knew Terrance was a cutthroat businessman when he needed to be, but this was ridiculous. "You're seriously talking to me about contracts right now?"

"You are what is best for my company. I need you with me. Why do you think I gave you all those perks when you renegotiated your contract?"

"Perks? More money, a car when I already had a company driver, two weeks vacations that I hardly ever took because I worked fifteen hour days. Those perks?"

"Well . . ." Terrance seemed a bit flustered. She didn't mean to seem ungrateful, but she was well within her rights to quit.

"Just a minute." Emma stood and walked to the door. She opened it and called for Harry. He came in and Emma took her seat once again. "Harry, as my attorney, can you explain to Mr. Hunt why I am well within my rights to resign from my position at Hunt Consolidated if I choose?"

35

"Mr. Hunt, according to Emma's employment contact, she can resign her position at Hunt Consolidated if she agrees to not take employment at a competitor for five years. Currently, Emma is considering employment at a company that would not fall into the competitor category. Therefore, she is well within her rights to terminate her contract with Hunt."

Emma smiled at her big brother. He nodded at her then gave her a wink.

"My lawyers will need to examine your contract. I don't want to let you go, Emma. I'm sorry, but if it comes down to it, I will fight for you."

Emma got a tiny thrill thinking of Terrance fighting for her, but her mind was made up. "We'll be ready."

One way to survive an event where the whole town is involved is to have a De Lacy by your side. Emma couldn't find Nell and Annie was glued to Harry's side, so Emma chose to hang out with the youngest De Lacy, Seamus.

The two huddled together in the corner of the MacLean living room in an attempt to avoid all the mourners, but with a camera crew watching her every move, it was a little hard to do.

"No more LA then?" Seamus asked and casually slung his arm around Emma's shoulder.

"Nope," she answered the twenty-year-old younger brother of her dreams.

"Bummer. I really loved that pool at your apartment." Seamus took a drink from the bottle he'd been sipping on then wiped some liquid from the red scruff on his chin.

"You just like my neighbor's daughter prancing around in her bikini."

Seamus quirked one side of his mouth up in a half smirk and shrugged his shoulder. "Guilty. I like hot babes. I can't have you, so I gotta look somewhere."

"What about your friend? What's her name?"

"You mean Ellie?"

"Yeah. You guys have been joined at the hip for years."

Seamus was a bona fide genius. When his teachers realized he wasn't a brat, just bored with the work, they suggested his parents have him tested and see if the Boston School for the Gifted would be a better fit. He met Ellie Stanton on his first day there and had been her best friend ever since. Emma didn't know Ellie personally, but from the way the De Lacy siblings described her, she was a match for Seamus in every way.

"Nah. She's more like another sister. Besides, we're business partners. It would just be weird." Seamus tightened his grip on Emma's shoulder. "You sure you don't want to give me a go? I am in my sexual prime." He nuzzled her ear with his nose.

Emma moved away with a laugh. "Number one, you are way to young for me. Number two, I used to change your diapers. And number three, you cannot hit on a woman at her mother's funeral."

"I made you laugh, though, didn't I?"

Emma leaned back into Seamus' arm. "Yeah, you did."

Emma escaped the cameras and the town of mourners after two long hours. The air on the back deck seemed to bring clean breath back into her lungs. Once she took a few large gulps, she realized how much she missed the scent of the east coast water wafting through the breeze.

She sipped the tumbler of Irish whiskey she brought out with her and used the moment to think about her mother. Days at the beach. Weeks spent working on school projects together. Bedtime stories. College graduation. The mayoral swearing-in ceremony. All the smiles. The image of her mother's devastated face when she walked into Emma's hospital room twelve years earlier came out of nowhere.

A tear slipped down Emma's cheek as she remembered what little her brain retained of the horrible day. One moment, she ran toward her car, afraid to be late to school. The next, she woke up in an ambulance. Brief flashes of the events of the attack stayed with Emma, but her mind blurred the colors and sounds. She recalled the pain with perfect clarity. Ropes burned into her skin where they restrained her. Her bones lit on fire with each break. Most of all, her breasts throbbed when her assailant bit into her flesh, leaving a permanent reminder. Her memory loss seemed to be due to a blow to the head and concussion. Even after twelve years of therapy, nothing came back.

"Penny for your thoughts, Emma Jean."

Emma gazed up into the hazel eyes of her first love. A warm smile complemented the rest of his comforting features. Six foot three with sandy blond hair and a muscular frame gave Emma an old familiar feeling of safety.

"Derek. Hi."

He sat down next to her on the wooden steps of the deck. "How are you holding up?"

"Still processing everything."

Derek slipped his arm around her shoulders and pulled her in close. "That brain of yours is working overtime again."

"Always."

He slid his left hand into hers and she felt something unexpected. She picked up his hand and skimmed his naked ring finger.

"Oh, I guess Annie never mentioned my divorce."

Emma gasped in surprise.

"No. She didn't say anything." Emma didn't want to imagine Derek's picture perfect life. She asked her family and friends not to mention him either. Even though her romantic feelings for him disappeared long ago, she still wasn't comfortable hearing about his love life.

He threaded his fingers through hers. "Sarah Beth didn't like small town life as much as she thought she would. She took a job in Seattle a day before she filed for divorce. I haven't heard from her since we finalized everything six months ago."

"Wow." Emma's mouth gaped open in utter shock. If any man needed the label of husband material, Derek would be that man. He delivered the total package. Ryan-Gosling-gorgeous, charming, and intelligent. He worked as a history teacher at Marblehead High, lived in a beachfront home, and possessed phenomenal bedroom skills.

"I don't want to talk about me. What's going on with you? Did you really get fired?"

"Yes and no." She reached for her drink and took another sip. "Irene stormed into my office and fired me without authorization. I talked with Terrance earlier today. He said he wanted me to stay. Blah, blah, blah. I told him I resign, and Harry backed me up. I've got another job offer doing something different, but I'm not going to finalize anything until Harry talks with Terrance's lawyers."

"Another job as an international businesswoman?"

"Not quite, but I'd be based out of Boston."

"You're coming home?" The hope in his voice made her heart hurt.

No matter how much she loved Derek at one time, they'd never rekindle their relationship. One horrific attack and twelve years of threats scared her enough to stay away from a romantic relationship with him for good.

"I think so."

"Good to know."

The magazine selection at Harry's office sucked. Emma read an old article about how she hooked up with a Hollywood heartthrob. She laughed at the possibility. The guy acted like the typical A-lister and dropped one name after another on the two occasions they bumped into each other. Just another example of how the press got her life so wrong.

"Is he still on the call?" Emma asked Harry's secretary, Jocelyn, for the tenth time.

"Yes. Don't worry, he's got this." Jocelyn came out from behind her desk and sat down next to Emma. "I know those contracts as well as he does. He made sure you had an out. The competition clause is exactly what he needs. We got a copy of Aaron Russell's offer just in case. Relax."

"Thanks, Jocelyn. If I want to make this change,

sooner is better than later."

Jocelyn patted Emma's shoulder. "A workaholic like your brother."

"No MacLean ever walked away from a hard day's work."

"I believe you."

Harry opened his office door and popped his head out. "Jocelyn, do you mind calling out for some lunch? I'll be tied up with Emma for a couple of hours."

"Sure. Pizza from Romano's?"

"God, yes," Emma moaned. "I need comfort food right now. A big slice would hit the spot."

Harry smiled and held back a laugh. "Order two large Sicilian's. We can divide up the leftovers."

Emma's mouth watered just thinking about the spicy sauce, gooey cheese, and authentic Italian meats finding a new home in her belly.

"Come on in. I'll give you a brief rundown before the pizza gets here."

Emma got up and walked into Harry's office with Al and Ben following behind. She took a seat on his couch, and he took the chair beside her, several folders littered the coffee table in front of them.

"First of all, they are letting you out of your contract."

Emma didn't realize how much tension she held in her body until she let it go in that moment. "Did you give them a copy of Aaron's offer?"

"Yes. Terrance insisted. He seemed pretty pissed."

"What? Because the offer came from Aaron or because he lost?"

"A little of both, I think." Harry stood when his fax

machine beeped. He picked up and examined the first page. "I guess they expected this outcome. You need to fill all this out and sign them to make your resignation official. You get to keep the SUV, and there are some other provisions you'll walk away with."

"And the show? Did you speak with the network too?" The contract with the network gave her little wiggle room.

"Yes. That is what took me so long." Harry sat in his chair and let the fax machine continue to spit out dozens of sheets of paper. "You are on the hook for the rest of the season, some promotional stuff, and the reunion special. After you fulfill those commitments, you're done."

Emma turned toward Al and Ben. "I do love you guys. This is so much harder than I expected."

The guys smiled and continued to do their jobs.

"There is also this." Harry opened a folder and handed her several pieces of paper clipped together at the top.

Emma scanned the papers, and all the air flew out of her lungs. "This is a joke."

"No. The money is part of what they deem your bonus for this year and also your share of the last deal you completed." Harry flipped the page to show her the details.

Emma worked hard at Hunt. Not for the money or any of the so-called perks, but because she loved how much her work made a difference. She never imagined herself making more than ten figures a year, but her bank account proved she did. The amount detailed in the paperwork stated upwards of eight figures.

"What am I going to do with all this?" She swayed in

her seat at the thought of managing so much money.

"Get a life. Take a vacation." Harry moved from his chair and sat next to her. "Since you want to do this thing with Russell, and the whole deal is time sensitive, you won't get a real vacation anytime soon. Promise me you will schedule some time for yourself to relax. You can start having girl's night with Annie and Nell again. They both miss you."

"I miss them too. I'll think about it." She let her head rest on Harry's shoulder. "I need to pack up my place in LA."

"Take Dad with you. He needs a little breather. The trip would be good for both of you."

"I think you're right."

"Emma," Aaron answered with hope in his voice.

"I can start Wednesday of next week." She bit down on her lower lip in an attempt to keep her nerves at bay.

"Excellent," he sighed in apparent relief. "I'd like to keep you a surprise until the broadcast the following Monday in Boston. We can get together and sign the contracts on Wednesday."

"Sounds perfect. I'll email you a few change requests. I'm heading out to LA with my dad to pack up my apartment. I'll be staying with him while I'm not traveling, at least for a while." The whole conversation seemed so surreal to her. She never imagined her life turning out this way.

"Safe travels. We'll meet at my office Wednesday morning. I will leave a pass with the front desk. I don't think the press will suspect anything since you've come to my office before."

"What about the wrestlers and the rest of the staff?" She hoped to come into as little discord as possible.

"I want them to be surprised too. We will be airing several segments on the show and online with the wrestlers and commentators speculating on whom they think should be the new GM. They all think you'll be someone inside the company." He released a hardy laugh. "Oh, think how surprised they will be."

"I'm excited to meet everyone. People are so different when the cameras turn off. You understand the cameras will follow me until the end of next month?"

"Not a problem. By the way, you need to start thinking about your entrance music."

"Entrance music?" Aaron and all the wrestlers entered to specific music, but not Curtis Sharp.

"Yes, you deserve a little flair whenever you appear."

The perfect song came to her instantly. "What about the Nerdy Girl Nation theme song? I'm sure we can get permission to use it." Garrett wrote the song specifically for his show, but she was sure he would be honored for her to use the song to make her entrances.

"Brilliant. You think Garrett Green will keep his trap shut until your big reveal?"

"Yes, he's actually a fantastic guy."

"If you say so. With you in my corner, he might lay off me."

"Sure thing, Boss."

"I love the sound of that."

"Get used to it." A wide smile spread across her face. She made the right decision.

The ding of Rob's cell phone alerted him to a new email as

he rode the elevator up to Aaron Russell's office. He pulled the phone from his pocket and searched through his email. One email from an unknown address caught his eye. He opened what he thought might be a fan letter. Oh, how wrong he was.

Rob walked out of the elevator in a slight haze. Aaron's assistant waved him over to the seating area to wait. He took a seat in one of the plush leather chairs before he read the email from *the* Nerdy Girl herself, Emma MacLean.

Rob,

Thank you so much for the beautiful gift. We decided where to plant the tree. when the time comes.

Time for me to make a confession of my own. I am still a big IWA fan and follow your career as well. Gosh, I can't believe we met twelve years ago. The day I met you ranks as one of the best days of my life for so many reasons.

I'm glad you're in the area since I'm coming back home. I'm sure you can relate to how difficult it is to find a friend you can trust when your in the spotlight. After everything going on lately, I'd love to catch up sometime soon.

I'm taking a little time to get my life together which means I'm packing up my life in LA. The cameras are still on me through the rest of this season. If my career goes the way I'm contemplating, they will still be around, but not as frequently.

I'll email you or give you a call once I get settled.

Emma

"Holy shit," he whispered but still got the attention of Aaron's assistant. "Sorry."

He didn't believe what was happening. Emma would be back in Boston and wanted to catch up. She might not mean catching up the way he'd dreamed about, but the possibility existed now.

"Rob," Aaron called from his office doorway.

Rob got up to his feet and walked over to Aaron to shake his hand. "How are you today? Good mood, I hope."

"Excellent and one of the reasons I want to talk to you. Come on in." Aaron moved, and Rob entered the office. "Hold all my calls," he directed his assistant.

Rob settled on the couch while Aaron sat in the armchair to the right.

"This is a bit unusual for the two of us to meet one on one, but there are a few things I would like to discuss with you that cannot leave this room." Aaron loosened his tie and unbuttoned the top button of his shirt.

"This sounds serious." Rob flexed his fingers and tilted his head to the side. Something big was about to happen, but from the impression he got from Aaron's relaxed demeanor, he didn't think it was a bad thing.

"You're aware of all the problems Curtis Sharp caused?" Rob nodded. "I offered the position to someone outside of the company with an intimate knowledge of the IWA and our history."

"What?" Aaron all but promised Rob the position. The entire nation of IWA fans wanted Rob in the role.

"Yes. With all the fans chanting for you to take the position of GM, I thought you should be the first person I needed to consult on my plan."

The fans envisioned Rob as a leader, never afraid to stand up to Curtis Sharp. Their encouragement made Rob want the job too.

"What do you need from me?" Rob uttered through clenched teeth.

"I believe this person will get a tremendous reception, we've got to keep some conflict going. I would like to pit the two of you against each other and find out where things go."

"Am I going to fight this guy?" Whoever the guy was, Rob wanted to make sure if they got into the ring that the guy grasped at least a basic knowledge of what a real fight was. He'd lay the guy out flat if the same current of adrenaline ran through his veins.

"Did I say the job went to a man?"

That gave Rob reason to pause. "A woman?"

"I think she is exactly what this company needs to flip us upside down and give you all a chance to earn those checks I keep signing."

Rob wasn't sure how to respond, so he said what he thought Aaron expected of him. "How do you plan to pit us against each other?"

"I want you to keep up the hype. You believe the GM job should be yours. Even go so far as you announcing some plans for when you would ultimately take over the position. If all goes well, I will make the announcement during our event here in Boston. We will be doing promos the entire week before, building anticipation. The PR department is working on the campaign. We want an ad featuring you with several different shadows to leave everyone guessing."

Rob nodded. The new direction could make the next few weeks interesting. "When do we get started?"

"Tomorrow. I think Gwen wants you in a tux for

some of the shots."

The IWA lead photographer, Gwen Stanton, always made Rob look like a million bucks but never requested a tux before.

"I think I can handle a tuxedo."

"I want to thank you for being such a good sport about this. You'll be rewarded."

"Is that right?"

"Absolutely," Aaron echoed with authority. "Now, you said there was something else you wanted to discuss."

With everything Aaron threw at him, he almost forgot his reason for coming.

"I wanted to ask a favor."

Aaron nodded. "I guess I owe you one."

"You're friends with Emma MacLean, right?"

Aaron froze in his seat. His reaction confused Rob, but Aaron slowly answered the question.

"Yes. Why do you ask?"

"We met several years ago and we've been following each other's careers over the years. You heard her mother passed away?"

"Yes, a tragedy."

Rob ran his hand through his hair before he swallowed the small lump in his throat. "I sent my condolences to Emma recently and I was wondering if you might . . . I mean it might be a little awkward for me . . ."

"I don't think I've ever seen you this flustered," Aaron laughed. "I spoke to Emma myself this week. She will be at the event here in Boston. I would be happy to arrange some time for you to chat."

Rob chose his words carefully. "Thanks. We haven't seen each other in person in years. I'm . . ."

"Were the two of you together?"

"No, no." Rob shook his head. "She was dating someone at the time."

"Not now, though?" Aaron asked.

"No. I'd like the chance to get to know her again."

Aaron smiled one of his brightest smiles. "I would be happy to facilitate in any way I can."

"I'm Rob and I'm an alcoholic."

"Hello, Rob," the room of strangers answered back.

Rob surveyed the basement room of the Methodist church twenty miles from his apartment. Out of his list of meetings, the church only came up twice in his rotation so far.

"Nine years sober." The small group gave him a round of applause. "I thought stopping wouldn't be a problem. Not for me. My friends drank as much as I did, maybe more, but none of them wanted to stop. I slipped a little further every day, details of my life got lost. After one scary blackout and I checked myself into rehab. I realized if I wanted to achieve the life I dreamed of, I needed to take drastic measures.

"That brings me to today. I work hard. I sacrifice. Today, I found out the promotion I worked so hard for went to someone else. These are the moments I struggle the most. I gave up drinking to be able to do this job and find out I'm still not good enough. Days like this make that one beer or shot of vodka pretty tempting."

"We all have those days, Rob." The meeting leader, Joe, stood and addressed the room. "The twenty years of sobriety I struggled for brought me more downs than ups. We need to remember how much that one beer or shot would not only affect our lives but the lives of those around us. In your situation, the promotion you want might come up again down the line. But if you choose to take a drink, you could put it in jeopardy."

Joe wrapped up the meeting and followed Rob as he got a cup of coffee.

"You got a good sponsor?" Joe asked and poured himself a cup.

"On speed dial." Rob laughed then took a sip. "Days like this happen every once in a while. I'm glad I can find a meeting and pull my sorry ass back up."

"I know this is only your second or third meeting here, but this is a good group of people. You'll be safe here. No leaks, I promise." Joe lifted his brow.

Rob understood. Joe recognized who he was. He read the story a so-called friend from Rob's AA group in Baltimore leaked to the press.

"Thanks, Joe." Rob shook Joe's hand.

Joe pulled a card from his pocket. "Here's my number, just in case you can't get ahold of your sponsor. Please, come back anytime."

Rob took the card and smiled. He recognized the sincerity in Joe's eyes. Joe was a man he could trust.

"Ah, the nerd cave. Saving the best for last?" Mick joked when he walked into Emma's private office. The walls were covered with framed posters while the shelves held hundreds of books and collectibles.

"I didn't want the cameras in here. This room is the only one I kept private." Emma brought in several boxes and set them next to a large roll of bubble wrap.

Emma and Mick packed up most of her apartment in LA over two days. They finally came to the last room. Surrounded by her most prized possessions, her home office was the only place Emma ever felt like herself.

She began with her figurine collection. From her first edition Lando Calrissian to her newest Thor collectible, they were all precious in her eyes. Small boxes held all her character Lego Minifigures. Emma sighed at the sight of each one in their separate plastic prisons, wondering when she would be able to display them again.

"Added a few more over the years," Mick spoke in awe while he thumbed through a pile of plastic sleeved comic books.

"This is my nirvana, Dad. This room is the real me." She wrapped Lando and placed him in his box.

"Your mother and I always worried about what you were going to be when you grew up."

"What do you mean?" Emma asked while her father sat on the floor beside her.

"With Harry, he showed us earlier on he would follow in your mother's footsteps. The law was in his blood. You? Something new and different every day." He laughed as if flipping through years of memories in his mind. "One day you couldn't get enough of astronomy. The next, sculpting. There were all the comic books and science journals. We were sure you'd never be able to narrow your choices down." He took her hand in his. The conversation turned down a more serious road. "After your attack, you changed. Obviously you would after the ordeal you went through, but we never thought you would pack most of yourself away." He motioned to the room packed with Emma's real personality.

Emma couldn't stop the tears at the thought of the vicious attack. She didn't remember the attack itself in her conscious mind, but the memories seeped into her nightmares constantly over the years. Therapy and hypnosis attempted to bring the memories forward, but the evilness lived in her dreams. She would wake to remember flashes, but never enough to know who hurt her with such vicious cruelty.

"I never asked you directly, but was the attack the

reason you broke things off with Derek?"

"Sort of." Derek was wonderful and supportive, but she could never be honest with him about that night. A week after graduation, she tried to break up with him. Derek wouldn't give her up completely, and they created a few special moments over the next few years.

"We were going to different schools and I was so skittish about everything. Derek needed someone stronger." She tried to concentrate on wrapping all her Iron Man action figures.

"I hope this new job isn't going to hold you back, Princess. I would love to catch you sculpting in the workshop again. The cameras won't be on you all the time. Why don't you let your hair down, relax, and start dating again."

"Dad, please. Let's not get into my love life."

"I'm saying, don't hold yourself back anymore. People will love the real you."

She rolled her eyes. Such a dad thing to say. Secretly, she hoped he was right.

"Get the hell out of here!"

A shocked Emma walked into her friend's gym to find him screaming at an equally irate man.

Mitch stood in front of Emma while Al and Ben recorded it all from over her shoulder.

"Bill?" Emma called in a firm but worried tone.

Her friend, Bill Bell, and the other man turned toward the sound of her voice. Emma's stomach flipped and acid billowed when she recognized the man. The former IWA General Manager, Curtis Sharp, stood before her.

Emma stepped around her father to address Curtis.

"Mr. Sharp, I'm surprised to see you here." Emma hoped the shake in her voice went unnoticed.

"Well, well, well. If it isn't Terrance Hunt's former lap dog. You looking for another juicy bone?" Curtis sneered.

Emma put her arm out to hold her father back. "I came to visit my friend." She walked around Curtis to hug Bill.

The retired IWA wrestler's hugs helped her through several bad days over the past five years. "Sorry about him," Bill said and pulled her into his arms.

"Don't worry about it. I hoped I could show my dad around and get one last workout in before we leave." She pulled back and gave him her warmest smile.

"Sure thing." Bill held his hand out to Mitch. "Nice to meet you. I'm so sorry for your loss."

"Thank you," Mitch said while they shook hands.

"You work out here?" Curtis scoffed.

Bill slung his arm around Emma's shoulders and grinned. "Emma is the best amateur female wrestler I've ever seen."

"Is that so?" Curtis' eyes sparked with a wicked gleam.

"Don't get any ideas, Sharp. She's not into working for douchebags." Bill tightened his hold on Emma's shoulders. "He's trying to poach some of my guys for Ring Royalty."

It didn't surprise Emma one bit. Curtis Sharp appeared as slimy in person as he did on television. The idea he would go to work for the IWA's biggest competitor was no out of the scope of his bottom feeder ways.

"She doesn't strike me as a girl who knows the

difference between a Diamond Cutter and a Pile Driver." Curtis quirked his eyebrow up on one side, begging her to prove her worth to him.

"If Janice is around, you can watch us spar and decide for yourself." Emma unzipped her hoodie and slipped it off to reveal her blue Under Armour racerback tank top. "Mr. Sharp, you obviously don't realize I started wrestling about two minutes after I took my first steps. It's in the MacLean blood. We're fighters. Since I moved to LA, Bill brought me under his wing and taught me a few things."

A girl about the same height and weight as Emma came strolling in. "Oh, hell." She threw her hands up. "Is Emma here to kick my ass again?"

Emma laughed and pulled her friend into a warm hug. "One last time."

Janice pushed Emma back playfully. "Fine. Consider this your going away present."

The women got into the ring dominating the center of the large room. Bill got in the ring to help Emma wrap her hands.

"I'm going to miss you."

"Oh, I feel like we'll be seeing each other again soon." She winked at him then looked at her father. Mitch stood to the right of the camera, his arms folded across his chest with a huge grin on his face.

Hands wrapped and ready, Emma and Janice were ready to show what they were capable of.

Ten minutes later, Emma had Janice in a submission hold she liked to call a Car Bomb. Janice tapped on the mat and Emma let go. She stood and helped Janice to her feet.

"I won't miss that, but you will be buying me dinner

the next time you're in town."

"Of course." Emma pulled Janice in for a sweaty hug while her breathing returned to normal. "I plan to be back at the end of the month. I'll take you to Spago."

"God, yes!" Janice joked.

The women said their goodbyes and Emma walked to the ropes. She leaned her forearms against them and quirked her brow at Curtis. "What do you think, Mr. Sharp? Do I know my way around the ring?"

"Maybe, but you'd never make it on the professional circuit."

"Ah ah." She wagged her index finger at Curtis. "Never say never."

"Excuse me. We're here to meet with Aaron Russell. I'm Emma MacLean." Emma, Rob, Al, and Ben waited at the front desk of the IWA Corporate offices for the secretary to acknowledge them.

"Yes, Miss MacLean. Let me get your passes." The young woman eyed Emma with a distinct distain before she got up to retrieve their passes.

Emma saw nothing wrong with her casual clothes. Aaron told them all to dress comfortably since he would be taking them to the training facility after they finished their business. Her dark hair was pulled back into a loose ponytail, and she wore her black-framed glasses with only a touch of lip-gloss on her lips. As for her outfit, she wore her purple and black trainers, a pair of black yoga pants, and a lavender short-sleeved tee shirt. The guys were all dressed in similar attire, tennis shoes, jeans, and tee shirts.

"Take the first elevator to your right to the fifth floor. The entire floor is the executive offices. Mr. Russell's is at the end of the hall."

Emma nodded and smiled. "Thanks, I've been here before. I remember the way."

The receptionist tried to hold back her sneer, but the snide expression slipped through as Aaron stepped off the elevator.

"Emma. Harry. So glad you're here." Aaron brought Emma into a friendly hug before pulling back to shake Harry's hand. "Come on up. Lunch is all set up for us. Afterward, we can head over to the training facility."

"Can't wait," Harry said while he put his arm around Emma and led her to the elevators.

Emma and Harry sat across the table from Aaron, the attorney for IWA, Craig Dawson, and the head of Human Resources, Patricia Finley. They went over her contact point by point; everything was exactly the way she wanted.

Even with the certainty she was doing the right thing and moving forward with her life, her hand shook while she signed the documents in triplicate. When she finished and released her pen from her fingertips, she heard the pop of a cork from the opposite side of the room.

"This is cause for celebration," Aaron exclaimed before he poured them all a glass of champagne. "This is a far cry from our usual contract signings. There will be no broken tables or chairs today." The rest of them laughed. "I thought I would mark this occasion with a special toast. To Emma." They all lifted their glasses. "I have seen you grow over the last four years from a shy and soft spoken young lady into a strong and determined woman. I hope the journey you take with us here at IWA will continue to strengthen your character and fill your life with excitement and laughter."

"Here, here," Harry said with a clink of his glass to Emma's.

They all clinked glasses and took a sip of the decadent champagne before Emma spoke up.

"The shy and soft spoken girl still exists, but as you say, I am determined to make this work. I have so many ideas already."

"Good to hear." Aaron put down his glass. "Let's get over to the training facility to check out some of the wrestlers because you are going to pick all the fights for our event next week."

Emma sputtered a bit. She didn't expect to be taking control so soon. "You're serious?"

"Yes. You've studied the storylines going now. I trust your judgment. Tell me whom you would like to fight and we'll make it happen. Plus, I want you to be out with the commentators during the main event."

Emma's heart began to race at the thought of sitting ringside. She thought commentating would happen eventually, but she never dared to assume wearing the headset would be at her first official event.

"You are the boss," she said with a nervous laugh.

Four rings were set up in the main training facility room, and wrestlers sparred in each one. Aaron detailed the facility mainly for Harry and the camera's benefit when her focus drifted to one particular ring.

Rob "Bobby" Breyer was a magnificent specimen, as a man and a wrestler. At six foot two, two hundred and twenty pounds, he was perfection in Emma's opinion. His usually slicked back dark hair was free of any product and covered his face while he sparred with his opponent, Chance Robicheaux.

She turned her attention back to Aaron as she heard her name.

"What?" she asked.

"I was wondering if you would like to get in the ring with Cherry. I figured she could show you some moves."

Aaron's grin spread wide across his face at the sight of abject horror on Emma's.

"I . . . Uh."

"She can," Harry spoke up. "And she will. Don't let her fool you. She's been around wrestlers all her life. Even trained with one of the best. I think she might be able to show Cherry a thing or two."

Aaron called Cherry Spencer and her tag-team partner, Peaches, over to the group while Harry became the recipient of the Emma MacLean death stare. Harry promptly laughed the expression off and took Emma's glasses from her face.

Emma gathered every ounce of courage in her at the moment and took Aaron's hand to help her into the ring.

"Cherry, I'd like you to meet a friend of mine, Emma MacLean."

"Wow," Cherry exclaimed. "Honored to meet you. I am a big fan."

Emma accepted Cherry's outstretched hand to shake. Cherry had a similar build to Emma and the same dark hair. The two women differed only in skin tone and eye color. Where Emma's skin shimmered with only a slight golden hue from her occasional trips to the beach, Cherry glowed with a natural caramel tone due to her Cuban ancestry. Emma always thought light brown eyes like Cherry's would've suited her better, but her entire family sported the ice blue color of the MacLean clan.

"I'm a fan of yours as well. I loved the submission hold you put on Steffi in your last match," Emma said with an edge of excitement.

"I can show you if you'd like. Peaches?"

Emma was formally introduced to Peaches and the

three ladies got down to business.

Chance practiced a new move with Rob. At the last second, the ring next to him with female trio caught his eye. Rob laid Chance out flat.

"What the hell?" Rob exclaimed while he extended his hand to help Chance to his feet.

"Look who is in the next fucking ring."

The sight before him would make any straight man strain in his shorts.

Cherry sat on the back of Peaches to show a submission hold to none other than Emma MacLean.

Rob swallowed a few times to rid the dryness in his throat. He hadn't set eyes on the raven-haired beauty in person since he was a teenager. After her email response to his condolence and offer of friendship, he'd prepared for this moment. Being in the same room with her again was exhilarating, yet a little overwhelming.

"What do you think she's doing here?" Rob's voice trembled at the thought of coming face to face with her. He'd readied himself for Monday since Aaron told him she would be there. Nothing ever seemed to work out the way he'd hoped concerning Emma.

"She's tight with Russell. Seems like she still has the camera crew with her. You should probably put a shirt on."

Rob glanced down at the sweat trailing down his chest. The world admired his shirtless chest on national TV weekly, but he wasn't sure he wanted the next impression he made on Emma to be of a sweat-drenched mess. He grabbed a towel and his shirt while Chance hopped out of the ring and walked over to the other one.

"Perfect!" Cherry instructed. "You're a natural." Cherry turned her head to Aaron. "You think we can convince her to fight in a real match?"

Emma laughed as she got off Peaches and helped her up.

"Never say never, Emma." Harry cocked his eyebrow at her.

Sometimes she hated how well her brother got her. He would pick this moment to remember her childhood daydream of becoming a women's champion. Harry would use this as an opportunity to share it with the world if she didn't shut him down.

"Enough of your mouth." Her eyes drifted from her brother to the crowd of people who gathered around the ring.

Emma's heart leapt into her throat. Rob Breyer stared right at her with a brilliant smirk on his face. Sweat drenched hair, crystal blue eyes, killer smile, and a body currently making her lady parts ache rattled her entire being.

"Good to see you again, Emma." Rob offered his hand to help her out of the ring.

"You too, Rob." She immediately backtracked. "I mean, Bobby."

"Rob is fine." She realized she held his hand a bit longer than she needed to and reluctantly pulled away. "It's been a while."

"Twelve years." Emma lost herself in his eyes, but the real world intruded when Aaron spoke up.

"That's right, you two know each other," Aaron mentioned with a sideways glance at Rob.

"Emma was part of one of the most important days of my life." Rob's smile intimated something sinful. She needed to set things straight.

"What he means is I was there the day he won the national wrestling championship against my boyfriend."

Rob turned to Aaron and continued the story. "I met her and her boyfriend, Derek, during the tournament. Derek and I were both shocked when we advanced to the final match against each other."

"Rob won the match after Derek put him through the ringer." Emma laughed at the memory of the two teenagers rolling around on the mat.

"Yes, but Derek got the girl." Rob's smile was genuine and caused a flush to creep up Emma's neck to her cheeks.

"Didn't last much longer," Harry quipped. "Not after—"

Emma smacked Harry on the shoulder. "I don't think this is the time or place to get into my lackluster love life."

"Oh, I don't know. I might be interested in hearing what an idiot my old pal Derek is." Rob walked over next to Harry like they were old friends.

Emma grabbed Harry's arm, pulled it around his back and forced it upward. "Don't you dare."

"I give! I give!" Emma let go as the crowd around them laughed. "I taught you well, young Padawan."

They proceeded on the tour with several more people in tow, including Rob and Chance. Before she left for the day, Emma got a moment to herself when Peaches led her into the women's locker room to freshen up.

She used the restroom, reapplied her lip gloss, and

deemed herself camera-ready once again.

When she opened the door, Rob's muscular arm pushed her back inside and closed the door.

"Hey," Rob whispered.

"Hey," she whispered back and wondered what was going on.

Rob cleared his throat before he began. "I wanted to get you alone for a minute to tell you how good it is to see you again."

"I think we did this part back in the ring."

"Yeah, but I also wanted to see if you might be free for dinner tonight."

Emma's heart swelled at the thought, but she remembered the job she just finalized. There were several couples working for the company. What would happen if . . . She realized she was getting ahead of herself and needed to respond.

"I would love to catch up, but things are crazy for me right now. Plus with the cameras, any man I'm seen with is painted as my soul mate." She laughed but was saddened by how true her words were.

The disappointment was clear on his face. The same expression he had when she walked away from him twelve years earlier with Derek's arm draped around her shoulders.

"Maybe . . ."

"Maybe?" His eyes seemed to lighten a shade off their normal blue.

Emma reached into the front pocket of the jeans he had changed into and took his phone. After several taps, her number was programmed in under NERDY GIRL.

"This is my personal cell phone. Only a few people

have this number. I'm trusting you not to give this out."

"No. Never." His smile widened as she slipped the phone into his hand. "Can I call you tonight?"

She nodded and tucked a few strands of hair behind her ear. "I'm staying at my dad's until I get back on my feet. The cameras are usually gone by eight."

"Expect a call at five after."

"I'll be waiting." She wouldn't let herself touch him in case she couldn't stop, so she ducked out the door and went back out to meet Harry and Aaron.

9

"Dad, I had fun, but I swear I'm going to tape Harry's mouth shut one of these days." Emma recounted her wrestling lesson to her father and the camera while father and daughter shared a double meat lover's pizza in the MacLean kitchen.

"I remember the first day you got on the mat with Harry. He was eight and you were about three?" She nodded in agreement. "You wanted to take him down so bad. He was three times your size, but you were so determined. We couldn't keep you away from his practice. I kind of figured you dated Derek because of the whole wrestling thing."

"Ah, Derek. Funny you should mention him." She put her pizza slice down and wiped her mouth with her napkin. "You remember the guy he lost to at the nationals senior year?"

"Yeah, a kid from Baltimore, right?"

"You remember The Baltimore Bruiser."

Mick's eyes went wide at the realization. "Bobby Breyer?"

"Yep. One and the same." She took a drink of her local microbrew. "He was at the training facility today. He's the one who sent the oak tree kit."

"No kidding?" She nodded. "Wow. It was, what, twelve years ago?"

"Almost. Feels like a lifetime, though. Then Harry had to mouth off about how Derek and I broke up."

Mick took a sip of his own beer. "He's the vice-principal over at the high school now."

"He didn't say anything when we talked after the funeral." Derek had been a natural leader in high school. When he told her he was going to major in secondary education, she wasn't at all surprised.

"Mrs. Mosley had her baby over Christmas break and decided not to come back, so the school board promoted him in January."

"Is he still coaching the wrestling team?"

"Sure is. All those boys are top notch. Some of them would be naturals in the IWA." Mick took a bite of his pizza before clearing his throat to speak. "He's single, too."

"Dad. Derek and I were over a long time ago."

"Right." Mick wiped his face with his napkin. "I still don't quite understand why you gave up on him. He was good to you."

"We weren't meant to be, Dad."

Her father stared at her long and hard. He always seemed to know what she was feeling or thinking with the exception of her relationship with Derek.

Mick gathered their plates and set them in the sink. He came over and kissed Emma on the forehead. "No one deserved what they did to you, but pushing everybody away didn't do you any favors, Princess. You're going to need to stop pushing one of these days." After a light caress on the cheek, Mick left Emma to her thoughts.

That time in her life was one of the most difficult she'd ever experienced. High school had not been easy for Emma by any means. She was tall and rail thin until her junior year when she seemed to grow curves overnight. Her shy nature and nerdy pursuits made her easy pickings for the popular crowd. Especially queen bee, Maria DeFazio.

She felt a common thread form when she and Derek were paired on a chemistry project together their junior year. They became more as wrestling season came around and Harry helped out with the squad. Derek had always been friendly towards Emma, but never showed any romantic interest until one day after practice. She was caught off guard when he kissed her while she was waiting for Harry outside the wrestling room. He asked her out as soon as he broke the kiss and she nodded through the fog he created.

Emma and Derek had plenty of trouble from outside forces during high school, but they didn't let any of it separate them. The end of their senior year, everything went to hell when both Emma and Derek were nominated for Prom King and Queen. Emma was called names, bullied, and even had her locker destroyed. When Derek won King and Maria won Queen, Derek refused to dance with Maria. A few days later, Emma was kidnapped, beaten, and violated with hardly a memory of the entire ordeal. Derek stood by her every step of the way, but with her fragile state, she didn't think they would last.

When he returned home on break during her college years, they would hook up until he met Sarah Beth the fall of his senior year. Letting Derek go was one of the hardest things she ever had to do, but she eventually did. One thing her relationship with Derek taught her was to keep her private life private. Until the disaster with Patrick, she had succeeded with a few men. She wondered if she and Rob could be . . . something more.

Rob glanced at the clock every few minutes for over an hour, waiting for the moment to call. He felt as if he had walked across every square inch of his apartment at least a hundred times.

Finally, his phone displayed five after eight and he pushed the button to dial Emma's number.

"Hello, Rob."

He smiled and released the majority of his anxiety with her greeting. "Hey, Emma. How are you?"

"Good. I had dinner with my dad before the cameras left."

"I can't even imagine having the cameras on you twenty-four seven." He sat in his favorite chair hoping the soft confines would help relax him a bit more.

"There are only a few more weeks left of filming. I want to be me again."

"You mean it's not really you on the show?" he teased.

"It is but not if that makes sense. I flip a switch every time I step in front of the cameras. I'm sure there are differences between Bobby and Rob."

He agreed with her there. "Several. I would love to fill you in on them."

"Fill me in?" she giggled and he realized how suggestive he sounded.

"I mean I'd like to get to know you." Time to bite the bullet and tell her what he wanted. "You said things are crazy and I understand the craziness. But, would you even consider, after filming is over and things are calmer, going out with me?"

He heard her blow out a long breath, which in turn had him holding his own.

"I would love to say yes."

His chest began to burn from the lack of oxygen and impending rejection.

"Tell you what, if after Monday you still would like to have dinner, I would love to."

He froze for a few seconds while dissecting what she had actually said.

"What happens on Monday?"

"Um, well . . . I've started a new job. The announcement is going to be made on Monday. I'm sure the media is going to go insane."

A new job he could handle. "You'll be based in Boston?"

"Yes, there will be some, ah . . . travel involved, but my home office will be in Boston. My dad and I packed up my apartment in LA earlier this week and I'm likely staying with him until filming is finished. I don't want my new place featured on the show."

"I get that." He remembered the shy, beautiful girl with a laugh he couldn't get out of his head. He understood craving privacy. Lack of had been the main reason he left Baltimore and moved to Boston permanently.

"I can't wait to leave my clothes all over the place and spend all day in my pajamas."

"I'd love to see those pajamas. Are we talking flannel or silk, because I think there is something so incredibly sexy about a girl in some plaid flannel."

She laughed the same uplifting laugh he remembered, making his heart soar. The sweet sound cemented his intentions. He didn't care what Monday brought; he would not let her get away again.

"You might enjoy my vast collection."

"I'm sure I will. I need to be honest with you, I've thought about you a lot over the years."

"I've thought about you, too," she admitted in a whisper.

"Back then, I saw how you and Derek were. But, there was something there between us, a connection."

"Yes, I believe there was. Maybe now is our time to explore our connection."

"Nothing would make me happier."

And Rob was happy, probably happier than he'd been in years. Every night at five after eight, Emma would answer and they would talk for hours.

Rob soaked up every ounce of information she put forth. He learned her favorites and offered his in return. They liked a lot of the same music and movies but differed when the subject turned to their favorite comics. She worshiped at the altar of Stan Lee and the Marvel universe where he was more of a DC kind of guy. Except when it came to Captain America. Rob considered you un-

American if you disliked the Captain.

Not only did they talk in depth about their likes, but they also shared a few hardships as well. He confessed how life was not as picture perfect being Big Bobby's son. She had been vague at first but ended up going into a little detail about how she was bullied up until she left home for college. He hated that she still seemed to carry all the pain of the past with her.

When he hung up with her on Sunday night, he vowed to do whatever he could to keep away the pain. He had been half in love with her for years. In one more day, he would be all the way there.

10

"Listen up," Aaron called out to the group of IWA staff gathered backstage. "This is the last night you will have to deal with my ugly mug for a while. Seeing me at every event over the last couple of weeks has been eventful for all of us. I lost my focus and allowed Curtis Sharp to take advantage of the situation. Not anymore. After tonight, your new GM will be working with me to make this organization the best we can possibly be. They will also take over these pre-show sessions, so no more of my rambling."

Rob gave Aaron his props. The man stepped up and took the reins when Curtis Sharp screwed things all to hell.

"I've heard grumblings about holding back our new GM's identity for too long. The truth is this person signed on the dotted line within the last week. This person will be an asset to this organization and their leadership will bring us to the greatness it deserves."

Chance clapped Rob on the shoulder. "What the hell is he talking about?" he whispered.

"Things are about to change, my friend." Rob grimaced and turned his attention back to Aaron.

"This is a little unorthodox to run the show like I am tonight, but I swear the secrecy will be worth it. I will astound all the fans and critics by the end of this night. Join me in making IWA history!"

The wrestlers all let out loud cheers and grunts in agreement.

"This has got to be important. Why would they have us in a tag team match?" Chance asked as he and Rob walked to the backstage entrance.

"This is a new direction. I met with Aaron the other day about where he's going with this." Rob heard the crowd's excitement from where they stood.

"Whatever Russell's got up his sleeve, I hope he knows what he's doing. I don't want to feel the wrath of Big Bobby." Chance shook his head and wiggled the rest of his body.

"You and me both." Big Bobby's reaction to Rob's transition back into a tag team faction wouldn't be pleasant. His father's dream for him had always been to be a singles competitor. The goal for Rob to become the heavyweight champion again seemed to be everything his father lived for. Rob wanted to enjoy his career and keep healthy enough to wrestle for the foreseeable future.

The Baltimore Bruiser's entrance music began to play. Time to turn on the charm and get the night started.

The crowd screamed and hollered when Rob entered

with Chance at his side. The pair entered the ring and Rob took a microphone to begin his speech.

"Welcome to Monday Night Mayhem!" The crowd went wild, but Rob got back on task within a moment. "Thank you all for coming to celebrate this momentous occasion in IWA history with us." The screams of excitement from the crowd were almost deafening. "Tonight, all the rumors will be put to rest. Curtis Sharp's tyrannical reign of the IWA is over and the new regime will begin. First, we wanted to hear from your IWA favorites about the change taking place tonight." Rob and Chance turned their attention to the jumbo screen where a series of clips began to play.

Several members of the IWA came on screen speculating on all the changes they were hoping for. Most believed Rob would be the force behind the changes.

The clips came to an end and Rob began to speak once again. "I want to thank all you for your support these last few weeks as we all make this transition. The future of the IWA will be safe in our new leader's hands and I am personally going to guarantee you will be happy with their direction."

The crowd's celebration halted when Aaron's theme music began to play.

Aaron began to speak into his microphone before he even entered the ring. "Thanks for warming them up for me." The crowd laughed and cheered. Aaron entered the ring with his microphone by his side. "You ready for this?"

Rob shook his head with a laugh. "Probably not."

Aaron placed his hand on Rob's shoulder and squeezed. "Before the end of the night, you *will* be a happy man." With a wink, Aaron began his introduction of the new GM, who the hell ever she was.

"I think I'm going to be sick." Emma put her head between her knees to hold off the nausea.

"You're nervous," Harry said while he rubbed her back. "A few more minutes and the security team will be here to escort you to the staging area."

"A few more minutes," she repeated as she brought her head back up and turned her attention to the monitor with a live feed of the event.

The broadcast showed a montage of several IWA wrestlers voicing their opinions on the next GM's identity. Some came up with ridiculous suggestions. Most thought Bobby Breyer was a sure thing. Not one suspected the former Huntress.

At that moment, Rob and Chance were in the ring, preparing to celebrate the announcement of what the crowd thought would be Bobby being made GM. Rob controlled his bravado, but she worried about the crowd's reaction. The new twist in the show's story would pit Emma against Bobby for taking a job the fans believed was perfect for him. Rob knew this, but not who his new nemesis would be.

Rob and Chance continued gearing up the crowd when Aaron's entrance music flowed through the arena.

Six security guards surrounded Emma to conceal her identity from anyone in the area.

"You can do this," Emma chanted to herself. She waited with her eyes closed while she listened to Aaron make his announcement.

"Gentlemen. I know you are all anxious to meet our new GM and you will. Let's get a few things straight."

Aaron cleared his throat before he continued. "The old regime is finished. We are changing the way we run things around here. With the new direction comes new leadership. I've had the privilege of experiencing many in-depth discussions about the future of the IWA with the person I have chosen to help lead us. Over the last few days, this person has shown me what I already believed with absolute certainty: I had picked the perfect person for the job. Ladies and gentlemen, let me introduce you to not only the new General Manager of Televised Events but also the Executive Vice-President of Talent and Creative for the International Wrestling Association."

One elongated guitar note later, the crowd hushed. She listened while her own video montage began to play on the huge video screen.

The security guards stepped away from Emma to allow her to enter the staging area. "Good luck, Miss MacLean."

"Thanks," she whispered to a security guard before climbing the last few stairs. She flipped her internal switch. "You can do this," she muttered to herself.

Her entrance music blared with a Joan Jett type vibe. The kick-ass, chick power anthem was exactly what she needed to calm her nerves and give her the confidence to make her way down the ramp.

The crowd erupted in cheers as they realized the woman walking toward the ring was Emma MacLean. Before she was even halfway there, she heard her name chanted loudly throughout the arena. She was the picture of confidence as she high-fived several fans and waved to the crowd.

Once she climbed the ring's steel steps, Aaron held

out his hand to help her into the ring. It was an odd action to fit through the ropes with her three-inch heels, stretchy black skirt, and curve-hugging sleeveless purple blouse. After she was all the way in and standing upright, Aaron pulled her into a hug and told her she would be brilliant. He handed her his microphone and gave her the go-ahead to introduce herself to the IWA fans.

"You surprised?" she asked the crowd who responded with cheers. "A good surprise, I guess." They got even louder and chanted her name again.

"First, I want to say thank you to Aaron Russell for the chance to join the IWA. As some of you might remember, I've been a hardcore wrestling fan for years. When the opportunity arose to be part of an organization I spent most of my life following, I couldn't let it pass."

Emma quickly glanced at Rob in full Bobby mode with complete shock on his face. His black suit, crisp white shirt, and loose blood red tie sent a different sort of shock straight to her core.

She returned her focus to the crowd. "Now, for my first official act with the IWA, I want to announce tonight's lineup." Aaron gave her a nod of encouragement before she continued. "These times are changing. I'm going to shake things up a bit. There will be matches tonight and on Tuesday, a tournament for each of the IWA Championship belts. The winners in each category will go on to the semi-finals next Monday in Chicago. The finals will be held the week after in Kansas City. We will all see what these men and women are made of when the winner of each tournament faces a champion in Los Angeles at the Breaking Rules event." She went on to announce matches for those competing for each belt.

"And finally, since these two gentlemen seem to work so well together, they will be our second match in the tournament for the tag team title. Bobby Breyer and Chance Robicheaux against the Vertolli Brothers." Chance slapped Rob on the shoulder after Rob made a slight choking sound.

Emma's theme song played again while Aaron took her hand and helped her out of the ring. She chatted with him as they walked back up the ramp and into the backstage area.

"You were amazing!" Harry scooped her up and twirled her around before he set her back on her feet.

"I thought I might lose my nerve there for a minute, but once the adrenalin started pumping, it was like ruling the boardroom." Emma took a few more deep breaths as she came down from her high.

"Break time is over," Aaron said as he placed his hand on the small of Emma's back. "I need to talk with you and Bobby off camera for a moment."

Just when she thought she had calmed down, her nerves shot back up.

Emma turned her head to see Rob and Chance approach them. Aaron stepped aside and took a minute to talk to Troy about how he needed a few minutes alone with Emma and Rob.

"Smokin' hot intro, Miss MacLean. Shocked the hell out of this one." Chance hit Rob hard on the back.

"Thanks, Chance." She caught Rob staring at her with a slight upward curve of his lips. "I think Aaron needs to steal the two of us away for a minute."

Emma's usual cameraman had his camera pointed downward and was not recording. Rob leaned in to whisper in Emma's ear. "You owe me dinner."

She nodded with her own small smile when Aaron came up behind her.

"I've got the two of you for ten minutes off camera, then back to business." Aaron led the two of them into a lounge area they used to film backstage interviews throughout the broadcast.

"Emma, we've discussed how this is going to go this evening, but this is all a surprise to Rob."

"You can say that again." Rob plopped down on the leather couch behind him.

"Sorry," Aaron told Rob. "Keeping Emma's new position a secret was a necessity for her as much as for the organization." He motioned for Emma to take a seat next to Rob. "When I realized the two of you already knew each other, I thought this would work to our advantage."

Emma smoothed her skirt out beneath her and sat next to Rob.

"While the reaction Emma received here by the crowd in Boston was positive, many of Bobby's fans might not be as happy." Aaron paced back and forth in front of them.

"What is the next step?" Rob asked Aaron before he glanced to his side for a peek at Emma.

Emma was about to speak up and tell Rob about the plan they'd worked on when Aaron stopped pacing and spoke first.

"I want the two of you to be the next power couple of the IWA."

"A what?" Emma squeaked. "We never discussed this."

Aaron's smile grew wide at the shock evident on

Emma's face. "Don't worry, Emma. I think this new direction will work to our advantage."

Emma sat back, crossed her arms over her chest and scowled at Aaron.

"There's my feisty girl. Don't worry, we won't be going too off course at first." Aaron laughed and sat down in the chair across from the couch.

"Why don't you let me in on this new plan of yours." Rob seemed eager to hear Aaron's new plan.

"While I still want to pit the two of you against each other at first, after I saw Bobby's reaction when you entered, I think the fans could tell there was an attraction there. This can work for us. Bobby's internal struggle losing the job the fans wanted for him to a woman he's insanely attracted to."

Rob smiled and nodded. "He's not too off base there."

Emma shook her head at Rob's comment, but the smile never left her face. "Fine, he's conflicted and I'm only interested in doing my job. And?"

"I have a few more ideas, but not much we can openly discuss until Emma's full-time filming ends." Aaron glanced at his watch and saw their time was almost up. "I'll give you two a few minutes to talk alone. I'll see you both after the main event." Aaron went out the door and closed it behind him.

"Oh, hell." Emma dropped her head on the back of the couch. "I can't believe he's doing this. Flirt on camera? Perhaps, but I don't think I can handle any PDA's." The thought of being somewhat intimate on camera terrified her more than wrestling did.

"Emma, look at me." Rob took her hand and pulled

her closer to him.

Emma gave him her attention, but her concentration wavered after a few seconds of staring into his brilliant blue eyes.

"This can work for us." He cupped her cheek and continued to gaze into her eyes.

Emma had already made up her mind. If Rob still wanted her after the announcement was made, she would go for it. One big problem still needed to be addressed.

"My last day of filming *Hunt for Life* is in three weeks in Los Angeles. The press will be going crazy after tonight. Adding a real relationship to the mix will be pandemonium. If we can keep the IWA side of us front and center until then . . ."

"Yeah?" He scooted over a little closer.

She placed her hand on his chest, slipping her fingertips across the silk tie he was wearing around his neck. "Yeah."

At the moment before a first kiss, a few things usually occur. Each person may experience a shortness of breath, increased heart rate, and even sweaty palms. When Emma found herself at the moment with Rob's lips mere millimeters away from hers, none of the usual chaos surfaced. Her body was enveloped in warmth and completely at ease.

When their lips touched for the first time, her stomach flipped at the feeling of fire flowing throughout her body. She moved her hand from where she'd gripped his tie to the back of his neck and felt the hairs at his nape stand on end. A moaned escaped her when his tongue pressed against the seam of her lips. She opened them to him for what seemed like mere seconds before the roar of the crowd in the arena alerted them time was short.

"Fuck," he whispered as he touched his forehead to hers. "I don't think I can hold back with you kissing me like that."

"You've waited twelve years."

"Twelve years too many. I should have kissed you when I had the chance."

"You understand why I didn't let you." Emma moved away from him and stood. "Soon, I won't stop you." She walked over and opened the door. With another flip of her switch, she was off to make her first official night with the IWA a success.

11

"Emma MacLean," Emma answered her cell phone in the midst of the chaos of her first night on the job.

"Well, well, if it isn't the first lady of wrestling."

"Garrett Green. You watching the show?" Emma asked as she walked through the back halls of the arena.

"Yes, ma'am. Can I get an exclusive?"

The screen playing the broadcast told Emma she needed to get to the backstage area in time to go out for the main event.

"Call me about nine tomorrow morning and I can give you a phone interview. I'm sorry, my schedule is booked until the end of the week." She hustled her way, her heels clicking as she sped up.

"No problem, Gorgeous."

She ended the call and got to her spot in time to hear

Rob's voice as he began a pre-match rant.

Rob had changed from his suit to his fighting gear, a pair of dark blue grappling shorts with matching kneepads and boots with no shirt.

He took the microphone and began what would become the start of his fake feud with Emma.

"I've heard all night long how the new direction Miss MacLean has us going in is going to change the face of the IWA. What you haven't seen is the direction I can take us, starting with canceling this ridiculous tag team match." The crowd begins to boo and shout their disapproval. "There is a reason I have not competed in a tag team match for over a year. No offense, Chance." He smacked Chance on the chest. "I am a singles competitor and should be competing in a number one contender match for the heavyweight title."

As planned, Emma's music began to play and she sauntered toward the ring.

Rob struggled to keep his mask in place. The sight of her long, tanned legs brought images of them wrapped around his waist. The sway of her hips made him think of running his fingertips across the soft skin there. The bounce of her ponytail had his fingers itching to wrap the silky strands around his hand while he . . .

Rocked back into the moment, Rob composed himself when Emma dipped between the ropes and entered the ring. With her own microphone in hand, Emma straightened and began her retaliation speech.

"Mr. Breyer." She sized him up with an authoritative air. "I watched you over the last year in match after match. Some you've won and others you lost. The one thing I noticed specifically is your confidence. Some might call you overconfident. I would call you arrogant." Emma smiled while she got hoots and hollers of approval from the crowd. "This match tonight is to remind you this organization is not based on one member's success, but on the team of talented individuals. Therefore, your match will begin with Chance in the ring so you can't attempt to dominate this match. Give your partner a chance and work together if you want to succeed tonight."

With a turn of her head and the swish of her hips, she exited the ring and walked over to the commentator's table to take a seat. With a flick of her wrist, Emma signaled the bell to begin the match.

"Bobby, get your head in the game and get the hell out of the ring," Chance whisper yelled and pushed Rob into the corner.

"Right." He leered at the advancing Vertolli brother. "Good luck." Rob ducked between the ropes before Chance took on their opponent.

Chance danced around ring for a few seconds before one of the brothers attacked. A bounce off the ropes, a shove into the corner, and a well-placed kick to the chest and Chance dominated the match. An attempted pin by Chance was thwarted and Rob was tagged in. Switched into fight mode, Rob went after the bigger Vertolli.

Getting the edge over the brothers wasn't as easy as Rob had thought. He eventually had to tag Chance back in and was surprised when Chance got the pin within a minute, winning them the match.

The referee lifted Chance and Rob's arms while the announcer declared their victory.

Rob peeked over to the commentator's table and saw

the smile on Emma's face. He let a smirk of his own cross his lips before he played up the victory with Chance for their fans.

"Right on time," Rob mumbled at his ringing cell phone. Exactly one hour after winning his first tag team match in over a year, his father called to give his opinion of the night's events. "Hello, Dad."

"Bobby."

Rob cringed. He had gotten used to the fans calling him Bobby over the years, but his friends and family had always called him Rob, except his father. To Robert Breyer Senior, he would always be little Bobby.

"What did you think of the match tonight?"

"Horseshit!"

Rob rolled his eyes and sat down on a bench beside the bus transporting the wrestlers to the airport. "Tell me how you really feel, Dad."

"You should be in a heavyweight contender match, not Cosmo. You've won twelve more matches than he has in the past year."

"Dad, this is the direction Aaron wants to go. On camera, I might not be happy, but I think Chance and I are a good team. We can earn those tag team belts."

"You told her tonight, you are a singles competitor. The woman needs to get a few facts straight. First she takes your job, now she is making you compete with Chance," Robert Senior huffed. "He has a long way to go before he can even come close to your skill."

"Dad, I've got to get going. We're loading up to go to the airport."

"Buffalo tomorrow, right?"

Rob shook his head once again. His dad knew Rob's schedule almost better than he did. "Yes. I'll be back in Boston on Wednesday."

"Your mother's birthday is coming up. She would love for you to make a visit."

A visit to Baltimore was not on his top ten list of things to do anytime soon. The trip would be for his mother, though. Despite her poor taste in men, Rob loved his mother dearly. The thought brought Emma to his mind. How was she handling her own loss?

"I'll see what I can do. Tell her I'll call her soon."

"Safe trip, Son." The call disconnected.

"Your dad pissed?" Chance asked as he plopped down next to Rob on the bench.

"Yeah."

"Fuck him. He can't control you anymore and it's killing him. We were on fire tonight. Don't think I didn't see you giving the side eye to our new GM. What's going to happen there?"

One side of Rob's mouth curled upward. "Time will tell."

12

The flight to Buffalo was only a little under two hours, but for Emma every moment counted. She had so much she needed to do before her head hit the pillow at one of Buffalo's finest hotels.

"Here are tonight's numbers from the broadcast. The arena numbers aren't in, but they usually take a day or so to get the information." Emma's new assistant, Kelly Merchant, rattled off and handed her a tablet programmed with the schedule of her new life.

"Thank you, Kelly. These first few weeks will be an adjustment, but I think working together will help me get the hang of everything pretty fast."

Kelly let out a sigh of relief and sunk back into her seat. "I'm glad I still have a job. When Mr. Sharp was fired, I was sure I'd be next."

Emma had been given glowing reviews on Kelly's work since Kelly had joined the company two years earlier. "Why would you think that?"

"Sharp was always making threats. It was implied more than once, if he went down, I'd be going with him."

Emma sensed there was more to the story, but decided not to push. Her own experience with Curtis Sharp made her realize he was as much of a prick to Kelly as he was to everyone else.

"If you can help me get through this before we land, there is no way I'll be able to go on without you."

Kelly released a short laugh and went through the Monday night ritual with her new boss.

After the pilot announced they needed to fasten their seatbelts in preparation for descent, Kelly and Emma had their report finalized and ready to send.

"What a crash course. Last time I crammed like that was when I worked on my Master's." Emma pinched the bridge of her nose after she removed her glasses.

"You'll have the IWA turned around in no time." Kelly took Emma's hand and squeezed.

Emma's heart flipped a bit at Kelly's kind words. It had been so long since any female colleague had offered her any good words. Irene never gave her an ounce of praise. In Emma's mind, Irene's actions were out of jealousy. It didn't mean the lack of acknowledgment didn't sting.

"Thanks, Kelly. I don't have the best record with female co-workers."

"Ha. Irene Hunt was a bitch. She treated you like trash for no reason except you were doing your job better than she did hers."

The cameras were off at the moment, but Emma still didn't want to say anything to condemn Irene. "She has her faults. I'm sure with me gone, things will get better. She needs to realize Terrance loves her."

"Wow, I would never stand up for someone who fired me. You're too nice."

"Not nice, just . . . I know her game and I played with her for a long time. She needs to move on and so do I. Hopefully after a good eight hours of sleep."

They both laughed right before the plane touched down on the runway.

After the plane taxied to the terminal, Kelly and Emma gathered their things. Emma felt a hand on her shoulder as she slipped her new tablet into her messenger bag.

She turned to find Rob in the aisle. "Hey."

"I was wondering if you had a second before the cameras come back on?"

"Sure." She excused herself from Kelly and made her way to a deserted galley area where they would be able to talk in private for a moment.

"Tonight went well," Rob stated. He took her hand in his and backed her into the corner of the galley.

A jolt of adrenaline shot through her veins with his touch. "All as planned, I guess. How do you feel about you and Chance?"

"We've always worked well together. I don't think there will be a problem there." His fingertips caressed up and down her arm bringing goose bumps to the surface of her skin.

"But?" she whispered. She had a feeling he wouldn't pull her aside to talk about his performance in the ring.

"My father called me."

Images of Robert Breyer Senior flooded her mind. He was one of the greatest wrestlers of his time. He was also the biggest SOB in the business. She had seen his attitude toward Rob first hand when he won the national tournament back in high school. While Emma and Derek's own parents praised him on how well he did despite his loss, Robert Senior dressed down Rob on all the mistakes he made. The scene was difficult to view and even more disheartening to see one of her idols fall.

"I guess he's not too happy."

"My dad is never, what I would call, happy." Rob's eyes closed and his fingers threaded through hers.

She squeezed his hand to get his attention and he opened his brilliant blue eyes. "This isn't about him. This is your life and your career. You are an amazing athlete and, as far as I can tell, a pretty wonderful guy. You've been out of his shadow for a long time, maybe he doesn't want you to be."

Rob seemed dazed by her words. A look of complete awe crossed his face. Emma began to return his smile when his lips were suddenly on hers. Her base instincts took over and she moved her fingers to grip the hair at the nape of his neck.

He pushed her further into the corner while her tongue slipped into his mouth. His length hardened against her stomach and a low moan escaped her lips.

His hand on her cheek triggered her to slow her kisses down. A few more soft pecks were traded while his thumb rubbed underneath her eye.

"Three weeks and you are mine for a whole two days."

"What?" She pushed him back a bit to get a look at him.

"You promised me a date and we have years of catching up to do. Once the cameras are off, you and I are going to disappear for a few days to get reacquainted."

She gulped. Sex. He meant sex and lots of it. No man had tended to her in over a year. With what Rob pressed against her pelvis, she imagined him to have a lot of skill. The way his muscles moved while he stocked around the ring would be nothing compared to how they would feel beneath her fingertips as he moved inside of her.

"It's a date." God help her, the experience would probably be the best date of her life.

13

Four hours of sleep wasn't enough for Emma. After a large yawn, she gulped down her room service coffee. Time to switch on the public persona and get her interview with Garrett Green out of the way.

After she downed half of another cup and felt human again, her phone rang with Garrett's ringtone.

"Morning, Garrett," Emma answered with a chipper tone.

"Hello, Miss Boo. You ready to give me the dirty?"

Emma let out a genuine laugh. One thing Garrett was always good for.

"I'm ready, Mr. Green, whenever you are."

A few more formalities and they were ready to go live.

"The biggest surprise in IWA history has been the

bomb Aaron Russell dropped last night on Monday Night Mayhem. No one expected America's favorite huntress to become the new general manager, especially not the apparent heir apparent Bobby Breyer. I, for one, want to get the scoop from my favorite nerdy girl, Emma MacLean. Morning, Emma."

"Good morning, Garrett," Emma replied in her best sing-song voice.

"You've had an interesting night. Why all the secrecy? Who knew you were joining the IWA?"

"Only three people in the organization. The secrecy was Aaron's idea."

"The announcement came as quite a shock to a lot of people. No one more than the Baltimore Bruiser, Bobby Breyer. There are rumors flying around about Bobby's reaction. Did the Baltimore Bruiser know he was losing out on the job to a woman?"

"Mr. Breyer was informed of my position with the IWA when I walked out into the arena last night."

"Strange how Breyer's initial reaction was more shock than anger. You would think the moment he realized he lost the job to you, he would have been stomping around the ring."

Emma held back a laugh. "You can speculate all you want Garrett, but the only person who can tell you what he was feeling is Bobby Breyer."

"Can you score me an interview?"

Emma let the laugh go. "I'll see what I can do."

"An inside source said you, Aaron Russell, and Bobby Breyer disappeared from the cameras for over ten minutes for a private pow-wow. Any comment on what needed to be discussed off camera?"

Emma blushed as she thought of those ten minutes and her first kiss with Rob. Then she remembered their second kiss on the plane and how she was ready for a third, fourth, and fifth as soon as possible.

"Emma?"

"Yes, sorry. Mr. Russell wanted to discuss a few details in private with Mr. Breyer. I wanted to make sure both of us would get on the same page. After the events later in the evening, you can assume we are nowhere close to an agreement about the future of the IWA."

"But he won his tag team match. He and Chance move on to the semi-finals. Shouldn't he be happy?"

Emma remembered how she had decided to answer the question when she and Aaron had gone through a barrage of possible inquiries the weekend before.

"I believe Mr. Breyer won't be content with only one win. Now he will be able to show the IWA fans he is a team player as well as a leader."

"One last question."

"Only one?" Emma quipped.

"The last look between you and Breyer is being analyzed frame by frame all over the internet. Fans are saying there is some definite sexual tension between the two of you. Care to comment?"

Damn, she thought she let the mask slip a bit in those last moments. Obviously, Aaron's power couple idea wasn't going to be hard to sell.

"Tension, yes. Sexual, no," she answered in a confident tone.

"Oh, come on, Emma. We've been watching both of you for years and neither of you has ever seemed so sexually frustrated."

"I'm sorry, but from my side of the fence, it was a little bit of joy. I was right. Breyer is a hell of a wrestler, but together with Robicheaux, they would be unstoppable."

"But—"

"Nope, sorry. I have things to do and people to see in Buffalo today."

"Good luck on your first official full day, Miss MacLean. I *will* be talking to you soon."

They wrapped up the interview and Emma ended the call. She turned to see her ever-present camera crew and realized stripping and jumping back in bed wasn't an option. Buffalo awaited her and she couldn't afford to disappoint.

"It's your show. Go get 'em," Aaron encouraged Emma.

She gathered what courage she had built while she visited with her new co-workers throughout her first day with the IWA. Time for her to lead her first pre-show meeting. The understatement of the evening was her frazzled nerves, but she had a job to do and she was going to do it.

"Good evening, everyone." She cleared her throat while the room quieted. "I got a chance to talk to most of you today one on one. Thank you all for being so welcoming."

"Sharp was a right prat!" Barry Hanson, the British Baller, called from the back of the room. A loud round of applause and hollers followed.

"My dealings with Mr. Sharp lead me to agree with your assessment, Mr. Hanson." Emma curled her lips into a crooked smirk. "I hope if I ever leave the company, I won't be accused of being a right prat."

She glanced over to see Aaron smile before her gaze landed on Rob. His arms crossed over his chest and he was as handsome as ever, especially with that grin on his face.

"You've all been informed of the card for tonight. I'm so thankful you're all on board with the direction we are taking. We want the fans to get a terrific show, but I want you all to enjoy a healthy competition. The complaints I heard about my predecessor was about the way he intended the direction of each match was too predictable and stale. We're going to shake things up, rock this company's foundation, and let you all leave your mark. Now, get out there and do your best."

Emma turned to find Aaron's arms outstretched for a hug. The gesture should have felt weird, but he was such an old friend, it just wasn't.

"You're amazing. I haven't been this excited for a long time. Well, except last night of course."

The Internet had been all a buzz since the big reveal the evening before. If she thought her picture was everywhere before, she was certainly mistaken now. Kelly had calls come in from NBC, ABC, Fox, CBS, Bravo, CNN, and the BBC. All wanted the interview she had given Garrett Green, who was over the moon since he scooped them all. There were talks to hire her own media assistant to handle all her agent and Kelly were unable to keep up with. Someone based in the office full time sounded like a fabulous idea since Kelly would travel with her most of the time.

"I'm glad I'm helping. This is only the beginning. I have major plans for your company, Mr. Russell."

"And, that's why I hired you."

Cherry ran up to the two of them and gave Emma a quick hug. "You were fantastic! Barry hasn't spoken in a meeting for three years. He never has more than a few words to say. God, his accent is sexy."

Emma tipped her head back and laughed. The adrenaline along with the new friendships she created had her riding a high she had never experienced before.

"I won't stand in your way," Aaron announced. "He's a big puppy dog." He patted Cherry on the back and walked over to talk with some of the trainers.

"Oh, wow. I can't believe he said that." Cherry shook her head with embarrassment.

"You know they say it's always the quiet ones who are so good in . . ." Emma winked.

Cherry laughed and retorted, "You must be a wild cat then?" She lifted her eyebrow in question.

"I've no complaints." She tried to sound confident, but heat flooded her cheeks confirming otherwise.

"None from him?" Cherry nodded to Rob.

"Oh, no. We're not . . . We haven't . . ." Emma stopped before she dug herself any deeper in front of the cameras.

"Only a matter of time." Cherry smacked Emma on the butt.

Emma tried to act shocked, but a giggle escaped, breaking her facade. One more glance at Rob and she was certain. *They* were going to happen and she had a feeling her wild cat would come out like never before.

Rob, Cherry, and Cosmo were seated at a table in the ring at their Buffalo event. Rob had the microphone and addressed the crowd.

"You see here before you three of our semi-finalists. Some of you recently reached out to us with questions about the future. The three of us decided what better way to answer these questions than to ask our new GM, right here, right now." The crowd roared at the prospect of Emma being questioned. "Ladies and Gentlemen, put your hands together for our new General Manager, Miss Emma MacLean!"

Emma's intro music and video began to play as she appeared at the top of the ramp. Rob was supposed to control his reaction, but she was so tempting, it was hard to keep the desire off his face.

Cosmo, the six foot nine, four hundred and twenty pound heavyweight semi-finalist, helped Emma through the ropes and handed her a microphone.

"Thank you to those who welcomed me to the IWA. I appreciate all your support and can't wait to answer some of your questions." Emma stood while the three wrestlers stayed seated. "Why don't you start, Cosmo?"

"Miss Emma, Michael from Vermont wants asks how your experience in the board room qualifies you for this job in the ring."

Rob sensed she was nervous, but she pulled herself together with what seemed a well thought out answer.

"When Mr. Russell offered me this position, I thought the same thing. What did I have to offer the IWA? When I read over the job description and talked with Mr. Russell, I began to understand why he wanted me for this company. Many of you might think I'm only standing here because of my association with Terrance Hunt. Yes, I did meet Mr. Russell through him, but my love and appreciation for this company began long before our first meeting."

Emma dipped her head and pushed her hair behind her ear before she returned to her answer.

"I remember watching Big Bobby Breyer fight Hank Fieldstone for the first heavyweight title when I was ten. I had been watching my brother wrestle for years and once I found out people made a living traveling all over the world doing something they love, I was hooked. I vowed right then and there to become a Bombshell Champion. Twenty years later, I'm no Bombshell, but I get to help men and women on their roads to glory.

"So, I stand here today with all the knowledge I gathered over the years and place it at the IWA's disposal. I want to take this company into a new age. There are so many exciting things now in development. Over the next year, things are going to change for the better and the IWA will be stronger than ever."

The crowd went wild. Their excitement was so contagious, Rob found himself wanting to question her on those developments. Instead, he shook his head with indifference to the crowd.

Cherry spoke up with the next question. "Angela from Kansas City asks if you would ever get in the ring yourself? I know for a fact you have some mad skills, so?"

Emma shook her head as telltale signs of a blush crept up on her cheeks. "I had fun the other day with Cherry and Peaches while they were showing me some of their holds, but I'm not sure if I would actually be able to compete on your level. We can spar sometime, but I don't think I'm anywhere near event ready."

"Your brother seemed to think otherwise," Cherry

spoke up.

Emma rolled her eyes as Rob held in the chuckle desperately fighting to get out.

"My brother was one of the reasons I fell in love with this sport. I learned a lot from him and a few others. He would also like nothing more than to embarrass me. I have no doubt if he had the chance, he would push me into this ring. It doesn't mean I'd be ready to fight."

The crowd began to chant Emma's name, but when Rob stood with a microphone in hand, they quieted in an instant.

"One last question, Miss MacLean."

"Yes, Mr. Breyer."

The way she said his name caused his heart rate to jolt more than the cross body slam he received in his match the night before. He was careful to keep his composure while he asked his question.

"Jason from Dallas asks who your favorite wrestler is. Past or present, doesn't matter."

Emma stared into his eyes. She understood he was challenging her. A small smile and a nod of acceptance brought the answer out of her.

"So many men over the years. Ken Crusher, Salvo Bartolini, even Big Bobby Breyer could be a contender. The one person who comes to mind had the most drive, an insatiable desire to win at all cost, yet be man enough to accept when he has been defeated." Emma turned to address the crowd. "Someone who held an IWA title for four hundred and eighty-nine days the first time and hundreds of days after during his nine title runs."

Rob's blood ran cold. Only one man held the title nine different times. As the name came to the forefront of his mind, Emma spoke it aloud.

"William J. Bell. The one and only, Washington Warrior."

Rob swallowed hard. This was not good. Bill Bell was his father's biggest rival. While some of the wrestlers were friends off camera, Big Bobby and Bell were anything but. Emma declaring Bell as her favorite wrestler sent a message straight to his father. Even though he was supposed to be appalled by her choice, he was rather proud of her gutsy selection.

"I will continue to answer questions throughout the week from fans, but you all came here tonight to see your own favorites in the ring. I think it's time to give these people the show they paid for." Emma smirked and handed Rob her microphone.

Holy hell, Rob thought. Her mere presence had turned him on before. Now, she scorched him down to the marrow in his bones. She presented a side of herself, just like he did every time he stepped into the ring. His father be damned, he had fallen hard for another side of Emma MacLean.

"Speak of the devil," Rob muttered before answering his phone. "You catch the show, Dad?"

"Who the hell does this Emma MacLean think she is? Is she calling me out? Because if she is, I will be there next Monday night." Robert Senior huffed and puffed after his quick rant.

"All part of the show. If you want me to talk to Aaron about you coming on next week, I can." The idea was a disaster in the making, but Rob was sure he would calm down if he met Emma.

"You do that. It wasn't like this in my day. Scripted and choreographed. Such a disgrace to the sport."

Rob shook his head as he continued to walk through the corridor of the arena. Things were different from when his father was the top man. His rivalry with William J. Bell was real, down to the broken bones and bloodied lips. Watching the two men was like art. What they had was unadulterated hatred, which was expressed every time they were within feet of each other.

"Dad, things are different now. It's still spontaneous, but we plan for certain outcomes for the safety of the wrestlers."

"Right." His father wasn't convinced.

"I'll talk to Aaron and Emma and call you in the morning."

"Fine. Chicago on Monday, right?"

"Yes. On to St. Louis Tuesday."

Rob saw Emma with her assistant and found the perfect opportunity to interrupt. "I've gotta go, Dad. Talk to you tomorrow." He hung up before Robert Senior spoke another word.

"Can I get a moment, Miss MacLean?"

Emma's head popped up at his question. She froze for a fraction of a second before she glanced at the cameras then back to him.

"It's fine."

"All right. What can I help you with, Mr. Breyer." She folded her arms beneath her breast.

"You've gone and stirred up a whole lot of trouble with your answer to my question tonight."

Emma raised her eyebrows before she adjusted her glasses. "I suppose you are going tell me what kind of trouble I'm in."

"My father seems to think you issued him a challenge. He is prepared to be in Chicago on Monday night."

Emma's arms fell limp to her sides and the color drained from her face.

"Should I—" She cleared her throat. "Should I get my gear ready? Cherry seems to think I could do well in the ring."

Rob lifted the corner of his mouth while he tried to swallow his laughter. She seemed nervous about meeting his father again, but she was still trying to make a joke.

"I don't think things will go that far, but I will say I wouldn't mind seeing you in the ring. I'd take a tumble with you, show you some moves."

Emma relaxed at his attempt at humor. "I'm sure you would." She shook her head and the color returned to her cheeks. "I think having your father in Chicago is a fantastic idea. Kelly can arrange flight and accommodations. Would your mother be coming as well?"

"Yes, I would think so."

"I'll make the call personally in the morning. See you back in Boston."

Rob nodded and walked further down the corridor, wondering how exactly he would introduce Emma to his mother.

14

As the plane taxied at Logan International Airport in Boston the following morning, the captain gave the go-ahead to turn back on electronic devices. Emma grabbed her cell phone and dialed the number she needed, hoping the conversation would be somewhat civilized.

"Hello?" a soft, but firm voice answered.

"This is Emma MacLean. Can I speak with Robert Breyer, please?"

"Miss MacLean," the woman answered back with enthusiasm. "He's not in. I'm Lisa Breyer, Big Bobby's wife."

"So wonderful to talk to you, Mrs. Breyer."

"Surprising to hear after the conversation you had with my son last night."

Emma's voice caught in her throat.

How do I respond to that?

"Oh, hon, I understand how things are. I was a wrestler's wife and manager for way too many years. I'm sure you meant nothing by it. But Big Bobby does take things a bit personal."

"Your husband is one of the reasons I called. I wondered if Big Bobby, and you of course, would be willing to come out to Chicago next Monday for the show. I'm not so sure I want to square off with Big Bobby, but the guys think I can handle him."

Lisa laughed at the comment. "I'm sure you can. If Big Bobby could be half as charmed as my son seems to be, I think you'll be all right."

"Charmed?" Emma got caught in the moment. Had Rob told his mother about her? What did she think of her son and his new boss?

"Oh, Emma. My boy was crazy about you after one meeting."

"I'm not sure what you mean." Being coy was her only idea of how to get information at the moment.

"He came home after he met you in Boston. He was supposed to be with Big Bobby for three more weeks, but after he met you, things were different. He said meeting you was like finding the woman you never knew you needed and grieving when you lost her. It was a few months before he snapped back. When he saw you again at the regional finals, he got heartsick all over again."

"I never meant to cause him any pain. I was in a relationship both times I met him." Rob was the one who got away, but she never realized he felt the same way about her.

"You aren't now."

"No, ma'am."

"And the way my boy looks at you now, is the same way he looked when he would talk about all the wonders of Emma MacLean. A mother recognizes those kinds of smiles. He's fallen for you again and I don't think he's the only one."

Lisa had Emma pegged. She'd never even met the woman, but Lisa already had an insight into Emma's soul.

"You might be right," Emma whispered. She shook her head a bit to rein in her thoughts. "About Monday. Do you think you'll be able to come?"

"We'll be there, hon."

"Excellent. We'll take care of your flight and accommodations. My assistant, Kelly Merchant, will give you a call with all the details."

"Can't wait to meet you. Tell my boy to give his mother a call ever once in a while, will you?"

"I will. Thank you, Mrs. Breyer. I'll see you Monday."

"Bye-bye, hon."

Emma slumped back in her seat when she ended the call. The plane taxied to the gate and the passengers gathered their belongings.

"You all right?" Kelly asked as she touched Emma's hand.

"Yes. I'll be squaring off with Big Bobby on Monday night." Emma shrugged and gave Kelly a weak smile.

Kelly didn't seem surprised at the news but appeared as nervous as Emma at the idea. "God help us all."

"I'll get the Breyers' travel plans finalized and give them a call. You have the photo shoot tomorrow with Gwen and Bobby. Do you need me to be there?" Kelly asked Emma as they gathered their bags from the luggage carousel.

"No." Emma pulled up the handle on her suitcase. "I'll meet you back at the office when I'm done. It will be nice to sit behind a desk again."

She heard Ben snort and glanced over to her camera crew. The boys hated sitting with her in the office in LA. With any luck, her office at IWA headquarters would be entertaining enough for the rest of the shooting schedule.

Emma and Kelly parted ways when they reached the curb where Phil waited next to a black Chevy Escalade limo.

Emma stopped short at the view and was almost knocked over by the crew behind her.

"Phil? What the . . ." Emma asked her driver while he stood with a grin.

The back door of the limo opened and out popped a familiar head.

"Annie?" The sight of her sister-in-law was not what she expected.

Annie got out of the limo and pulled someone out behind her.

"Nell?" Emma placed her hand over her mouth at the surprise. Nell had avoided her since the loss of the MacLean matriarch. She had been told Nell was at the funeral but never saw her.

A curvier version of her twin sister, Nell was just as beautiful as Annie, but one hundred times more insecure.

Emma saw Nell's nerves come to the surface as the crew surrounded them. A bob of her throat, a hesitant step, and Nell walked into Emma's open arms.

"I'm sorry," Nell whispered.

Emma swallowed hard and held on tight to her

friend. Even though they hadn't spoken, she knew Nell felt the same loss.

Emma pulled back from Nell with tears in her eyes. "What are you guys doing here?"

Annie wrapped her arms around the other two ladies. "We are going to celebrate. First we are off to the spa for a day of pampering and beauty to get you ready for your first IWA photo shoot. Then, we are off to dinner at O'Rourke's."

"O'Rourke's?" Emma questioned. O'Rourke's was *the* bar to go to in Marblehead. Annie tended bar there while Harry was in law school, so Emma and Nell always felt comfortable hanging out there.

"Yes, O'Rourke's. Teddy O'Rourke is running the place now and the food is so much better. Plus, where would I want to celebrate both of my sister's new jobs at?" Annie smiled and glanced at Nell.

"You?" Emma asked Nell.

"Yes, I was offered the director of the teen program position at the Boston Public Library. I start in two weeks." Nell's entire face lit up as she told Emma she had finally gotten her dream job.

"So, you'll be moving to Boston?" An idea sparked in Emma's mind.

"Eventually, I don't think I have time to get moved before I start. The commute is going to be awful."

"I know what we can do." Emma ushered them all into the limo, bags, friends, and crew. The ladies began to formulate a plan to make one of their teenage dreams come true.

"Please tell me we can get massages every week," Annie

moaned as the three ladies sat down at their table at O'Rourke's. "I think they're in order after all your flights home."

Nell and Emma nodded in agreement. Once they had both gotten over the fact they were almost naked in front of a stranger, they both let themselves enjoy the full body massage.

"I'll make sure "massage with my BFF's" is on my calendar every week," Emma replied. "I think one of the places my real estate agent suggested is not far from there."

Nell took a sip of water before shaking her head. "I'm not sure I'm comfortable with you buying a place and letting me live there."

Emma took Nell's hand. "You'll be doing me a huge favor. I will be out of town three to four days a week and I'll need somebody to take care of the place. We've always dreamed of living together in Boston. I can afford my own home. You can't believe what someone paid me for my apartment in LA. Way over asking price just because I lived there."

"I insist on you letting me pay for some things. Groceries and laundry stuff for sure." Nell took another sip of her drink.

"We'll work everything out." Emma smiled and caught the hint of excitement in Nell's eyes.

"It will give me an excuse for me and Sam to make day trips into the city. While Emma's traveling, I can help you get settled." Annie loved being a stay at home mom, but a project like a new house to put together was a chance for her to spread her decorator wings once again.

It was all coming together. Emma was learning the

ropes of her new job. She would be able to move out of her father's house and create a home with one of her best friends. Another plus would be a private place for her to entertain a certain wrestler she had her eye on.

Their meal was filled with a lot of laughs and wonderful stories from their youth. The cameras captured every moment, including the bevy of men who stopped by the table to say hello.

One man stood out from all the others.

"Hello, ladies. Good to see you, Emma."

"Derek. Hi." She got up from her seat and gave him a big hug.

He held her tight for a moment before he pulled back and gave her a soft kiss on the cheek.

"Please, sit." Emma sat and Derek took the seat next to her. "You forgot to mention you're a vice-principal now. Congratulations."

"Thanks. It's been challenging learning about all the students instead of the ones in my classes or on the team."

"How did the wrestling team do this year?" Emma asked as the idea her father had posed about a visit to the team came to mind.

"They're a terrific bunch of kids and did better than they did last year, so I'm pretty happy."

"I know school is over, but do you think they would be up for a visit from some of the IWA?"

Derek's eyes widened. "Really? I mean, it's not the reason I came over, but they would love meeting them. We're doing voluntary workouts all summer long so it would make their summer so much sweeter."

"Some of them are in town on Friday. I'll see if I can set something up if you want to give me your number."

"Sure." Derek pulled out his wallet and retrieved a card with his office number at the school and jotted his cell phone number on the back. "Give me a call when you figure things out or if you just want to talk."

"Okay."

Derek got up and leaned down to give her another kiss on the cheek.

"I'll give you a call."

"Talk to you soon," he replied before he walked away.

Emma turned her attention back to Annie and Nell, who stared at her with their evil twin smiles.

"What?" she questioned.

"You *know* what." Annie kicked Emma under the table. "It's so obvious he's still hung up on you."

Emma's blush covered her cheeks. "He's a wonderful guy, but I don't think we could make a go of it again. Besides, he might be seeing someone."

"He's not," Nell stated as if it were fact.

Annie and Emma turned to Nell with questioning looks.

"And how would you know?" Annie asked.

"He goes to my gym. Girls talk in the locker room about coming there just to ogle him. Several of them asked him out, but as far as the rumor mill goes, there hasn't been anyone since Sarah Beth." Nell shrugged.

"I'm not anxious to go back to the high school, but it would be nice for the kids to visit with some of the wrestlers."

"Uh-huh. One wrestler who has seemed to get under your feathers?" Annie nudged her sister who nodded in agreement.

"I'm sure I haven't the slightest idea of what you're talking about," Emma replied before her cell phone rang. The caller ID told her Rob was calling. With the cameras watching she had to act professional.

"Good evening, Mr. Breyer."

"Oh, so all business tonight, Miss MacLean?"

"Yes. What can I do for you tonight?" She hoped he would catch on to the fact the cameras were still rolling even though it was past their regular eight o'clock cut-off time.

"I needed to confirm some details for the photo shoot tomorrow. Gwen wants us there at seven, right?"

"I believe so. Oh, and I talked with your mother this morning. Kelly has set up the travel arrangements for your parents to be in Chicago on Monday."

"Yes, I got an earful from my mother already. She can't wait to meet you."

Emma bit down hard on her lip to keep herself from slipping up in front of the cameras. "I look forward to meeting her as well."

She heard Rob laugh on the other end and gathered he understood she was stifling her answers.

"While I have you," she said, "I was wondering if you were free Friday afternoon. I was hoping to get some of the wrestlers together to visit the wrestling team at my old high school."

She heard him flip a couple of pages. "Nothing I can't move around. Chance is in town. Who you like me to see if he can join us?"

"Yes, please check with him. I'll see you in the morning."

"Good night, Emma."

Lindsey Gray

"Good night, Rob."

Emma ended the call and found the twins smiling at her again.

Annie turned to Nell. "Can you say triangle?"

"Tri-an-gel," Nell stated in three separate syllables.

"No triangle." Emma set her phone down on the table. "Derek and I are just friends and Rob's . . ." She tried to think of a way to explain the situation in line with Aaron's plans. "He's growing on me."

"Bet you'd like him to grow something in you," Annie added with a laugh.

"You are terrible," Emma retorted with an embarrassed laugh of her own. "I think you should go home and back to your hubby. Maybe you'll stop thinking about my love life and focus on your own."

"Believe me, there is nothing wrong with my love life. God, Harry can still go for hours. And his tongue—"

Emma clasped her hands over her ears. "No. No. No. That's my brother you're talking about." She removed her hands and shuddered at the thought.

"Fine. You get yourself a hottie so we can talk about him. Bachelor number one." Annie pointed to a table by the door where Derek sat with a friend. "Or bachelor number two." Annie pointed to Emma's phone.

Emma never saw herself with Derek again. She knew it wasn't even possible. As for Rob, he was the one setting her on fire. His touch, his kiss, his whispered words during their late night phone calls. She wanted to share all those details of with her two best friends, but she wasn't sure how.

15

"Seven AM looks good on you," Rob remarked when he sat down in the stylist chair next to Emma.

"Thanks," Emma snorted. She wore a hoodie with her favorite pair of worn jeans and a purple tee shirt with *Bazinga* printed across the front. With little sleep and even less time, she threw her hair up into a messy bun. Along with her black framed glasses, she seemed more like a nerdy teenager than a sophisticated reality star.

"I just wanted to say sorry about the question the other night. I really wasn't meaning to stir anything up with Big Bobby. Bill is a good friend and I have a lot of respect for him." Emma gave the entire speech while playing with her hoodie strings and avoiding eye contact with everyone in the room.

"You know Bill?" Rob asked.

"Um, yeah." She glanced up to see the confusion on Rob's face. "He owns a gym in LA. I've been training there for about five years."

"So, Harry really wasn't kidding when he said you have skills in the ring?"

"Bill seems to think I'm pretty good. I just do it for me mostly. It's hard enough going into the ring in a skirt and heels. I don't think I could do it in the scraps of material the Bombshells do."

They both turned when the door opened and saw their photographer, Gwen, approaching.

Rob leaned in close enough to whisper. "We will talk about this later."

"You two ready to do this?" Gwen asked when she approached them.

Emma leaned in to check herself out in the mirror. "Might take a couple of hours and several layers of makeup. Hope you cleared your schedule."

Gwen laughed along with Rob. "Don't worry. Angela has everything she needs to get you together. Tom is getting your suit, Rob. Make yourselves comfortable." Gwen patted both of their shoulders and left to set up her equipment for the photo shoot.

"I need coffee to get comfortable," Emma moaned while she rubbed her temples.

"Lucky for you, I picked some up on my way over." Rob held out a large to go cup of coffee to her.

She turned and accepted the drink with a smile. "Thanks."

One sip of the warm, rich liquid calmed her nerves.

"Ahhhh. I didn't drink any this morning. I could kiss you for this."

"I wouldn't be opposed to kissing you. I'd kiss you even with coffee breath."

She turned to Rob and took in his smile with his dimpled, unshaven cheeks. Beyond him, she saw the camera lens. The early hour and his alluring blue eyes made her forget millions of people would eventually see their exchange.

"Not today, big boy." She attempted to laugh it off.

"That's not never." He winked at her.

I'm so screwed.

The black Gucci suit, white shirt, and black tie suited Rob better than anything he'd ever worn for a photo shoot. Yet when he saw Emma walk on the set, his collar and pants tightened.

She drove him crazy with all the purple she wore. The tee shirt and matching tennis shoes at the workout facility, the purple blouse on Mayhem, the *Bazinga* tee shirt, and the gown she just walked out wearing.

She seemed a little uncomfortable with the slit up to her mid thigh on the left side of her dress. She kept patting her thigh in what he assumed to be an attempt to preserve her modesty.

"You are stunning." Rob took Emma's hand and twirled her around. He heard a few clicks and assumed Gwen already snapped a few photos.

Emma let out a squeal before Rob brought her into his arms. "You're pretty sharp yourself."

"Perfect," Gwen called. "Now, let's get some with the bell."

Rob led Emma over to stand in front of a white wall where a cherry red ring bell hung. They each took turns ringing it, moving and turning when Gwen instructed them to. Some stern glares toward each other and away mixed in with a few shots of Rob acting smitten while Emma's back was turned to him made a perfect first shot of the two of them together.

Time flew and Rob was sad to see Emma walk back to the dressing room to remove her dress.

"Come see some of these shots," Gwen called to him.

Rob loosened his tie and walked over to where she had set up her laptop. A few clicks and Gwen brought up a proof sheet of the photos.

"Holy shit!" Rob focused on the first several shots Gwen had taken before she posed them. The way Gwen captured the image of Emma's dress floating through the air mesmerized him. The ease and joy on her face, as he held her hand above them, was priceless.

"Pretty fine, Rob," Gwen commented while she enlarged the shot he'd admired.

"Me? No. She's . . ." He brought his hand to his throat and rubbed while he swallowed hard.

"Well, well, well. Is Bobby breaking his dry streak?" Gwen chuckled and she crossed her arms in front of her.

"For her, absolutely." Rob's last serious relationship was so long ago. At least before he met Gwen three years before.

"You're serious?"

Rob turned to catch her surprised expression. "Do you think I'm incapable or something?"

"No, I thought this thing between you two was part of the story. From what I see here, I can honestly say I've never seen you look so good. Happy is new for you."

"I think I like it too."

"Go get changed. My sister is going to work her magic on these real quick to give you and Emma an idea of what we're going for."

Rob turned around to walk back toward the dressing room and froze at what he saw. He had assumed the cameras had followed Emma, so the sight of the lens fixated on him caught him off guard. After a few slow steps in the right direction, he hurried along wondering how much the camera caught.

"This thing between them is real?" Troy asked Ben when he called to relay how the photo shoot went.

"It appears genuine. Al and I agree there is something more here."

"Fantastic! This is going to make the season finale ratings go through the roof. Film as much of the two of them together as you can. You know how to push the envelope, don't you Ben?"

"Yes, sir."

"Send me all you have by the end of the day." Troy hung up with a huge smile on his face. A juicy romance was just what *Hunt for Life* needed after the whole firing thing blew up in his face.

Irene assured him Emma's employment contract was unbreakable. Firing the nerdy girl was sure to be gold and skyrocket the ratings. Things didn't turn out quite the way they planned. Emma was supposed to make a fuss and come back, fueling the rift between her and Irene, not quit. Thankfully, Irene spent plenty of time on her knees or in his bed to make up for it. Now, if he could just find a way to spin Emma's latest romance, things might get back on track.

"You are amazing, sis."

Gwen stared at the computer screen where the photos were displayed that her younger sister, Ellie, edited.

"You wanted the best on this one. I had some time. Not a problem." Ellie clicked a few more places on the screen and adjusted a few things at Gwen's instruction.

The shoot was special in more ways than one. Not only was Gwen able to document a blossoming love story, she was able to share it with her little sister.

At nineteen, Ellie Stanton was the most sought after graphic designer in Boston. A college graduate at seventeen, Ellie had started a graphic design firm and garnered praise from all over the world. Gwen had tried to bring Ellie with her on several important shoots to help edit some of the photos as quickly as possible. Unfortunately, this had only been the second one Ellie attended. Gwen was glad Ellie had chosen to come for this particular shoot, one where she would finally meet Emma MacLean.

Emma gasped. "Is that me?"

"It sure is," Gwen replied.

"You are so talented, Gwen. Can you take all my photos?"

Gwen laughed at how serious Emma sounded. "I can't take all the credit. This is my sister, Ellie. She's a genius and can edit much faster than I can."

Ellie stood and wiped her palm on her jeans before she offered her hand to Emma. "It's nice to meet you. I'm a big fan of yours."

"Thanks so much." Emma smiled and shook Ellie's hand.

"Ellie is a big supporter of the Nerdy Girl Nation. Her design firm has co-sponsored several events for the Boston chapter." Gwen said with pride.

Realization seemed to dawn on Emma's face. "Stanton Designs, of course. I can't believe I didn't put two and two together. You're the one who has put up with Seamus all these years. Thanks for that, by the way."

Emma and Ellie began a lively conversation about their similar pursuits. Gwen was never happier to be right about introducing the two women. She hoped Ellie would finally come out of her shell with a nudge from Emma.

"We are waiting for Mr. Breyer," Phil informed Emma while he helped her into the SUV.

"Okay." Apparently she didn't have a say in whom her driving companions were anymore. She didn't mind, but traveling in a confined space with Rob and the cameras was bound to be trouble.

"Sorry, I had to take a call." Rob settled into the seat next to Emma, the dash camera aimed directly at the two.

"Are you going to the training facility?" Emma kept an eye on the traffic in front of them.

"Yes. It seems I need a little more training since I have some pretty competitive matches coming up." They hit a bump and his thigh pressed against hers for a few seconds. "Sorry. Um . . . I'm meeting Chance. Phil said it wouldn't be a problem to give me a lift."

"Not a problem at all. I'm ahead of schedule for once since the shoot didn't take as long as I had planned. I need to get a few things done this afternoon so I can be home on time."

Rob shifted in the seat, turned his body toward her

and draped his arm across the seat. "Something special?"

She stared at his uplifted brow and the quirk of the corner of his mouth before she responded. "Oh, dinner with the family. I haven't got to spend much time with my niece and nephew lately."

"You're the fun aunt?"

"I'm not sure fun is the right word. Charlotte seems to think I'm pretty cool. Sam's still a baby, so he likes anyone who feeds him or changes his diaper when he needs it." She laughed a little thinking about the few times she had changed Sam. He was the first boy she'd ever changed a diaper on and boy, was he a completely different experience from changing a girl.

"So, kids? You see yourself having any?"

Emma gulped and felt her palms dampen. He was asking about their possible future without asking directly, the sneaky bastard.

"Well, yes, of course. I would love to with the right man."

"And what qualifications would this man need to father your children?"

Her throat went dry in an instant.

He's asking me this in front of the cameras. Is he crazy?

"I don't think this is an appropriate conversation." What could she say? She sure as hell wasn't about to admit he ticked off every box on her baby daddy checklist.

"Sorry, I'm curious. You were with the tightass, the one who wore the fake Gucci suits, for like a year, right?"

"Yes. Patrick." She rolled her eyes. What an utter waste of space he was. After the crap he pulled with her and Terrance, he would be lucky to get a job writing for a neighborhood newsletter.

"I wondered if he was the kind of guy you'd want to make babies with."

The twinkle in his eye told her he was doing it on purpose. He was trying to rile her up on camera and get a reaction out of her.

"A big no. He was only interested in what I gave him and not at all what he could give me."

"So, answer my question."

"What do I want in a father for my children? A husband?" He nodded and she ventured to be as honest as possible. "Someone I can be myself with, I guess. I want a man who can put his wife and children first. Family is so important to me, especially since I lost my mom. He'd have to love them too."

"What about you?" He slid closer to her, his knee touched her thigh. "Loving you is important as well."

Christ on a cracker, she thought. They hadn't even been on a real date yet, and he was talking about babies, love, and marriage. She thought while they already had a toe in the fire of Hades, might as well jump in with both feet.

"Of course. I wouldn't be able to marry someone I didn't love." She took her opportunity to turn the tables on him. "What about you? Any wife and kiddos in your future?"

"With the right woman. I can't wait to be a dad. I'm ready for the football practices, ballet lessons, bedtime stories, and all the rest. I loved certain parts of my childhood, but I would do things differently with my kids. Once I say I do, I don't want to be separated for weeks at a time like my parents were."

"What would you do differently?" she asked before she thought what his answer might be.

"When I was little, my dad was traveling a lot. We went around with him during the summers at first. The separation wasn't good for any of us. Mom was still my dad's manager and doing everything with him hundreds of miles away was hard. When I was about to go into third grade, we pulled up stakes and went on the road with dad year round. I was sort of homeschooled on the road for several years."

"I had no idea."

"Yeah. A bunch of the wrestlers had kids around my age. The mothers would take turns with each subject. My mom did most of our English and Math, but some of the others would do History and Science."

"A little traveling school?"

He nodded. "Not much different from what child actors do on a set, I assume. It was fun, but I don't think I'd want the same life for my kids."

"Noted." It slipped out of her mouth before she could even think. Heat rose up her neck with embarrassment.

"Would you be interested in applying for the position? I can assure you, the benefits package would be amazing."

Emma gritted her teeth at the way he knew how to push her buttons, especially in front of the cameras. She thanked God and all that was holy when Phil pulled into the IWA parking garage. "And this conversation is over." She gathered her bag and what little she had left of her composure before Phil opened her door.

"I'll get you an application. I'm sure you're more than qualified."

It took everything she had in her to get out of the car

without emitting another word.

16

"I have never had a more awkward conversation in my life," Emma lamented to Annie while they prepared dinner in the MacLean kitchen. She was glad Ben and Al were off for the night. All she needed was them to catch her rehashing the conversation with Annie.

"The guy has balls." Annie tasted some sauce from the pot she stirred and smiled. "This is ready."

Emma stirred the pasta she was cooking and took a piece out to taste. "This is too." She took the pot over to the sink and drained the water.

"I guess you're not ready." Annie wiped her hands on a towel and crossed her arms in front of her chest.

"For kids?"

Annie nodded.

"Not in the next nine months. In the next couple of years? Sure. I would like to have a husband first."

"It's not like you don't have options, sweetie." Annie smacked Emma on the butt with a towel when she passed behind her to get a serving dish.

"Don't say Derek. Our ship sailed a long time ago." A pang hit Emma in the chest. Derek entering her life again was nice, but she was afraid to go there again for more reasons than one.

"There's Rob, too."

"Ugh," Emma grunted. "We work together. I'm supposed to keep things professional. The conversation we had today was so far from it."

"Be friends first. You and Derek were friendly before you got together."

"Please, do not compare this to anything I had with Derek." Emma plopped down on a kitchen stool with a huff.

"Listen to me. I have limited experience with men since I was lucky enough to meet my soul mate while I was still in diapers." Emma rolled her eyes. She remembered how Annie would always wonder off from wherever they were playing to go find Harry when Annie and Nell came for a play date. "But you showed me those pictures from this morning. Your face lights up when you talk about him. You're falling for Rob and that's okay. Falling can be wonderful, but the fall is only part of the adventure."

"Yeah, there is the crashing and burning part at the end."

Annie swatted Emma with the towel again. "Stop being so cynical. Take a chance. You want to."

"What I want is irrelevant at the moment. I need to

focus on getting through the next couple of weeks, starting with tomorrow." Going back to her alma mater still gave her chills, but she would do it for the sake of the kids. "I've got Rob, Chance, Cherry, Peaches, and Cosmo coming with me tomorrow. Rob and Cosmo don't get along, so I'm praying they can keep it together."

"It's not as bad as his dad was with Bill Bell?"

"No." From what Rob explained, Big Bobby and Bill were still fighting as recently as a few months ago. "Say a little prayer for me, will you?"

"I'll add you to my list."

Emma answered her phone after she slipped into bed. "You are totally on my shit list."

"Come on, baby," Rob cooed. "I didn't plan to talk to you the way I did, but I'm glad we talked."

"I can see the tabloids now. Ugh!" She punched her pillow in clear frustration.

"Emma, I'm sorry the subject came up the way it did, but I'm glad I know now. This isn't a short-term thing for me. We have a lot to learn about each other still, but I'm in this for the long haul."

Emma hugged her pillow to her chest. "I need to keep reminding myself this is only for a few more weeks."

"Right. After LA, we are going away for an entire week. I've cleared your schedule with Aaron and Kelly. If anything urgent comes up, you can do it over the phone or computer. If Chance and I advance to the tag team title match at Breaking Rules, I'll need some time to recuperate."

"Do I get a hint?" An entire week wrapped up in each other's arms sounded heavenly but where would he take her for his grand seduction?

"Chance's family owns a B&B with a full-service spa outside of Atlanta."

"Seems pretty convenient since we are due in Atlanta the following week." He must not want to go back to work until the last possible second.

"I reserved the deluxe package. We can lounge in bed, eat room service, even get a massage if we want."

"Sounds like heaven." She lay down on her bed and stretched her whole body out. The mere thought of any type of activity in a bed with Rob made her skin warm.

"It will be." He laughed and caused her girly bits to tingle. "Get some sleep and I'll see you tomorrow afternoon."

"Don't remind me. I can't believe I'm doing this." The closer the day came, the more foreboding she felt about the visit her alma mater.

"Not ready to go back to the good old days with Derek?"

"Not many of them were good." A pang hit her chest so hard, her scars tingled beneath her breasts.

"You forget, I met you when you were in high school. You were the most amazing girl I'd ever met."

He sounded sincere, but her old insecurities crept up on her. "You didn't go to my school. The way people reacted to Derek and I dating was like I drowned their puppies after murdering their cats. School sucked most of the time, but the last few months were like a living nightmare."

After her attack, Emma's life only got worse. One of her classmates started a rumor she had made the whole thing up and injured herself to get sympathy. It made things almost unbearable. If not for the principal and her teachers letting her finish the year from home, she wouldn't have passed her finals.

"I'm so sorry for everything you went through. You don't need to go with us. We can go on our own." The concern in his voice was evident.

"No, I made a promise to Derek. I'll meet you there at four."

"If you're sure?"

"Yes, I'm sure."

"All right. Goodnight."

"Goodnight." Emma ended the call and plugged her cell phone into the charger.

The conversation hadn't gone as she planned. She hoped the memories of that horrific time in her life wouldn't bring the nightmares back. A sure way to bring them back was to look in the box in her closet. The box she took with her throughout her various moves. She slipped out of bed and dug the wooden box out of the back of her closet. The lid creaked when she opened it, but not so loud her snoring father would wake up.

Each folder was labeled with a date. The first folder was dated just a few days after her attack. She picked up a tissue and pulled the paper out of the folder with it.

The same sloppy handwriting adorned every threatening letter within. Every threat include a picture of herself, her family, or her friends. Each letter differed slightly from the last, but the main idea came through loud and clear: stay away from Derek McInerney or she wouldn't survive another attack.

Emma tried to stay away from Derek, but those first few years were hard. She loved him so much and needed the support he so willingly gave to her. The fear won out though and because of it, she eventually let him go.

Every time a new letter arrived her logical mind screamed for her to go to the police, but the threats stopped her every single time.

Emma returned the letter to the folder, closed the box, and returned it to the closet. Her hands were shaking by the time she got back in bed. She was so tired of being afraid. Afraid to turn over the letters, afraid to show affection in public, afraid to be the real Emma in front of the world.

Her mind would never rest without a little help. She went into the bathroom, grabbed a sleeping pill, and swallowed the little white tablet with a gulp of water. Curled up in a ball under her cool sheets, she eventually fell into a dreamless sleep.

"Hey." Cherry grabbed Emma's arm and pulled her back from the group on their way to the wrestling room. "Are you okay?"

"A little overwhelming. I haven't been back here since I graduated."

Cherry threaded her arm through Emma's. "Were you bullied, too?"

Emma stopped in her tracks. The woman was twenty-five and in fabulous shape. Why would anyone bully or pick on Cherry?

"You think I always had this body?" Cherry waved her hand in front of herself.

"Well . . . Yeah."

"Not even close. I didn't sprout up until I hit

134

eighteen. I headed right to the gym and I worked my ass off for this body. I still imagine those bitches' faces on every opponent."

Emma never supposed Cherry could be a victim of a mean girl squad. The cruelty from her own female tormentors she handled rather well. The guys were the ones who came up with sick and twisted ways to hurt her.

"I'm gonna get you in the ring with me, Emma. We are going to work out some of this shit. You need good work out, girl."

"Thanks. Help me get through today. Please."

"Of course." Cherry wrapped her arm around Emma's shoulder and hugged her new friend.

"Split into two groups and spar," Derek told the boys on his wrestling squad. "Hopefully, our guests can give you guys some pointers to get us to regionals again next year."

Derek walked over to join Emma, who was taking the scene all in.

"You're great with them. This has always been your calling."

"Thanks." Derek slipped his arm around her waist, skyrocketing her nerves. "And is this your calling? Working for the IWA?"

Cherry and Peaches instructed a couple of the boys with a move while Cosmo let another boy put him in a submission hold. Rob and Chance chatted with a couple of the kids and showed off their muscles.

"So far, so good. This has been a unique experience, but I think working with Aaron is the right choice for me. I love being home. I've missed my family so much. I wish it could've happened a little sooner. My mom would've . .

." She stopped herself before she got too emotional. Derek had seen her devastated before, but she wasn't ready for him to see her so distraught again.

Derek pulled her in close and kissed her temple. "Fate has a twisted sense of humor sometimes, but we're all still here for you. I'm still here for you."

The knots in her stomach tightened and the queasiness took over. If she didn't get out of there for a minute, she feared what might happen.

"I need a minute. Mind if I use the bathroom next to your office?"

"Go ahead. I'm going to catch up with Bobby. I still can't believe how he turned out." Derek shook his head before they parted.

The cameras didn't follow her as she went into the bathroom. She splashed a bit of water on her face; her despondency swirled through her head. One glance at her reflection in the mirror told her she wasn't ready to relive any of her high school days.

"Just get through today," she told herself. A motto she had repeated every morning before going to school as a teen.

She was patting her face with a paper towel when she heard the door creak. Assuming Cherry or even Rob was coming to check on her, she didn't bother turning around. When she didn't hear anything after a moment, she turned toward the door.

A sheet of paper hung on the back of the door, blood red letters scrawled across it.

Stay away, bitch!
I won't ask you again.
This is your final warning.

Emma clasped her hand over her mouth to keep the sob from escaping.

She never received threats in person, always through the mail. A letter delivered there could only mean one thing, her attacker was there.

"Keep it together," she chanted through her soft sobs. She took a piece of tissue, removed the note from the door, and tucked it in her purse. Her legs wobbled and she let herself fall to the floor.

After a few moments, she was able to grab the basin and pull herself to her feet. The movement caused instant nausea. She turned and vomited, almost missing the toilet.

When there was nothing left of her lunch to lose, she stood and gazed in the mirror. Her lips and cheeks were pale while the vessels in her eyes shimmered bright red. She turned on the faucet and cupped her hands to catch some water to drink.

There was a soft knock on the door a moment later. "Emma? Are you okay?" Cherry asked.

Emma had no idea what to say or do, but she wouldn't be able to get out of there by herself. She turned off the water before she answered.

"Can you come in, Cherry?" She sat down on the edge of the toilet seat.

"Sure." Cherry opened the door and found a pale, distraught Emma. "Oh, sweetie. You're sick."

"Yeah." Emma brushed her hair out of her face and felt the sweat from her clammy cheeks on her fingertips.

"We're wrapping things up. Can you get up?" Cherry offered her hand to Emma.

"I think so." She wobbled a little when she stood. Cherry dampened a paper towel and handed the wet blob to Emma. "Thanks."

After a little clean up, Cherry helped Emma out of the bathroom and into the hallway where they found Rob with the camera crew.

"Everything okay?" Rob asked. Emma saw he moved his eyes up and down her body with concern.

"I just need some rest."

Rob looked confused but he kept silent.

"I was telling Emma we were about done. We should get her to the car." Cherry said and continued to hold Emma's trembling form upright.

Emma saw Derek enter the hallway and note her pale complexion. "Em?"

"Hey, I'm gonna cut out on you. I'm not feeling well."

Derek removed Emma from Cherry's arms into his. Emma winced at the emotional pain the movement caused.

"You need some of chicken soup? I can whip up my mom's recipe."

"Thanks, but no." She pulled back from him. "I think a shower and bed are best now. I hope the kids had a good time."

Derek smiled. "This made their year. Thanks again for coming."

"No problem." She moved to grab onto Cherry's

arm, but Derek stopped her.

"I'll call you soon."

Emma nodded, took Cherry's arm, and started for the car with Rob and the camera crew trailing behind.

"Troy, I'm not feeling well and need to be alone for the night. Can we give the guys the rest of the day off and start back up in the morning?" Emma begged the producer of *Hunt for Life*. She needed some time to get herself together after a much-needed cry fest.

"Only because I don't want Ben hearing you hurl. We all know he can't hold it in once someone starts in front of him."

Emma relaxed somewhat. A little time alone was just what she needed.

"Thanks so much. I promise they can film me in the morning even if I'm still a hot mess."

"You owe me one. Dinner when you're in LA?"

"Sure. Talk to you later." Emma ended the call and heard Ben sigh in relief.

"Yeah, they don't need both of us puking on camera." Emma placed her phone in her bag. "Phil, can you drop me off at home and take the guys back to the hotel?"

"Yes, Miss MacLean."

Emma relaxed back into the plush leather seat and prayed Phil would drive the quickest route home.

18

Emma noticed Annie's car in the drive before she entered the house. "Annie? Dad? I'm home. No cameras tonight."

Annie walked in with baby Sam resting on her hip. "How did the trip to school go?"

"The kids had a wonderful time, but I'm not feeling so hot. The crew has the night off while I recuperate." Emma took Sam's outstretched hand in her own. "I wish I felt up to some playtime with my favorite guy. Maybe tomorrow?"

"Sure. I came over to use your oven. Ours went out and the new one won't be installed until Monday."

Emma nodded as she remembered. "The community center carnival is this weekend."

"Yeah. Otherwise, it wouldn't be a big deal."

"It's fine. I'm going to shower and go to bed." Emma

squeezed Sam's hand before she let it go.

"I'll check on you before I leave. Mick is doing a special cruise tonight and said he'd be late."

"Thanks for telling me."

Emma walked to her room and shut the door behind her. She dropped her bag and stripped while on her way to the bathroom.

The water warmed within a minute of her turning on the tap. As she stepped under the spray, the warm water began to take the tension in her body away. If only it would take the worries in her mind as well.

"Annie, right?" Rob asked the redhead who answered the door at Emma's house.

"Yeah. You're Bobby Breyer."

"Yes. I was wondering if I could check on Emma. She seemed pretty sick when she left the school." Rob held a bottle of ginger ale and some cheese crackers in his arms. He hoped the food enticed Emma enough to tell him about her sudden illness.

"Come in." Annie opened the door a bit wider to allow Rob to walk through. "She's in the shower. You want to wait in the kitchen with me?"

"Okay."

Rob followed Annie into the kitchen where he saw dozens of trays of treats on the counters and a playpen with a little boy snoozing in it.

"Who's this little guy?" Rob asked while he set his stuff down on the only uninhabited counter space.

"My son, Sam. Don't worry about being too loud. Once we get him to sleep, he's oblivious to the world."

Rob laughed. He envied the kid. Not a care in the

141

world besides who was going to feed and change him.

"Nice for you and Harry?"

"So nice. Our daughter was horrible when she was his age. It's one of the reasons we waited so long to have another."

"Emma told me about Charlotte. Eleven?"

"Yes." Annie plated another dozen cookies. "When did you and Emma find time to talk about us? She hasn't said anything."

"The cameras aren't around, are they?" He hadn't seen them when he came in and assumed they wouldn't be in Emma's bedroom waiting for her to come out of the shower.

"No. Since she's sick, they are off for the night." Annie placed her spatula on the counter and turned to him. "What are you two up to?"

"God, I wish she would've gotten a chance to tell you."

Annie crossed her arms in front of her chest, tilted her head a bit to one side, and stared at him, waiting for a response.

"We've been getting to know each other. Did she tell you we met back in high school?"

"Yes, at an IWA event. I was so mad I didn't get to go."

"Well, we connected back then, but she was with Derek. But now she's single."

"You *are* sneaking around!" Annie smiled and seemed rather proud.

"Not sneaking. Waiting until the time is right. We agreed we didn't want to start anything in front of the cameras."

"So you've been calling her every night? I was with her the other night when you called."

"Guilty," he said, happy he was finally able to talk to someone about it.

"She told me about the conversation you had in the car yesterday." She grabbed a hand towel and smacked him with it. "What the hell were you thinking?"

He laughed at Annie's protectiveness. "I wasn't. I was trying to play my part while getting some answers to a few questions I had."

"Your part?"

"Yeah, I guess she didn't tell you about that either." He ran his hand through his hair and dislodged it from the product he had in it. "Aaron wants us eventually to be a kind of power couple. I was interested in Emma way before the announcement, so Aaron decided to change up his original ideas for me. The plan is for something big happen at the event in LA. Not sure what yet, but it's also her last day shooting *Hunt for Life*, so I'm sure everyone wants it to be good."

Annie slumped against the counter.

"This is just like her."

"In what way?" Rob was a little confused by Annie's statement.

"She always keeps anything of a romantic nature away from us. After she and Derek broke up, she never wanted to talk about any of her relationships. She didn't tell me about last year's loser until it was almost over. A couple of the others I found out about way after the fact." Annie shook her head with a frown. "She's my best friend. I hear about everything else in her life, why not this?"

"I have no idea."

Annie seemed on the verge of tears and Rob had no idea what to do.

"When filming is done, don't let her keep you a secret from us. Harry is a huge fan of yours and I'm sure Mick would love to meet you. Nan will love you too."

"I'll be here for Sunday dinner every week if you want." Rob smiled and Annie perked up.

"We do family dinners on Thursdays."

"Thursdays it is."

"I heard the water go off a few minutes ago. I'll go check on her." She gave his forearm a squeeze and left the kitchen.

Rob sat down at the kitchen table and stared at the sleeping boy. He felt an urge to pick up Sam and hold him in his arms. If he and Emma could get their shit together, one day he hoped to hold his own child in the same kitchen.

"Come in," Emma called as she ran her towel over her wet hair.

"Feeling better?" Annie asked as she came in and sat on the bed across from Emma.

"A little." The shower had helped physically but hadn't done anything to wash away the memories. How was she ever going to move past it? She thought by helping to educate kids and adults about bullying through the Nerdy Girl Nation, she was healing. When she found the note on the back of the bathroom door, she turned back into the terrified teenage girl she had fought so hard to get away from.

"I know something that might help."

"What?" Emma let her towel rest around her neck.

"Your boyfriend is in the kitchen. He seems worried about you."

"Rob's here?" Emma smacked her hand over her mouth the instant she realized what she said.

"Yes, he is. He already explained, but you don't get a pass. You and I will be talking about this away from the cameras. Soon."

"I'm sorry."

Annie patted Emma's hand. "No, you're not. You've always kept the guy stuff to yourself. Not anymore. I've already given him a standing invitation to Thursday dinners. You can't keep him away from us."

"Okay." Emma scrunched up her face and her bottom lip trembled. Annie was her best friend. Why couldn't she confide in her like normal woman would?

"Enjoy some time with your guy. I'll come get everything before I go to the community center tomorrow." Annie patted Emma's hand again before she stood and left the room.

Emma moved back to the bed to sit up against the headboard. The conversation wouldn't be easy, but someone needed to know.

"Hey," Rob said as he peeked in.

"Hi. Come in."

Rob entered and closed the door behind him. "Gifts." He held up a bowl of cheese crackers and a glass of what appeared to be ginger ale.

"Thanks." She took them from him and set them on her bedside table. "Sit."

He sat on the bed facing her and took her hand in his. The towel slipped from around her shoulders when he pulled at the end.

"I feel like something else happened today. You were so pale and shaking when you walked out with Cherry." His voice caught in his throat. "Tell me what happened."

"It's a long story."

"We've got all night."

Emma stood up and got her purse. She brought it back to the bed and dug the note out with a tissue.

"This note was put on the back of the bathroom door while I was in there." She laid it out on the bed with care.

"What the hell does this mean?"

Emma took a deep breath and slowly let it out to calm her nerves. "I told you how bad it was for me in high school, right?"

"This has to do with something that happened twelve years ago?"

She nodded. "It's not the first note like this I've gotten, but it is the first one delivered in person."

"What?" He took her hand in his.

"After Derek and I were nominated for Prom King and Queen, the bullying reached a whole new level. My childhood nemesis, Maria DeFazio, also got nominated. She did everything she could to make sure I wouldn't win. Prom came and she and Derek won. When Derek refused to dance with her, she stormed off. Before we left, she confronted me for making a fool out of her. It was the first time I fought back. I ended up with a black eye and a ripped dress. The principal broke us up but made sure to tell our parents we would be meeting with him the next week." A tear ran down her cheek when she thought of what she needed to admit next.

Rob pulled her into his arms and she held on tight as she buried her face in his chest.

"Come on, let's lie down." He lay down on his back and settled her into the nook of his neck. "Better?"

She hummed and snuggled in closer.

"Can we please stay like this while I get it all out?"

"Okay." He began to make slow, soft strokes up and down her spine with his fingertips.

"Mom and Dad both had early days so they were going to meet me at school. I got out the front door and halfway down the walk when someone hit me from behind and knocked me out. When I didn't show up at school, my parents came home to find me. They found my car still at home and my keys embedded in the grass beside the walk."

"Scared the hell out of them, right?"

"They told me they called the police right away. By the time they had everything organized for a search, I had been found."

"I don't want to ask, but I'd like to know."

She wiggled in his arms and brought her leg to drape over his. "I don't remember much, just flashes. None of them good."

"Oh, baby." His grip was like a vice, but the tight embrace was exactly what she needed to get the last of the story out.

"The doctors say I blocked the whole thing out. I've spent years in therapy trying to remember, but I don't dredge up anything more than I did right after the attack. I only remember a lot of pain and huge hands. The only clear memory I have is of waking up in the emergency room."

"How did you end up getting there?"

"I guess someone took me to school and laid me next

147

to the principal's car. He found me and called an ambulance then even rode with me to the hospital."

"Were you in the hospital long?" His fingers trailed up and down her spine in a soothing motion.

"Just overnight. They were able to set the break in my arm without surgery. There was not much they could do about the broken ribs, but a plastic surgeon came in to see about the . . ." She swallowed hard then whispered. "The bite marks."

"Oh, God." His arms wrapped tighter around her. "Where?"

"All over," she choked up. Not very many people knew about the marks. Just the doctors, her mother, Harry, and Derek knew all the details. She couldn't bring herself to tell her father. "All over my breasts. They had no suspects to compare the bites to and the dentals didn't match anyone listed in their database. As far as I know, the case is still open."

"I know you're scared, but please tell me you're going to get these notes to the police."

"I think it's time. But I don't know if the notes were really the worst part." She shifted to get a tighter grip around Rob's body. "Each note had a picture enclosed. The first had a picture of me asleep in my hospital bed after the attack. Over the years, pictures of my family and friends were included. The creepiest was a picture of Sam when he was just a few days old."

"Sick bastard." He squeezed her tight then kissed her forehead. "I'll be with you every step of the way if you want." He laid another kiss on her hair and nuzzled at her temple. "Are these threats the only reason you're staying away from Derek?"

"No." She turned to rest her head on her elbow. "This, you and me, makes me nervous, but happy in a way I don't think I've ever been. Right now, I need to be in your arms and sleep. Can that be enough for now?"

"More than enough. Let me get comfortable." Rob got up from the bed a slipped off his shoes, socks, and jeans. He crawled back into her arms in his tee shirt and boxer briefs. "Good?"

"Perfect."

"What time will the cameras be here tomorrow?"

"I'm not sure. Early I expect. I've got to help with the carnival tomorrow. Why don't you come with me?"

"If you're sure."

"Positive." She gave him a soft peck on the lips before she snuggled back and gave in to her complete exhaustion.

19

Sleep didn't come at all for Rob. Emma was restless, and he had to soothe her several times.

Emma told him about the bullying when she was younger. She should've never suggested they go to the high school. They could've arranged for the kids to come to the training facility instead. Emma should never set foot on the campus again, not when some sicko could get to her so easily.

Emma rolled over to find him still awake.

"What time is it?" she asked.

He lifted his head to glance at the red numbers on her alarm clock. "A little before one."

"Did you hear my dad come in?"

"No." He lifted his hand and moved the hair away from her face. "You are so beautiful like this."

She let out a soft laugh. "You mean a sleepy, restless

mess?"

"Absolutely. I love the rumpled look. I wouldn't mind seeing you like this every day. It would mean spending days in bed, but I assure you, I'm willing to keep you company." He leaned in and kissed her, turning her on her back. He hovered above her and caressed her cheek with his fingertips.

"I've never spent days lounging in bed unless I was sick." She trailed her fingertips from his jawline to the back of his neck.

He moved his pelvis against hers. Soft moans reverberated off the walls as he continued the slow thrusts. With thrusts came kisses. With kisses came tongues. With tongues came fire.

"I think," he panted. "I think you might be coming down with a fever. We should spend the weekend in bed." Their abdomens were now skin on skin. He moved his hand to stroke her rib cage.

She moved her hands to the exposed skin of his back and squeezed. "If you keep touching me, we might have to."

"I'll touch you wherever you want." He moved against her again, harder than he'd ever been.

"Keep going." She pushed against his back to urge him on.

"Fuck. I've thought about you like this so many times."

She pushed down a little harder on his back and lifted her pelvis. "You've thought about dry humping me in my bedroom at my parent's house?"

"Not exactly dry, are we?" Her moisture soaked into his boxer briefs.

"You understand," his pace sped up, "ugh, what I mean. I've thought of you in your apartment in LA, on your dining room table."

Her lips formed an O shape.

"I thought about you in the dressing room where I kissed you for the first time. Oh, fuck. I've thought about that one a lot. Taking you up against the wall with your legs wrapped around my waist."

Her eyes closed and she released a loud moan.

The words were getting to her, so he decided to go in for the kill.

"Most of all, I've thought about all the things I could do to you in my own bed. My tongue would love you in places no other has loved before. I'd be so deep inside of you, touching that spot with the head of my cock, and you'd beg me for more. Will you let me worship your body in my bed?"

"Yes! God!" She brought her head up from the pillow only to slam it back down.

Her muscles quivered against him as she reached her peak. His lips crashed against hers, his hips thrust against hers. "So fucking beautiful."

"Rob," she whispered in a high-pitched sigh.

The sound of his name was all it took for him to find his own release. He had dreamed of her saying his name in the heights of ecstasy hundreds of times. Hearing her breathe it against his neck was a sextillion times better.

He moved off her, not wanting his sticky mess to get all over her.

"I don't . . ." He couldn't even find a word for what they had done.

"No one has ever talked to me like . . ." She turned

on her side and placed her hand over his throbbing heart. "I liked it."

"Yeah?"

"Yes, and up against the wall?"

"Uh huh."

"I'd like to try that."

Rob wanted to blurt out how much he loved her. Instead, he turned on his side and dove in to kiss her.

He thought they might be head for another round when he heard the sound of a loud motor pull into the drive.

They both froze.

"My car is in the drive."

She sat up and swung her legs over the side of the bed. "Guess that means I'm introducing my boyfriend to my dad."

"Boyfriend?"

"I think you've earned the title, don't you?"

"Yeah, girlfriend." He leaned over to peck her on the lips.

"Let me clean up a bit." She grabbed a pair of underwear and some sleep pants and went into the bathroom.

He stripped off his soaked boxer briefs and pulled on his jeans. The unusual sensation of free balling was one he would live with for the rest of the night.

Once they were both presentable, they walked to the door and she took his hand. When they walked into the kitchen, Mick MacLean had his head stuck in the refrigerator.

"We got any pizza, Em? I haven't eaten since this afternoon." Mick's head popped up from behind the door and noticed Emma and Rob there, hand in hand.

"Second shelf, I think."

"Right." Mick took the box out and placed it on the counter next to a tower of cookies and brownies. "Is there something I need to know?"

"Dad, this is Rob Breyer."

"Yes, but what is he doing in my kitchen at one in the morning?"

Rob squeezed Emma's hand as a sign of encouragement.

"Officially meeting you for one. Rob, this is my dad, Mick MacLean. Dad, this is my boyfriend, Rob Breyer."

"Oh." A smile spread across Mick's face. "Good to meet you, boyfriend Rob Breyer." Mick held out his hand for Rob to shake.

"You too, sir," Rob replied and shook Mick's hand.

"I got sick this afternoon and Rob came over to check on me. We fell asleep."

"You okay?" Mick's brow creased with worry.

"I'll be fine. Just needed a little break. The cameras won't be back until morning."

"Going back to the high school was a bit rough for her," Rob stated.

"I was worried." Mick scratched at the crease in his brow and Rob wondered if the movement was something all parents did when stressed. He'd seen his mother do it a thousand times.

"So, that's why he's here." Emma smiled and threaded her arm through Rob's.

"Would you mind if I talked to Rob for a moment?"

Rob didn't get a sense of dread like he did when meeting a girl's father, but something was different this time.

"I guess. Don't forget, we need to be at the community center by ten."

Mick nodded. Emma gave Rob a quick kiss before she yawned and walked back to her room.

"You want a beer?" Mick offered.

"No, thanks. I don't drink."

"Have a seat." Mick motioned to the kitchen table.

Rob sat down while Mick grabbed a bottle of beer and a piece of cold pizza.

Mick sat, took a bite, and washed it down before he began. "No bullshit, son. How bad was today?"

"Bad." Yes, the part with the kids seemed to go well, but the note took all the good away.

"Christ. She doesn't remember, but the last time she was there, she was loaded up into an ambulance."

Rob let his head fall back

"She tell you?" The man didn't need more than a few words to convey his own torment.

"Last night." Rob's hand closed into a fist. "I want to powerbomb the guy. What a son-of-a-bitch." He imagined smashing the guy's head into the mat.

"What?"

Rob was surprised to see the confusion on Mick's face. "I meant I wish there were something I could do outside the ring without getting arrested."

"You said him?"

Rob was now the confused one. "Yeah?"

"Did Emma say her attacker was a man? She said she couldn't remember, but we've always assumed it was the girls she fought with at the prom. The police could never find any solid evidence to make an arrest."

"I guess I assumed it was a man with the way she described her injuries. Whoever it was, he or she should be punished for what they put you all through."

"She's been in therapy ever since. I thought maybe after a while something would come back. In some ways, I'm thankful she can't remember. We wanted some justice but at what cost?"

Rob nodded his head in agreement. He began to see Emma's reason for keeping things to herself. She was in a no-win situation.

"The thing is, she never deserved any of their hatred. She was smart and beautiful and God, so strong. Yeah, she was shy, but that was no reason for bullying her the way those kids did." Mick's bottom lip began to quiver, but he tried to cover it by taking another drink.

"The moment I met her, I knew she was something special. Her smile, her voice, and her laugh, I don't think I've ever heard a more beautiful sound than her laugh."

"She gets it from her mom. Those two could giggle for hours." Mick sniffed back his tears before he grasp Rob on the shoulder. "You'll protect my girl?"

"Of course."

"Go get some sleep. We'll talk some more over breakfast." Mick stood and threw his empty bottle into the recycle bin.

Rob gave Mick the universal head nod and their conversation was over.

For a few minutes, he sat and thought the whirlwind of events of the last day. The woman whom he'd watched on television was far from the one asleep in the next room. She was beautiful but not perfect. But she was perfect for him.

20

By the time five am rolled around, Rob decided he needed to move to the couch in the living room. The cameras would be there soon but he didn't want to leave Emma's home yet.

A high-pitched scream woke him, caused him to roll off the couch, and hit his head on the coffee table.

"Oh, shit! Are you okay?"

Rob blinked a couple of times before he focused enough to see Emma's brother standing above him.

"You scream like a girl, Harry."

"Not me." Harry grabbed Rob by the hand and helped him up. "This is my daughter, Charlotte."

Rob turned to see a smaller version of Annie trembling in the corner.

"Charlotte," he acknowledged.

She let out a squeak before she slapped her hand over her mouth and ran down the hallway.

"She's a big fan and probably a little shocked to see you on her grandfather's couch."

"I see." Rob combed his fingers through his hair and found blood. "Could I trouble you for a bandage?"

"Sure, come in the kitchen."

Harry led Rob into the kitchen where he found Annie with baby Sam on her hip.

"Charlotte didn't maul you, did she?" Annie asked with a chuckle.

"No, banged it on the table," Rob replied as Harry pushed him onto a kitchen chair.

"The cut isn't big, but head wounds love to bleed." Harry slapped a small towel on Rob's head. "Hold this here."

Emma walked into the kitchen yawning. Her gaze went from Harry to Rob's head. "Oh, God! What did you do to him?" Emma rushed to examine Rob's wound.

"I'm fine." He kissed her hand. "Nothing new. I'll stop bleeding soon."

Emma's cheeks reddened at the sign of affection in front of her family. She had told Rob several times how difficult it was for her to show any affection in front of people.

"Something you wanna tell us, Em?" Harry crossed his arms in front of his chest with a slight smirk.

"Um . . . Rob and I are together now, but we, um . . ."

Rob stood and took Emma's hand in his. "What she's trying to say is we are together, but we don't want the world to find out yet because of work and the tabloids."

"So, how are you going to play this? We saw Ben and Al loading up on our way over. They should be here anytime." Harry raised his brow and waited for an answer.

Al and Ben were the reason he reluctantly left Emma's bed for the couch. A plan had come to mind as far as their professional romance was concerned.

"I came over last night because I was worried about Emma after what happened at the high school. She let me take care of her since Mick wasn't here and I slept on the couch."

Emma finished for him. "I've invited Rob to spend the day with us at the carnival." Emma gave Rob a soft kiss on the cheek and went to the fridge to get all the things she needed for breakfast.

When Ben and Al arrived, if they were shocked to see Rob there, they didn't show it. They handed both him and Emma mic packs and began to film like every other day.

"Winner. Winner. Chicken dinner!" Emma shouted after Rob knocked down a tower of milk bottles to win a prize.

"Ladies choice." Rob swept his arm in a grand fashion toward the stuffed toys hanging on the booth wall.

She smiled and searched for something she might like. Once she caught sight of a pillow the shape of the *Superman* symbol, she pointed it out to the booth attendant.

"That was the reason I stopped here." Rob rubbed the blue fur of the pillow in Emma's hands.

"Thank you. Nobody has ever won anything for me before. Some might think you're sucking up to the boss."

"Me?" He brought both of his hands up to rest over his heart. "I'm crushed you would think me capable of such a thing."

"Uh, huh." He was so darn adorable.

The whole day had been so much fun spending time together and being silly. They had started by helping Annie and Nell set up the bake sale. After too many tempting treats, they were given clearance to enjoy themselves for the rest of the day. After a lunch of hot cheese and soft pretzels washed down with cherry limeaid, they moved from game to game taking their chances.

They hadn't acted like anything more than friends, but Al and Ben seemed to be looking for intimate gestures.

"So, this is an annual thing?" Rob asked.

"Yes. My mother started this about ten years ago as a fundraiser to build the community center. One of the city councilmen owns the amusement rides so this is his big good deed for the year."

Emma hadn't been able to come for several years. Enjoying the carnival without her mother was bittersweet. She loved the games and rides, meeting with all the kids from the center, but the spirit her mother infused in the event was missing.

"Emma? Is that you?"

Emma cringed and froze at the sound of the woman's voice. Her fantasy that the woman died in a huge house fire or took a few too many Xanax before slipping into the afterlife was destroyed as soon as she turned around.

"Maria. You're looking . . ." Emma eyed her exquisite outfit along with the helmet hair cemented to her head. "Picture perfect, as usual."

"Sorry, I can't say the same for you." Maria tutted while her eyes roamed over Emma's casual jeans and a tee shirt.

Rob moved his hand to the small of Emma's back and laid a reassuring pressure on her.

"Maria, this is my friend, Rob. Rob, this is Maria. We went to school together." Emma pressed her lips into a thin line in an attempt to not let anything else out while the cameras were rolling.

"Oh, you're the drunk on that lame wrestling show Emma's working on." Maria titled her head and batted her eyelashes the same way she always delivered her nasty insults.

"Nine years sober and thanks for insulting our careers. What is it you do for a living?" Rob slipped his arm around Emma's waist and gave her hip a squeeze.

"I'm a stay-at-home wife. My husband and I are working on starting a family. He wants my body as stress-free as possible for a baby." She rubbed her flat belly and smirked.

"I didn't realize you were married. Who is the lucky guy?" Emma asked.

Maria held out her left hand to show a diamond encrusted wedding band. "I'm proud to say I'm Maria McInerney now."

"A McInerney?" Emma wasn't sure whom she meant then it dawned on her. "Oh, yes. I heard Paddy got married but I didn't remember who the bride was. Congratulations."

"Ew, no! Paddy's, like, fifty or something." Maria scrunched up her face in disgust.

"Sorry. My mistake. I can't think of another single McInerney besides Derek." Emma crossed her arms in front of her chest and tilted her head to imitate Maria.

"Still a bitch." Emma gasped in shock. She didn't

think she was being that obvious. "Since you haven't had a real man since Derek left your skank ass, I don't think you have any right to judge me."

Emma felt her fight or flight response coming on, but Rob held her in place with his hands on her hips. "I'm not judging you, Maria. The McInerneys are a wonderful family. Derek and I were actually together long after high school. We parted as friends. We're still friends."

"That's right," Derek said as he walked up to the three of them with a huge man at his side. "It's been forever ago, Maria. Just be a woman for once and drop it."

Maria got up in Derek's face. "I can't believe you kept seeing her after she pulled that stunt. How stupid are you?"

Derek put his hands on Maria's shoulders and gently pushed her away from him. "So, she broke her own bones and beat the shit out of herself? You're pathetic." Derek turned to the man beside him who seemed almost as angry as Derek was. "You better put a leash on your woman, Sully. This town does have laws about letting your dogs roam free."

Maria pushed Derek against the chest. "You bastard!"

Sully grabbed Maria around the waist as an expression of shock covered Emma's face. Never in a trillion years would Emma guess Derek's huge teddy bear of a cousin would marry the wicked witch of the northeast.

Sully was one of the nicest guys in the school. At almost seven feet tall at age fifteen, he did everything he could to make sure people weren't scared of his bulk. He'd never hurt a fly. Emma wondered how the hell he ended up with Maria.

"That's enough!" Sully barked. "Sorry, Emma." Sully

took his wife by the hand and led her back into the crowd. Emma couldn't believe Derek never thought to mention that the devil incarnate was now his cousin-in-law.

"Can you tell how happy I am she's part of my family? As long as she makes him happy, only God knows why she does, but I have to be okay with it."

"Hey. Harry is getting ready to go on." Rob pointed over to the staging area where Harry, Annie, and Mick stood.

"What is he doing?" Harry had taken on some last minute details since their mom passed, but Emma wasn't aware of any speech.

"I'll catch you guys later." Derek gave a little wave and disappeared into the crowd.

The lead singer of the band finished his song and motioned for Harry, Annie, and Mick. With a microphone in hand, Harry began to speak.

"Good afternoon, Marblehead!" The crowd cheered. "I'm Harry MacLean and this is my father, Mick, and my wife, Annie."

"Yo, Annie!" a deep male voice hollered from the back.

"We wanted to thank you all on behalf of the MacLean family for coming out today to support the community center my mother loved. Thanks to our new mayor, Rudy Babcock, and Councilman Weathers for all your hard work to help us raise thousands of dollars for the programs offered here at the center."

Harry turned to Annie, who nodded back to him.

"I wondered what my contribution to this town could be since my mother passed away. My father does boat cruise fundraisers every spring for the school system. My sister's foundation, Nerdy Girl Nation, provides supplies and computers for our teen outreach room here at the community center. I've offered legal clinics in the past, but I feel like I need to do more. Mayor Babcock has informed me he is not planning on running for the office in the next election. So, I'm officially announcing I will be running for Mayor of Marblehead for the next term."

The crowd erupted in applause and cheers. Emma stood stock still while the people around her got louder. First the showdown with Maria and now her brother announces he's running for office. She had no idea he had plans to run. He just turned thirty-five and had a thriving law practice.

"Emma?" Rob nudged her.

"Huh?"

"He's calling you up."

"Oh. Okay. Stay here, all right?"

"Of course." Rob shooed her away up to the stage.

She walked up the stairs and over to her brother's waiting arms. "You are so dead for springing this on me."

"That's what you get when I find your boyfriend sleeping on the couch."

Emma pulled back and sneered at him. Harry smiled. She couldn't stay mad at him for long so she gave him a kiss on the cheek. "Congratulations."

"Thanks. Now hug Annie. She's nervous about being a first lady."

Emma moved over to Annie's arms while Mick took Harry's place at the microphone.

"I'm sure Elaine is smiling down on us today. I know my son will be an asset to this town and will make a terrific mayor. He learned from the best. The preliminaries are coming up in a few months. Remember to vote MacLean on the next Election Day. Thank you all!"

21

"She was so beautiful, I tell ya." Emma's grandmother, Moira, squeezed Rob's hand and winked at Emma.

"Nan, come on. Stop," Emma pleaded from her seat next to Rob.

"No. He's the only young man you've brought home in years. I'm going to tell him how perfect my granddaughter is."

"Just one more story?" Rob asked. The time he'd spent in the MacLean household was better than any night in his own family home. He didn't want their time to come to an end; especially since the camera crew had already left for the night.

"Fine," she huffed.

"As I was saying, she was beautiful. Elaine and I worked for weeks getting the costume right. Halloween arrived and Emma became *Wonder Woman*."

"The gold wristbands and everything?" He asked.

"Oh, yes. The picture is on my mantle at home. I'll show you when you come for Thursday dinner next week."

"Lord!" Emma rolled her eyes.

Rob couldn't wait. Not just to see a young Emma as *Wonder Woman*, but for the real family dinner. He was the only child of parents who were also only children. His father's parents didn't approve of his career and his mother's parents didn't approve of his father, so both sets were scarce over the years. A big family dinner would be a first for him.

"Don't be embarrassed." He leaned in and kissed Emma's reddened cheek.

"Oh," Moira exclaimed.

"What now, Nan?" Emma asked as she cuddled into Rob's side.

"It's so nice to see the two of you so in love. Reminds me of my Michael and me." Moira got a dreamy look in her eyes.

"You and Gramps were so cute." Emma smiled, but Rob saw sadness there. They had talked about how close she was with her grandparents. The loss of her Gramps when she was thirteen devastated the whole MacLean family.

"I can see the two of you now. A great love story. I'm so glad I'm here to see you from the beginning."

Rob felt a flutter in his chest at the words and prayed she was right.

"I'm glad you're here, too. Now I can see what a knockout my Emma will be later on."

Moira's pale skin turned a bright shade of pink with Rob's words.

"Such a keeper. If you let this one go, make sure to drop him off on my doorstep." Moira winked again before she patted Rob's cheek.

The words of the sweet older woman socked him in the gut. If he and Emma were going to make a real go of it, there were a few things they needed to discuss. It wasn't the right time or the right place, but he wasn't sure his confidence would hold if he didn't do it then.

"You mind if I steal this pretty girl away for a little while?" Rob asked Moira.

"Only if you bring her back happier than she left." Moira laughed when Emma gasped.

"I'll do my best." Rob stood and offered Emma his hand. She took it and he led her back into her bedroom.

Rob shut the door behind them and took Emma in his arms.

"A spontaneous make-out session? I like the way you think." Emma slipped her arms around his neck and drew him down for a kiss.

A few pecks and a slip of the tongue made Rob's brain foggy. He knew he'd never get enough of her, but he restrained himself and pulled back.

"I really wanted to talk."

"Okay." They sat down on her bed. "What do you want to talk about?"

"About something Maria said."

"Ugh." Emma flung herself back on the bed. "Which part?"

"She called me a drunk. It occurred to me, we really haven't talked about it."

Emma pushed herself up to rest on her elbows. "I figured you'd tell me when you were ready."

Rob pushed Emma down flat, leaned over her, and laid a long, gentle kiss on her lips. "That is one of the many reasons I adore you."

She ran her fingers through his hair. "And you know what? You can tell me all about your past and I'll still adore you because it made you the man you are today."

Rob was a lucky son-of-a-bitch. He felt like he could do anything when she said things like that.

"I'm sure you've heard about what happened in Baltimore."

Emma nodded. "Some prick in your AA group recorded you talking at a meeting then released it to one of those tabloid shows."

"Yeah, I wish it had been any other meeting. I was struggling that day and shared more than I usually would." He remembered the day he'd come closest to falling off the wagon but rushed to a meeting instead.

"Nine years sober is a pretty big accomplishment." She flashed a small smile at him.

"At first I thought it was typical college stuff, then I wasn't making it through classes without a drink. I used to keep a water bottle full of vodka with me. My rock bottom moment came after the worst blackout ever. I went to a party and they were passing around this stuff, a hundred proof and tasted like Kool-aid. I remember the first drink, next thing I know I wake up in my buddy's room with a naked girl next to me."

"Oh, my God." Emma cupped his cheek. "You didn't . . ."

"No, she told me it was consensual. She confessed

she had wanted me for a long time. The big problem, she was my wrestling coach's seventeen-year-old daughter."

"Shit!"

"Yeah. I made her get dressed, my buddy's girlfriend made sure she got home, and I called around to find a good rehab in the area. I checked in that night and haven't drunk a drop since." He rested his forehead on her chest, the weight of his confession lifted off his shoulders.

"Would it be wrong of me to say I'm proud of you?"

"Proud?" He lifted his head to see her sincere expression.

"You realized you had a problem and you took the steps you needed to get yourself together. Nine years later, you're a successful athlete with a smoking hot girlfriend."

"I do, don't I?" He bent down and pressed his lips to her bare collarbone. "Don't you forget it."

"I won't."

22

The exhaustion of the week caught up with Emma on her plane ride to Chicago Sunday evening. She tried to sleep, but knowing Rob was only a few rows back distracted her thoughts toward meeting his parents.

Since she was such an experienced traveler, Emma fit all she needed into her carry on. When she saw Rob make his way over to the baggage claim, she felt compelled to walk over and act like she needed to wait for a bag to come through.

"Mom?" she heard Rob exclaim.

A tall, slender woman with light brown hair embraced Rob.

Emma grabbed Kelly by the arm. "I thought the Breyer's flight wasn't until the morning?"

"I booked them on a non-stop flight at eight

tomorrow morning." Kelly seemed as confused as Emma.

Robert Senior shook Rob's hand after his mother finished their long hug. Chance grabbed Lisa Breyer around the waist and swung her through the air.

Emma laughed at the scene and caught Rob's attention. His eyebrows rose in what she thought was an invitation to walk over, but she shook her head and helped Kelly get her bag from the conveyor belt.

As she got settled into the SUV, Emma heard her phone alert her to a text message.

Meet us for dinner in my room?

He had already met her entire family and half of her hometown. She had to meet his parents.

Text me your room number once you get settled.

She smiled when she received a response seconds later.

Have I told you lately how much I adore you?

Not lately.

I do. Don't worry. I'll hold your hand the entire time.

Until then.

"You're sure Troy is okay with this?" Emma asked while Al packed up his camera equipment.

"Doesn't matter. You deserve a break from us." Al

zipped up his bag and turned to help Ben with his equipment.

She realized how much the guys protected her since the horrible day back in Los Angeles. They had given up time with their friends and family to follow her around. The guys were doing their jobs, but she felt bad about all they had to deal with lately.

"I've been all over the place since I came back home and started this new job. Meeting Rob was not part of the plan, but it happened and I'm thrilled."

"And we are happy for you. Enjoy this time without us." Ben smiled a little and held his hand out for Emma's mic pack.

She slipped the pack out of her waistband and before she handed the contraption to Ben.

"Have a nice night and don't think about us for a while." Al opened the door to the suite.

"Right."

Emma walked out of the suite and down the hall to the elevator. She rode three floors up until she came to Rob's floor. The walk to his door seemed endless as all the 'what if's' flittered through her mind.

What if Robert Senior hated her?

What if Lisa changed her mind and thought she wasn't good for her son after all?

What if Rob realized his parents didn't approve and let her go?

She tried to shake off the unease of their impending meeting. A few deep breaths and an internal pep talk later, she knocked on the door.

"Hey," Rob answered and motioned for her to come in.

With the door shut behind them, Rob took Emma's hand and led her into the living room area of the suite.

"I usually share a room with Chance, but since this was a special occasion, I got this suite. Mom and Dad are still unpacking, but I ordered dinner to be brought up in about ten minutes."

"Okay," she whispered.

Rob slid his knuckle under her chin and lifted her gaze to meet his. "Everything's fine. My mom already adores you."

"But your dad . . ."

"You let me worry about him." Rob leaned in and gave her a soft kiss.

She relaxed into his arms and sat down on the couch with him. They talked about what their plans were for the week, starting with the show the next night.

"The plan is for your father walk in after you and Chance are in the ring. We can talk about what he wants to say, but at some point I will interrupt and come to the ring."

"I'm not reading from some damned script!"

Robert Senior made his entrance into the living room from the bedroom.

"Of course not, Mr. Breyer." Emma stood and straightened out her skirt. "We have some suggestions so we can segue to my entrance."

"Suggestions?" he asked and crossed his arms over his chest with a huff.

"Yes. We don't like the term scripted. Things seemed scripted when Curtis Sharp was in charge, but I don't make my wrestlers perform like trained monkeys. This is the direction Aaron and I decided on and we are going to proceed in hopes all will work out for the best." Emma's heart continued to pound in her chest as she finished her explanation. She had faced some intimidating men in her life in the boardroom, but facing off with Robert Senior brought on a whole new fear.

Will Big Bobby hate me forever?

"What suggestions?"

Emma turned and picked up her bag from the couch. She retrieved a few sheets of paper with the suggestions she had discussed with Aaron.

"Take a look and let me know." She handed the sheets to him.

"Fine. I'll read these *notes* after dinner and get back to you tomorrow. If you'll excuse us." Robert Senior motioned for her to leave.

"Dad, I've invited Emma for dinner," Rob divulged through clenched teeth.

Robert Senior's brow furrowed in appeared confusion when Lisa Breyer entered the room.

"Oh, Emma. I'm so glad your here." Lisa stepped forward. She ran her fingers through her hair to tame the wayward strands. "I wanted to thank you again for inviting us out here. This is the best birthday present ever."

Emma smacked Rob's arm. "You didn't tell me your mother's birthday was coming up."

"Not until Wednesday. I forgot. Forgive me?" Rob wrapped his arm around her waist and pouted.

She rolled her eyes and turned back to the Breyer's. Lisa had a smile a mile wide while a blood vessel throbbed in Robert Senior's forehead.

"Bobby. Explanation. Now!" Robert Senior demanded.

"Dad, Emma and I are seeing each other. You might not remember meeting her before, but we actually met her a couple of times several years ago."

Robert Senior squinted his eyes and stepped closer to Emma.

Emma's face became moist at the scrutiny and her glasses began to slip down her nose. She pushed them back up and Robert Senior's face unclenched.

"The girl you ran into in Boston. You're the reason my son left me early that summer." If it were possible, Robert Senior seemed angrier than he was the moment before.

"Dad, come on." Rob left Emma's side to stand in between her and his father.

"And now you're dating her?" Robert Senior scoffed.

"Yes." Rob puffed out his chest and stood eye to eye with his father.

Robert Senior gazed around his son at Emma. Inside she was a quaking mess, but she flipped her internal switch once again and portrayed the woman with a hard shell.

"I think this is wonderful if my opinion matters at all," Lisa piped up.

"Thank you, Mom."

Lisa turned her head to see Emma and gave her a wink and a smile.

Emma's nerves settled a bit at the knowledge at least one other Breyer had her back.

Their dinner of gourmet steaks arrived with little fanfare. Emma, Rob, and Lisa settled into an easy conversation while Robert Senior grumbled after every other bite.

Robert Senior set his glass down on the table with a

little more force than necessary. "And you?" He turned to Rob. "What are your intentions?"

Emma heard the disdain in the tone of Robert Senior's voice. The feel of Rob's hand grasping her own on her lap calmed her before he gave his answer.

"To do my job and live my life with Emma by my side."

"Aww," Lisa sighed.

"Dad, do you begrudge me the happiness you experienced with Mom all these years? You were married with a ten-year-old son by the time you were my age. Don't you think I deserve some happiness? I work hard and I think I've earned the right to enjoy my life with someone I care about."

Robert Senior took in his son's words. His face softened a bit as he turned his gaze to his wife.

"I want you to be happy, but you can't lose sight of your goals."

"I still have those goals." Rob brought their joined hands out from underneath the table and kissed Emma's. "They've changed a bit."

"Yes, tag team champion," Robert Senior sneered.

Emma gathered her courage and responded to him. "As I recall, some of your most famous finishing moves came from your tag team matches." Robert Senior tried to speak up, but she kept going. "Your Shake Brake move came out of your match with The Steel Baron against Bill Bell and Matthew Donahue. The Sideshow Slammer happened for the first time in your match with Dillon Haynes against Marcos and Miguel Cruz. And, oh, what about the time you won the tag team belts with Dorian Atwood and used the Tyrant Twist on Ward Poole and

Brett Wolf at the same time?"

Emma recognized the slight twinkle in Robert Senior's eye.

"You might be right but I don't want my boy distracted."

"I'm not here to hurt Rob's career. I want to see him succeed as much as you do." Emma felt like she was on the verge of a breakthrough with the man and wondered what would push him over the edge.

"You've followed the IWA for years, right?"

"Yes."

Robert Senior was silent for a moment before he began again.

"You know all about my career as well?"

"I do."

A wicked grin spread across Robert Senior's lips. Warning bells went off in Emma's brain at the sight.

Thus began the two hour-long IWA trivia session where Emma felt like she'd lived a weird combination of a game show and police interview nightmare. At the end of the night, Robert Senior seemed satisfied with her as the new GM of the IWA, but most importantly as his son's girlfriend.

Once his parents had retired to their room, Rob poured a club soda for Emma and sat with her on the couch.

"No wonder you've never had a steady girlfriend. I felt like I was taking the SAT's again." Emma sipped at the bottle of water he'd given her.

"Yeah. No one but you could've ever passed my father's test. I'm sorry he put you through that, but you held your own. I'm proud of you."

Emma turned and cuddled into Rob's side. "Thanks for standing up for me."

"Anytime." Rob moved closer and placed a light kiss on her lips before he'd pulled back. Emma groaned with disapproval. "If we start something tonight I won't be able to stop myself."

"Okay." Emma leaned in for one last kiss before she stood. "I need to get going. Big day tomorrow."

"Right." Rob stood and walked her to the door. "What time are you heading over to the arena?"

"Eight. Kelly and I need to work before my workout with Cherry and one of the match coordinators."

"Workout?"

"Guess I hadn't mentioned that yet, huh?" Emma noted the confusion on his face as he shook his head. "Aaron wants to get me in shape. I think he plans to put me in a match at some point. Never too early to start preparing."

"Really?"

She nodded. "I think fighting in a real match will be easier if I start out practicing in the empty arena. Maybe imagine I'm back at Bill's gym. Am I nuts?"

"No. You're not." Rob pulled her into his arms. "I can't wait to see what they come up with for your ring wear. Definitely purple."

She pulled back. "Without question." She gave him another kiss before she said a quiet goodnight.

Once she was back in her room, she stripped and fell into bed. Her dreams were full of purple-studded leather and knee-high black boots. If she ever did make her in-ring debut, she had a good idea of what she wanted to wear.

23

Sweat dripped from places on Emma's body she'd never sweat from before. Every muscle, every bone ached. She was stupid to think she could take a few weeks off and not hurt.

"Again," Lazlo, the match coordinator, yelled at Emma and Cherry.

"One more time, Emma." Cherry winked at her from the other side of the ring. "You got it in you?"

"I'm ready." Emma stared Cherry down.

Cherry ran at Emma full force. Emma grabbed Cherry around the waist and used Cherry's momentum to hip toss her to the mat.

The crowd of IWA talent and employees around the ring applauded and Emma helped Cherry up.

"Good job, girl." Cherry hugged Emma tight and

groaned. "Knocked the wind out of me."

"You okay?" Emma asked.

"I'm good." Cherry pushed Emma off and turned to bow to the crowd.

"I want a crack at her." Steffi, the reigning Bombshell Champion, stepped into the ring.

Emma's mind went on alert. Images of Steffi's matches and signature moves filtered through her brain.

"Just a few minutes," Lazlo cautioned before the two women began to circle the ring.

"How do you want to start this?" Emma asked.

"Wing it," Steffi answered.

The two continued to walk around the ring. They measured each other with every step.

Steffi lunged at Emma and the two held each other back by the shoulders. Emma decided to pull out one of her brother's favorite moves. She turned Steffi around so they were back to back, hooked their arms together, and flipped Steffi over her back and on the mat.

The crowd cheered again while Cherry and Peaches wolf whistled.

Steffi got to her feet and stretched her back. "Not bad. Next time we will work on submission holds." Steffi held out her hand to Emma.

Emma shook the champion's hand and realized she had made another friend.

"His name is Kieran Finley. Irish, but dark hair. He's been working the smaller circuits for about a year. We need him," Aaron insisted as he pulled up some film of the young Irishman on his laptop.

Emma recognized Kieran's potential right away. She

imagined him working well with several of their wrestlers. A belt belonged around Kieran Finley's waist.

"When can we meet with him?" She shut off the film.

"Within the next couple weeks." Aaron's voice dropped off.

"I feel a *but* coming next."

"Yes, there is a little complication."

Emma threw her hands up in the air with a huff. Her first possible acquisition for the company and there was a problem from the bang.

"What's the catch?"

"He's Patricia Finley's nephew."

"Oh." Big problem. They had family members who were wrestlers, but none were related to the human resources director. "I'm sure we can get some exemption if we sign him. Can we find someone who can deal with any of his HR concerns instead of Patricia?"

Aaron smiled wide and tilted his head to the side.

"Of course. You like making my job a little harder every day." Apparently, she would be adding HR specialist to her resume.

"It's your fault. You're so talented. You can do anything."

She laughed. There were many things she couldn't do and he knew about most of them.

"Don't think for one minute I didn't see your turn in the ring this morning."

Heat rose to her cheeks. While she was in the ring, she wasn't thinking about anything except her opponent.

"I think I did okay."

"You put Steffi on her ass. She hasn't been in that position in quite a while." Aaron laughed with a twinkle in his eye.

"You are up to something." Her stomach turned.

What the hell does he have in mind for now?

"Me." He pointed to himself. "President. You." He pointed to her. "Vice President. I have the right to keep a few things to myself."

"Fine. If I look like an ass in front of millions of people, I will put you on yours."

He clapped his hands together. "I wouldn't expect anything less."

Aaron did drive her crazy, but she did love and respect the guy more than most.

"Now, get a hold of Kieran's agent and set up a meeting as soon as possible." He handed her a folder with Kieran Finley's relevant details.

"Yes, Mr. President."

24

Rob was edgy. A scorching sizzle crawled under his skin and slithered through his muscles, making him feel the fire. His fire wouldn't be destroyed by a bout in the ring. Something was lurking on the horizon. He wished he had the faintest idea what the hell *it* was.

He felt his father behind him while he and Chance stood backstage and waited for their entrance music to begin.

"You got this, Dad?"

"I've done this thousands of times. Don't worry."

Rob turned toward his father. He looked better than he had in years. Robert Senior's dark brown hair with streaks of gray was short on the sides but messy on top and made him seem several years younger. Most of his physique had held up well since he'd retired, his chest still broad and his arms still hard as cannon balls. The black suit jacket, gray tee shirt, faded blue jeans, and Doc Marten's fit with the image Emma and Lisa had suggested. His dad's persona said laid back, yet classy. Something his tightass Big Bobby persona had never displayed. Rob prayed his dad pulled off the new façade.

"Now or never." Chance squeezed Rob's shoulder as music alerted them to get to the ring.

Rob turned to his dad. "See you out there."

Robert Senior nodded and appeared relaxed.

Chance and Rob received a huge Chicago welcome on their way to the ring. The duo even stopped to take a picture with a five-year-old set of twin boys. One had a Baltimore Bruiser shirt on and the other's shirt read, "Take a Chance on a Robicheaux".

The ring announcer brought the mic in front of him. "At this time, ladies and gentleman, we have a special guest we would like to welcome to the ring. He hardly needs an introduction. Eight-time heavyweight champion, three-time international champion, and four-time tag team champion. The only man to knock William J. Bell unconscious. Chicago, welcome Big Bobby Breyer!"

Big Bobby's theme music began to play and a new video montage flashed on the big screen above the entrance. The man himself strutted out with a confidence Rob hadn't seen in years. He waved to the crowd and high-fived several people on his way to the ring.

"He's doing great," Chance said as Rob watched his father's every move.

Big Bobby stopped to chat with the same twins Rob and Chance had. Before Rob figured out what was happening, Big Bobby had a twin sitting on each of his guns while he flexed. A happy father snapped several pictures before the boys were returned to their seats and Big Bobby shook their hands.

Rob let out a hardy laugh at the sight. It was as if he was seeing a whole new man strutting up to the ring. If he hadn't seen his father's swagger live and in person, he wasn't sure he would've believed it.

A mic was handed to Big Bobby when he entered the ring. He clapped Rob on the shoulder before he began.

"Great to be back in Chicago!"

Ear piercing screams came from the crowd. Rob was a little shocked at the reception but was overjoyed to see the wide grin on his father's face.

"I never expected to be in a ring waiting for my son to win a tag team match." Robert Senior rolled his eyes.

Rob froze. This was not the way it was supposed to go. He felt Chance move to his side and wait.

"The fact is my son is an amazing singles competitor." More screams of adoration came from the crowd. "Never in a million years did I see my son depending on a partner to help win a title. Especially not one like Chance Robicheaux."

Rob held his hand up to keep Chance from launching at Big Bobby. He didn't understand what his father was doing, but if Chance went after Big Bobby the match would be in jeopardy.

"My son has been living and breathing this existence since he could walk. He was pinning kids twice his size at the age of four and never did he need anyone's help."

Rob was about to launch at his father himself. Fortunately, Emma's entrance music began to play and she made her entrance into the arena. She waved and hit several hands on her way down the ramp, but she seemed to be in a hurry to get into the ring to dispel what Big Bobby had spewed.

With her own mic in hand, Emma entered the ring.

"We're so happy you're here tonight, Mr. Breyer." Emma smiled, but she was definitely pissed off. "And while we are happy you are here, we will not let you upset this match. These tag teams have worked hard to move on to this round and I will not allow you to physically or mentally disrupt this match."

"Hang tight, little lady. You didn't give me a chance to finish." Big Bobby winked at Rob and continued. "What I was going to say was I never imagined this partnership. After seeing for myself how well these two work together, I can't see those belts anywhere but around their waists after Breaking Rules."

A collective sigh was released from Emma, Rob, and Chance and the crowd went wild.

"Now, let's get this match over with so these boys can start training for a real match." Big Bobby turned and stared down the opponents, The Patton Boys.

Big Bobby extended his elbow to Emma to escort her out of the ring. She accepted with a somewhat shocked expression fixed on her face. The two donned headsets at the announcers' table to help commentate the match.

Chance stripped off his tee shirt and launched it into the crowd and smacked Rob on the back to get him to do the same.

Rob ripped his off and did his signature muscle ripple which excited the crowd.

Chance grabbed Rob behind the neck and put their foreheads together.

"I think that was your old man's way of saying he's proud of you. Now, let's do what we were born to and win this fucking match."

"You bet, brother." Rob moved back a bit and they bumped foreheads. Chance left the ring and the bell rang. "Showtime!"

"Done. Only twelve stitches this time." Dr. Marino snapped off his surgical gloves.

Rob laughed and rubbed the dried blood from his forehead. He sat up on the exam table to face Dr. Marino.

"Next time, let me know of any pre-existing head wounds before you go in the ring." The doctor crossed his arms in front of his chest and glared at Rob.

"Sorry. It was a little cut over two days ago. Smacked my head on a coffee table." He laughed again and shook his head. If Charlotte found out about this, she'd feel horrible. He'd need to give Harry a call and make sure she was okay.

"Will he live, Dr. Marino?"

Rob turned to see Emma enter the room with Al and Ben behind her.

"For now, but if he goes out into the ring with so much as a cat scratch, I'm kicking his ass."

"We do want to keep Mr. Breyer healthy." He sensed she wanted to reach out and touch him, but she held back.

"I'll keep track of all my nicks, I promise." The cut was almost healed. A kick to the head and a hit on the bare turnbuckle bust the tiny sliver wide open.

"You better." Dr. Marino put his hand on Rob's shoulder. "You are taking a few days off. You are off the roster until Kansas City."

"A whole week? How am I supposed to prepare for the final round?"

"Mentally, my boy." Dr. Marino left the room with arrogance, ticking Rob off.

"A whole week?" Rob asked.

"Better safe than sorry. Why don't you stay here for a couple of days, spend some time with your parents."

God, how he loved her. His palms itched to touch her. Later.

"We can take in a game at Wrigley Field. Go to the Brookfield Zoo. Oh, oh! We can go to Legoland!"

"Legoland?" Emma pouted.

"What if I promise to get you something?" He raised his brow in question.

"I have a lot of Legos. I don't know if you could find something I don't already have."

A challenge. He rubbed his hands together. "Oh, I bet I can find something."

Emma shook her head. "My collection is quite extensive. I even have my own Millennium Falcon. Charlotte and I put together the last time she visited me in LA."

"I'll get creative, but I think I can come up with something worthy. It's the least I can do for my new boss." He winked at her and she countered the gesture with an eye roll.

"Since you're not in any real danger, I've got work to do. See you back in Boston."

"Yes, I'll be back by Thursday. I have dinner plans." The dinner at her grandmother's house wasn't something he would miss. He'd dreamed about the home-cooked meal since the second Annie offered a standing invitation.

"So I heard." Her eyes twinkled while she smirked. "Have a safe trip and enjoy some time with your parents."

"I will."

Emma left the room, but Al and Ben stayed behind to give him a thumbs up before they left.

He lay back on the table and detected the throb of his scalp for the first time.

"Oh, thank God!" Lisa Breyer rushed to Rob's side with her husband close behind.

"Mom, I'm fine. You saw dad in much worse condition."

Lisa parted Rob's hair, unintentionally causing more harm than good. "Not too bad."

"The bare turnbuckle? I can't believe they haven't figured out a way to secure those things better." Robert Senior seemed more pissed than worried.

"Yeah, but I had a little cut I thought had healed. The turnbuckle busted it open again." Rob reached for the bottle of pain medication along with a bottle of water. He took two pills with a swig of water. "Good news is they are giving me a couple days off. If you can make arrangements, would you guys like to stay for a few extra days? I need to be back in Boston on Thursday, but I figured we can spend a few days here seeing the sights."

Tears ran down his mother's cheeks. "This is the best birthday present ever." Lisa hugged Rob tight.

Rob peered over his mother's shoulder to see his father's smile. Robert Senior mouthed "Thank you" which Rob responded with a smile and held on to his mother even tighter.

"This is the one," Rob told his mother as he picked up the

gift from the shelf.

"I never saw Emma as a Lego kind of gal. Are you sure she'll like this?"

He turned to his mother in the middle of the Chicago Legoland gift shop. "You have no idea how perfect this is. When I told her I was thinking of coming here, she actually pouted. When she lived in California, she would go to Legoland every chance she could."

"I like her." Lisa linked her arm through his and led him down the aisle.

"I do too. She's the one, Mom."

"I had a feeling." Lisa squeezed his arm and turned them down the aisle featuring all the IWA themed Legos.

"Robert!" Lisa hollered for her husband.

He turned the corner and caught up with them. "Wow. I didn't realize they had this much stuff."

"This is kind of cool." Rob looked at a large set with a wrestling ring and several minifigures, including him. "I don't have this one. I'm getting it." Rob took the box off the shelf and held it with Emma's gift.

"Hand me your phone," Lisa urged.

"What?"

"I want to take a picture and you can put it on insta whatever."

"Instagram?"

"Yes. What a silly name." Lisa held out her hand.

Rob handed over his phone and discovered his father trying to hold back his laughter. He handed Emma's present to his dad and held the ring set in front of him. Lisa snapped a few pictures of Rob and pulled Robert Senior into the picture.

"Okay, enough."

Lisa handed Rob back his phone and he scrolled through the pictures. He sent one off to Emma and told her she would be with him the next time he went Lego shopping.

She responded a few minutes later to tell him to name the date and she'd be there.

25

Emma laughed at the picture Rob sent her surrounded by Legos. At first, she never thought she would have anyone to share the nerdy part of herself with. God, how wrong she'd been. She was almost a little giddy at the thought of setting up her nerd cave in a new home. The things she would show him.

She shoved her phone into her bag and retrieved her keys.

"Dad?" she yelled after she entered the house. She dumped her bag and flipped off her shoes in the entryway. A loud round of laughter drifted toward her from the back deck. The cars in the street were her first clue to their visitors. Once on the deck, all was confirmed. It was poker night at the MacLean household.

"Hey, Dad." Emma kissed her father on the cheek

and surveyed the table.

"Good day, Princess?" he asked, never taking his eyes off his cards.

She placed her hands on Mick's shoulders and kneaded his tense muscles. "Not bad. I'm working on my first acquisition. I think this guy is going to be amazing. We're meeting for lunch on Friday."

"Good. Good." It came time for Mick to show his hand. "Read 'em and weep boys!"

"Royal flush?" Mayor Rudy Babcock whined. "You sure you aren't counting cards, Mick?"

"He better not be!" City Councilman, Bart Weathers, piped up. "Last time he did, he got a black eye and fat lip out of the deal."

The men groaned at what Emma assumed was a painful memory of one of their weekly game nights.

"I'm here tonight, so there is no cheating allowed. Unless you want to spend a night in lockup," Chief of Police, Jeremy Simmons, added.

"Hell no!" Harry exclaimed.

Emma laughed at the memory of her walking into the police station at the age of sixteen to find Harry in a holding cell. He only got brought in for being out on the beach after hours, but those few hours in a cell were enough to last a lifetime.

"You boys have fun. I'm wiped." Emma patted her father's shoulders to let him know she was done.

"Thanks. There is some mail on the counter for you." He was already dealing out cards for the next hand.

Emma poured a glass of club soda then set out to sort through the huge stack of mail on the counter.

"Bill. Junk. Junk. Junk." She flipped through one

envelope after another until her fingers felt the familiar rough envelope with her only her name scrawled across the front.

She didn't even notice she had dropped her glass on the kitchen floor until pain shot through her foot.

"Em, what—" Harry froze.

Emma's eye filled with tears when the glass pierced her foot, but she couldn't take her eyes off the envelope. She felt Harry come up behind her and help her into a nearby chair, yet her focus never wavered.

"What is it?" he asked.

She couldn't form the words. Every time she opened a threatening letter was just like the first time. The fear, the nausea, and the pain were all present even after so many years.

The envelope moved and she blinked once to clear the tears from her eyes. Harry tore it open before she could squeak out her protest.

"No," she cried in a hoarse sob.

"What the fuck is this?" Harry yelled.

Emma braced her hands over her ears while Harry yelled for her father. They would know now. She couldn't keep it a secret any longer.

"Oh my God," Mick whispered.

Emma slid her hands to her lap and raised her gaze to the papers trembling in her father's hand.

"Sh—" She cleared her throat to regain some volume in her voice. "Show them to me."

Harry and Mick exchanged looks. After a moment of silent staring, Mick handed it over.

Emma read the horrible words she knew would be there.

You fucking bitch! You had me fooled. All these years I thought you were keeping your promise. Now I find out your lying whore mouth continued to suck Derek's cock for years after our night together. You'll pay for breaking your promise. Maybe next time I'll sink my teeth into that juicy ass of yours before I wrap my hands around your neck to squeeze the life out of you.

She slid the letter to the side to reveal the photo. It was a picture of her tied to a chair with bloody bites marks visible on her breasts.

"I think I'm gonna be sick," Emma whispered. She clasped her hand over her mouth and held the papers out for her father to take.

Blood dripped onto the kitchen floor from the gash in her foot. She couldn't seem to care while the visualization of her tormentor's vile words filled her mind.

"Emma?" Mick squatted down in front of her. "Is this from the person who attacked you?" She closed her eyes and nodded. "Did you get letters like this before?"

She nodded again. "And pictures. Um, Harry? Can you get the wooden box on the top left shelf of my closet?"

"Sure." Harry walked out of the kitchen.

Mick wrapped a towel around her foot and applied pressure.

"Why didn't you tell me?"

The tears in her father's eyes broke her a little more. "At first, I was so scared he would come back. Then after I moved to California, he started threatening to hurt the family, even Annie, Nell, and the kids. I didn't know what to do."

Emma gathered Mick in her arms and held him while he cried on the kitchen floor.

Harry slipped in and placed the box on the counter.

Emma looked up to Harry. "They're all in there. Envelopes, letters, pictures, along with the dates and times I opened them. The last two are the only letters delivered by hand. The rest all came through the mail."

Harry opened the box and flipped through the folders. "Em, there is more than a hundred letters here."

"I know."

"We need to get Simmons in on this," Harry insisted.

Mick nodded in agreement. He slipped his finger under Emma's chin and brought her gaze to meet his own. "This guy isn't going to stop. We need to catch him."

Mick cleared out his poker buddies except Chief Simmons with promises of a fishing trip on his boat in a couple weeks. The Chief settled at the kitchen table with Emma, Mick, Harry, and the box of letters.

"We will start with fingerprinting and see if we get lucky with that. Yours are on file?"

Emma nodded. "They took a set after the attack. I never asked why."

The days following the attack were still blurry for Emma. She remembered a female officer and the sight of ink on her fingers but not a word of what the woman said to her.

"I never officially closed the case so I've always kept the files close to me." The Chief shook his head.

Emma did remember when Chief Simmons was the

Head of Detectives for the MPD and took on her case personally. He promised Emma he would get the little bastards and now Emma thought maybe she'd given him the evidence to keep his promise.

"Is there anything else you remember about that day?" he asked and took her hand.

"Just flashes. What scares me most is nobody knew about Derek and I until I said something the other day to Maria DeFazio. I guess I should say McInerney now." Emma still couldn't fathom Maria infiltrating one of the best families in town.

"We checked back then, she has a solid alibi. She and Derek were in the same class taking a test when you were found. Before that, she and her parents were in the principal's office most of the morning."

The four sat with matching expressions of frustration on their faces when Emma's phone rang.

She walked out to the entryway to retrieve it from her purse and answered it in time.

"Hey," she answered.

"Hey. You sound off. Everything okay?" Rob asked.

"I got another letter today." She tried to calm herself by tipping her head back and taking a deep breath.

"Shit! What did it say?"

"Doesn't matter." She sniffled and composed herself as much as possible. "Chief Simmons happened to be here with Dad for poker night. I gave him all the letters. They're going to get started right away."

"Oh, baby. It's for the best. They are going to get this guy."

So many people had uttered the same words, but she'd never believed them until they came from Rob.

26

Rob's flight had been delayed so he didn't get in until Thursday evening. He took a cab from the airport to Moira's house, which was conveniently only a few blocks away from Mick's house.

Annie opened the door before he got the chance to knock. "So glad you could come." She pulled him through the door with a hug.

The door shut behind him and he noticed Charlotte standing there.

"Do you like German chocolate cake?" Charlotte asked him.

"One of my favorites." He smiled and put his bags down beside the door.

"Mom and me made one for you to say sorry about your head."

Rob squatted down a bit and placed his hand on her

shoulder. "I already told you when I called it was no big deal. It doesn't even hurt anymore. Plus I got a few days off to spend with my mom on her birthday. Everything worked out."

"Come on, we need to eat dinner before we can think about cake." Annie pulled him into the kitchen.

An aroma he hadn't smelled in years filled his nostrils. "Oh, God," he moaned and took another whiff.

Moira came over and gave his cheek a pat. "I couldn't have your first meal with us be meatloaf. I do have standards."

"But this?" His gaze landed on the stove and surrounding countertop to find an authentic Irish meal. Corned beef, cabbage, potatoes, carrots, and some sort of rolls were ready to be gobbled up. "I'm going to be spending extra hours in the gym, but I don't mind."

"I like a boy with a healthy appetite. Annie, get him a drink while we wait for Emma to get here."

Rob checked his phone. "She's on her way. No cameras."

"Good. Nell's here and they make her uncomfortable."

Rob realized he hadn't met Annie's twin yet. He'd seen pictures, but they hadn't been introduced.

"Is Emma here?" Nell rushed into the kitchen with an open laptop.

"Not yet," Annie replied. "This is Rob. Rob, this is my sister, Nell."

Nell's cheeks reddened, but she put down the laptop and extended her hand. "Nice to meet you."

"You too." Rob shook her hand and compared the twins side by side.

Emma said they were identical twins. Both stood at the same height, had long, shiny red hair, big green eyes, button noses, and heart shaped lips. Annie seemed to be a slimmed down version of Nell. Both women gorgeous, but he thought Nell edged a little ahead of her sister with her lush curves.

Nell grabbed the laptop and turned the screen. "Emma's real estate agent sent me this listing. The house isn't even on the market, but she thought it would be perfect. I want to see if Emma has time to go look at it tomorrow. They are going to list it as a short sale on Monday, but if we can get it, we can close pretty quickly. We'll never find anything this good at this price."

Rob read through the specs of the house. It was four bedrooms, three and a half baths, a den, two-car garage, and a finished basement on a quarter acre for less than $600,000. He was sure Emma could afford much more, but why spend the money if you don't have to.

"This is amazing!" Annie jumped up and down with excitement.

Rob flipped through the interior pictures with the sisters and he had to agree. He saw Emma in the yellow house. He saw himself there. The yard was big enough for a dog to run around, maybe even a few kids. A house was something she could invest in for the future.

He pulled his lips up into a small smile. "Perfect."

"What's perfect?" Emma asked as she entered the kitchen.

"I found us a house," Nell stated with confidence.

Emma went to check the listing on the laptop.

Nell began to point things out and explain the situation. "And here's the den, a perfect office for you."

"The nerd cave can come out of the boxes," Mick added while he peeked over Emma's shoulder.

Emma smiled and Rob wrapped his arm around her waist. "What do you think?" he asked.

"You're right. I think this is the house for us. Thanks, Nell."

"Can you get away for a viewing tomorrow?" Nell questioned while she dialed the relator's number into her phone.

"After one. I have an early lunch meeting at eleven. I'm hoping to sign my first wrestler tomorrow," Emma beamed.

"This is a story I need to hear, but not without food." Rob's stomach growled. "See what I mean? What do we need to do to get this party started?"

Rob hadn't felt so full in years. The last time was when he went down to Atlanta to visit Chance's family. Mrs. Robicheaux stuffed him to the gills with down home, Southern cooking. Moira MacLean's meal was different, but every morsel was just as good.

"Did you save room for cake?" Charlotte asked Rob.

"A small piece, Miss Charlotte." He smiled at her and watched her whole face light up.

Charlotte got up from the table and scampered off to the kitchen.

"You've made her day," Annie commented. "You can't imagine how horrible she felt when she watched your match the other night."

"I'm always down for a piece of cake." Rob rubbed his stomach.

"You won't be disappointed." Emma threaded her

fingers through his underneath the table. "Charlotte wants to be a famous dessert chef or own a bakery. I think she's watched every episode of *Cake Boss* twenty times."

Charlotte came in with the most decadent piece of cake he had ever seen. One bite and he was sold. He was ready to help them set up a college fund to send her to the best culinary school.

The conversation continued around him as he devoured the cake.

"Kieran Finley."

The name brought him out of his chocolate haze. "What about him?"

"I'm meeting with him tomorrow. If all goes well, I'm hoping to get him to sign with us once his current contract is up."

Rob remembered Kieran. He had seen him fight a few of the former IWA wrestlers who were now working other circuits. He was good, young, but good. Rob understood their interest in him.

"I've seen a few of his matches online. He's pretty young." At only twenty-two, the kid still had some growing up to do.

"I thought about his age, but Kenny was only nineteen when he started. Kieran has way more talent than he does."

Rob nodded in agreement. Kenny Turgen had been around a bit longer than Rob but was still four years younger.

"Make him a good offer. He'd be a big asset," Rob assured her.

"I do have an inkling of what I'm doing, Mr. Breyer. Talent is something I have a skilled eye for." With a wink,

Emma took a bite of cake. She gave Rob every assurance she knew exactly what she was doing.

Emma took Rob back to her father's house after their monster dinner. Once they walked into her room, Rob shut the door behind them and placed his bag on the floor.

Emma ran her fingertip across the buttons of Rob's shirt. "I think I remember a little promise of a gift."

"I seem to remember the promise." He kissed the side of her neck, his two-day scruff rubbed beneath her ear.

"Ahhhhh, almost as nice as a new Lego set."

"Almost?"

She slid her arms around his neck and gave him a soft kiss. Her lips hovered a few centimeters in front of his as she spoke. "I do like Legos."

Rob pushed her back and watched her laugh at his expense. "At this rate, you're not getting anything."

"Come on, please. I'll be good." She sat down on the bed with a bounce.

He shook his head with a laugh and went to his bag to retrieve her gift.

"Now. . ." He balanced the wrapped box between his two hands and observed her excited anticipation. "I've got a lot of pressure on me at the moment. This is the first gift I'm giving you as your better half."

Emma rolled her eyes. "Come one, please. I had to be good all through dinner. I don't think I can wait any longer."

"Yes, you're right. You were a good girl. Remember, I will be giving you many more gifts and if I screw this one up, I've got several ideas for makeup presents." He handed over the gift and sat next to her on the bed.

She ripped into the package and saw the picture on the outside of the box. Her breath caught in her throat. "Really?"

"Yes. Do you like it?"

"Like it?" She cupped his cheek and brought his lips close to hers. "I love it." She placed several soft kisses on his lips and cheeks before she returned to open the box.

"Is blue okay?"

Emma took the blue Lego block alarm clock out of the box. "This is pretty perfect. My bedding is several shades of blue so it will fit right in. I can't wait to find a place of my own. I'm not materialistic or anything, but I miss sleeping in my own bed with my Egyptian cotton sheets."

"I can't wait to feel those sheets." Rob wrapped his arm around her waist and kissed her shoulder.

"The house we see tomorrow could be the one."

"I hope so because this talk of sheets has me hankering to get you between some." He nipped at the skin above her collarbone with his teeth.

"Soon."

27

After the huge family dinner, Emma was still stuffed the next day heading into her lunch meeting at Dooley's Irish Pub.

"Welcome, Miss MacLean," the barman called from the end of the bar. "Kieran be helpin' gettin' the meal together. Not often we get 'em in the kitchen."

"What's on the menu?" Emma took a seat on a bar stool and set down her bag on the bar. Al and Ben began to set up at the end of the bar.

"Lamb. Best thing you'll ever taste," he boasted.

"I am a MacLean, after all. Just because I don't have the accent doesn't mean I don't know a thing or two about the best recipes to ever come out of Ireland."

"Well, well." He sat a pint of dark liquid with a thick head on top in front of her. "Got a fiery lass here."

She picked up her pint and tipped the cool glass

toward him before taking a sip. The bubbles warmed her, flowed down her throat and settled in her stomach.

"God, so good." She smiled at her new favorite barman and set the pint down.

"Best in Boston."

Emma turned to find Kieran Finley walking out of the kitchen with a dish towel thrown over his shoulder.

"And you're the connoisseur, Mr. Finley?"

"I've tried a nip about every pint they serve in the place. This one here's the best." The barman set another glass on the bar, but with much less of the heavenly drink. "Don't drink much of the stuff meself, but a nip here and there never hurt none."

Emma felt at complete ease with the young Irishman. His accent flowed off his tongue with a sweet edge. The heavenly inflections only complemented his six foot four frame of solid muscle. The dark brown, almost black hair made his green eyes pop. The camera would love him and the fans would go crazy for him.

"Let's get down to business, shall we?"

Kieran led her to a table with both their drinks in hand. Al and Ben followed setting the camera up only a few feet from their table. Their food was brought a few moments later. They ate and drank and talked for only an hour, but the man was definitely IWA material.

"Can you spend a day in our training facility with some of our guys?"

"Name the day and I'll be there." He switched from laidback to eager and excited in an instant.

"How about tomorrow?" she asked and saw his eyes light up.

"On my list." He tapped his temple and smiled.

"I have a good feeling about you, Finley. Don't make me regret it."

Kieran shook her hand. "You've got my word. I won't be makin' you sorry, Miss MacLean."

Emma walked out with a feeling like she'd taken another step in the right direction. Kieran Finley was exactly what the IWA needed to shake them up a bit.

The moment Rob walked into the house Emma and Nell were thinking of buying, he felt at home.

The first floor was one big space. The kitchen, dining, and living rooms were all together. He imagined the huge family dinners in the dining room. The room was big enough for a table to seat sixteen.

Emma and Nell held onto each other and walked from one room to another with tears in their eyes. He saw both of them fall more in love with the house with each step they took.

"Well? You think you want to make an offer?" the realtor, he'd learned was named Gina Lombard, asked.

"When can we get an inspection done?" Emma asked.

"If I get the offer to the buyer today, I can call in a favor and get an inspector out here tomorrow." Gina was all smiles, as she should be. The inspection didn't matter; Emma would do whatever needed to be done to live in the house.

Emma turned to Rob. "I didn't ask what you thought."

He took her hand and pulled her away from Nell and Gina.

"You know what I see when I look at this house?"

She shook her head. "You making dinner in the kitchen with Annie and Nell while Charlotte frosts one of her cakes for our dessert. Over there." He pointed to the empty living room. "I see a big, comfy couch we can all lounge on for movie nights with popcorn fights. And out there." He pointed out the back window at the large back yard. "I see barbecues and birthday parties and a tire swing. I see a tree house and campouts and making some memories that will last forever."

"You do?"

"We might not be there yet, but we will be and I think this is the house where we all can be happy. Look at Nell." Emma turned to see Nell with stars in her eyes. "This can be a real family house. MacLeans, De Lacys, and even maybe a Breyer or two."

She grabbed him by the back of the neck and brought his lips down to hers. He responded with everything he had in him, knowing this kiss would be the first of millions they would share under her roof.

Nell's laugh carried over to the two and broke them apart.

Emma touched her lips and turned to Gina. "You got a pen?"

28

After the high of the weekend with the house inspection going so well, her offer accepted, and signing her first wrestler to a contract, Emma hadn't expected a low Monday night in Kansas City.

"How bad is it?" Peaches winced when the doctor prodded her knee for the hundredth time since she and Cherry left the ring.

Dr. Sorenson hated to give bad news, but by furrowed brow and sorrowful eyes, Emma surmised it wasn't good.

"You'll need an MRI, but I fear your ligament is torn."

Emma saw the tears well in Peaches' eyes. Months of rehab and an uncertain future were not what Emma saw for the talented woman who moments after her injury secured a Bombshell tag team title shot.

"What can we do, Emma?" Cherry asked at her tag team partner's side. "I can't fight for the titles by myself, can I?"

"You ladies have two options?"

Emma turned to see Aaron enter the room with a small smile on his face.

This is bad. Very, very bad.

"Only two, Mr. President?" Emma scoffed.

Aaron expression told Emma he was not amused.

"I will leave it up to you ladies, but I'd like you to hear my options." Aaron waited for a response and Emma nodded for him to continue. "You can forfeit the match and The Ramona's will get the title shot." Cherry stood to object, but Aaron lifted his hand to halt her. "Or." Cherry sat and crossed her arms. "You can choose another partner."

Emma rolled her eyes. She went through a mental list of whom Cherry had to choose from. The Bombshell division wasn't as big as the men's, so the ladies who weren't involved in matches or a natural enemy of Peaches and Cherry were few. She glanced up to Aaron and to find him staring at her. She turned her gaze toward Peaches, then Cherry and saw both the ladies were staring at her, too.

"No." Emma stepped back toward the door. "No. No. No. No. No. No way."

"You're ready. We've been working so hard," Cherry pleaded.

Emma felt her heart beat hard against her breastbone. She couldn't get enough air in her lungs, which might be causing the black spots blurring her vision.

"Whoa, girl. Don't freak out." Cherry grabbed Emma's hand and led her to sit in a chair next to Peaches.

Aaron handed her a bottle of water and she sipped at the cool drink while she tried to calm down.

"Hey." Peaches grabbed Emma's hand. "You can do this. Betty and Wendy won't know what hit them."

Emma attempted to let the idea sink in. Harry would be ecstatic and a little jealous. Her father would worry. Rob would be supportive. He might even help her out. She'd worked well with Lazlo and he kept telling her what a natural talent she was. She could almost hear Bill Bell's voice telling her to get her ass in the ring and give it all she had.

Every face in the room smiled with encouragement. Emma turned to Al and Ben and saw both of them nod to her. They sealed it. Those two had showed her the footage they had taken during her training sessions and pointed out all her best efforts. They had complete faith in her. With their approval, Aaron's suggestion, and pleas from Cherry and Peaches, she had no choice.

"I'll do it."

Cherry jumped on Emma's lap and hugged her tight. "You won't regret this. I've got your back. We will work our asses off this week. There will be no way we can lose."

"We can go out and make the announcement in a few minutes. The men's tag team match should be over soon."

"We'll need to go back to Boston tonight. I want to get started as soon as possible." Emma also didn't want to give herself any time to think about backing out. The sooner she started, the sooner she would convince herself she could actually fight live in front of forty thousand fans.

Rob and Chance entered the backstage area to find several of their fellow wrestlers ready to congratulate them. The only person Rob wanted a glimpse of at the moment was Emma.

After a few moments, he caught sight of Emma with Aaron. She wrung her hands together and nodded to Aaron when she spoke.

Al and Ben were there to catch every moment, but Rob decided he would take the risk. He grabbed Chance by the arm and pulled him over to Aaron and Emma with him.

"Congratulations, gentlemen," Aaron offered with a pat on Rob's back. "I didn't get to catch the end of the match, but I heard it was a fantastic victory."

Chance smacked Rob's bare chest. "This one got Vinnie on the ropes then jumped and pushed him back with both feet on his chest. When Vinnie bounces back, Bobby grabs Vinnie in a headlock and slams him to the mat. Easy three count."

"Ah, the old Diamond Cutter gets 'em every time." Aaron shook his hand. "We'll have more time to talk later, but Miss McLean and I have an announcement to make."

Rob gazed into Emma's eyes and saw turmoil there. He tried to silently communicate with her his worry but didn't get a chance. A few seconds later, she and Aaron were on their way out to the ring.

"What's going on?" Chance asked.

"I don't know, but I'm sure as hell going to find out."

Aaron's music played as the two of them made their way to the ring. Emma's mask slipped into place and the corners of her mouth lifted into a smile.

Just get through today.

Her motto ran on a loop in her mind the entire walk to the ring. When the two of them were in the ring with microphones in hand, the butterflies in her stomach seemed to turn into vicious bees stinging her in a constant steady stream.

"Only one match left tonight, but we wanted to address what happened earlier tonight in the Bombshell's tag team match," Aaron said and nodded for Emma to continue.

"Unfortunately, the injury Peaches sustained at the end of her match will keep her from competing in the Bombshell Tag Team title match with Cherry on Sunday." Emma heard the sound of the fan's hearts breaking.

"I gave Cherry and Peaches two options," Aaron announced.

"To forfeit the match and letting The Ramona's fight instead," Emma said. The crowd booed and screamed in protest.

"Or," Aaron spoke up. "Cherry could choose another partner."

A collective hush settled over the crowd when Aaron stretched his pause out for several seconds.

"Cherry has informed me of her choice and her new partner has agreed to participate in the match."

This was it. Emma felt like she would throw up any second. She swallowed hard and kept the false smile on her face.

"Ladies and gentlemen, making her in ring debut this Sunday night at Breaking Rules with Cherry in the Bombshell Tag Team Championship match is our own . . . Emma MacLean."

The sound of thousands of gasps hit Emma's ears before an uproar of applause soared through the arena. The crowd's instant support took a large weight off Emma's shoulders.

The rest of the segment was a blur, but she arrived backstage with the crowd's continued praise. The awaiting chair held her weight as she collapsed when she stepped into the backstage area.

Someone thrust a bottle of water into her hand and sat down beside her.

"We can do this Emma," Cherry whispered and took Emma's hand in her own. "We'll get started tomorrow. I've got faith in you."

"You're right. No problem. We can do this." Emma twisted the cap off the bottle and took a swig of the cool water.

She almost spit when she saw Betty and Wendy approach them.

"Just because you're the boss, don't mean we're gonna go easy on you," Betty uttered with obvious disgust.

Emma stood and looked Betty straight in the eye. "I wouldn't expect anything less."

"So we got it all straight. When you go down on Sunday, no hard feelings." Betty pasted a wicked grin on her face.

"Let the best Bombshell win." Emma kept eye contact with Betty and prayed her confidence wouldn't slip again.

Wendy pulled Betty back after a moment and Cherry put her arm around Emma. The pair walked to Emma's dressing room and away from the cameras.

"What's going on?"

Both Emma and Cherry were surprised to see Rob in Emma's dressing room.

"I'm fighting on Sunday. Aaron wanted me in the ring eventually, but Peaches' injury sped up the timetable." Emma's voice wavered a bit, but she kept her composure.

"I wouldn't have asked her if I didn't think she could do it." Cherry shot Rob a glare.

"Oh, I know she can," Rob exclaimed.

"You do?" Emma and Cherry asked at the same time.

"I've seen you. I know you're ready, but do you?" Rob lifted one eyebrow with his question.

Emma took a moment to absorb everything. Rob supported her. Cherry was sure they'd win. Bill told her years ago she was born to be in the ring. Aaron was behind the whole mess a hundred percent. Most of all, the fans seemed excited to see her in action.

She closed her eyes and took a deep cleansing breath. "I can do this."

"That's my girl." Rob grabbed her behind the neck and brought her into a ferocious kiss, taking away her cleansing breath in an instant.

"I knew it!" Cherry shouted and clapped.

Emma pulled back and placed her forehead on Rob's bare shoulder, her hand on his sweaty hip. "You're in so much trouble."

"I don't care. I'll make it up to you later." Rob pressed a kiss into her hair and pulled her into his arms.

Cherry shook her head. "I can't wait to see how this is gonna play out."

"Me too." Emma kissed the side of Rob's neck and squeezed him tighter.

29

"They can't go in." Aaron's assistant pointed to Al and Ben.

Emma turned away from Aaron's office door and studied the woman's expression. She seemed a tad terrified, but she didn't appear to be backing down.

"Mr. Russell said that any issues discussing private company policy were not to be filmed," the woman said with as much confidence she could muster.

Emma let her sweat for a few additional seconds before nodding and removing her mic pack. She handed it off to the guys and entered Aaron's office.

"What's this all about?" Emma questioned and shut the door. It was then she found a furious Rob seated on the couch.

"Thank you for joining us, Miss MacLean. Please sit." Aaron pointed to the couch where Rob sat.

Confused about what the three of them needed to speak about she hesitated, but when Aaron lifted his brow at her slight defiance, she sat next to Rob.

"As you both know, it is company policy for all wrestlers to provide a urine sample after they are out with an injury."

Emma held up her hand to interrupt. "If this is about Rob, he gave a sample and I watched while the tech did the initial test. Everything was negative."

"Yes, the initial test was, but after further testing, Mr. Breyer's sample came back positive for Methamphetamine."

"And it's complete and utter fucking bullshit!" Rob raged. He jumped up and paced while pulling at his hair with one hand.

Emma lost her voice at the sound of Rob's anger. She felt like she was in a parallel universe or something. Why in the world would Rob abuse drugs after being nine years sober? The answer was crystal clear to her. He wouldn't.

Emma's hands shook, but she tried to keep her voice even. "This has to be a mistake. Rob wouldn't touch meth or anything like it."

"Oh, he knows that." Rob turned back to point at Aaron. "Doesn't mean that he's not suspending me until further testing can be done."

"What? No!" Emma stood in outrage herself. "He and Chance have to fight at Breaking Rules."

"Emma, it is per company policy. You know it. The bright side of this is Rob had a random drug test less than thirty days ago and it was clean. Plus, he has never had a positive test before. I think something is going on here, but until we get additional testing done, my hands are tied." The wrinkle in Aaron's usually smooth brow conveyed his worry over the ordeal.

"Take my blood, hair, spit. Hell, I'll even jizz in a cup if you want me to. Jesus Christ!" Rob groaned and dropped down on the couch.

"I don't think that will be necessary. I will take you to a different lab. I've already contacted the director and I'm assured she will oversee the testing personally." Emma sensed there was something Aaron wasn't saying.

"What else?"

Aaron turned to meet her stare and she gave her own brow lift. Her assistant in LA had dubbed it as her don't-fuck-with-me look.

"Per policy, Rob is not allowed to have contact with anyone in the company until I inform him of the results."

Emma felt like she had been kicked in the chest. She knew what that meant and so did the men in the room. No contact between Emma and Rob.

"How long?" Emma said without thinking.

"Forty-eight hours," Aaron responded without pause.

Emma sank down and sat on the edge of the couch. Two days? It wasn't much time. They went twelve years, but that was before. Now, more than two waking hours without him seemed like an eternity. Two days would place them at Thursday. With a negative result, there would be plenty of time to get Rob to LA for Breaking Rules.

"I'll give you a few minutes and then I'll go with Rob to the lab."

Emma felt her head nodding but didn't notice Aaron slipping from the room.

"This is bullshit, just like you said. I hate it, but Aaron's right about the policy."

Rob threaded his fingers through her hair and brought her lips to his. The kiss started off rough, tongues thrusting and chests pressing hard against each other. Then Rob tapered off to slow and sensual kisses, the kind that made her thighs warm and her bra too tight.

His lips smiled against hers. He pulled back and caught her gaze. "When they have taken all my bodily fluids and everything comes up negative, I will reward your faith in me."

A quiver of her Kegel muscles told her she would be using them a lot more once those test results came in.

30

Kick.

Jab.

Punch.

Slap.

Pull.

Push.

Bounce.

Jump.

Pin.

Over and over and over.

Emma's body had been pushed to the brink and beyond. Cherry was right there with her and Lazlo in an attempt to make every move perfect. For the first time in her adult life, Emma felt like she wouldn't need her mask anymore.

"Holy shit, girl! You should've joined up years ago." Cherry lay flat on the mat after Emma pinned her again.

Emma rolled off Cherry and let her ache soaked muscles rest for a bit.

"I was kind of busy."

Cherry let out a hardy laugh. "Yeah, jet-setting with a billionaire. Rough."

"The job wasn't a picnic. Millions of dollars at stake every day. One keystroke could kill an entire deal. The pressure at times was unbelievable."

Emma remembered one of her biggest deals where nine hundred and sixty million dollars was on the line. A few signatures on the dotted lines and the months of stress were over. Her commission was nothing to sniff at either.

"But you're loaded now, right?" Cherry pulled herself up to sit.

"I guess. I've never needed much, so I invested a lot so I can give back. The Nerdy Girl Nation is so important to me. I remember when I went to my mom to ask her to help me start the organization. Even though she had committee meetings and budgets to balance, she would still Skype me at two in the morning when I needed to bounce an idea off her."

"Sounds like a wonderful lady."

"She was." Emma grabbed the middle rope to help herself off the mat. "I think she's watching over me now."

Emma hoped she was. She wished her mother could be there to see what Rob meant to her life. Elaine McLean had told her daughter many times her worries of the future. She wondered if her mom put in a good word with the man upstairs to give Emma the happily ever after she'd dreamed of.

"I've got some work I've neglected to get done and we've got a plane to catch in the morning." The next day she would fly back to LA to begin the press for Breaking Rules. She had interviews scheduled, dinners to attend, and people to schmooze with before she made her in-ring debut on Sunday.

"Don't work too hard," Cherry chided.

"I won't."

Emma dismissed Al and Ben for the night. They hated filming her in the office, so she saw no reason for them to come with her. Plus, there was still no word from Aaron on Rob's test results. She really didn't want them to be there when they came in. If she didn't hear something soon, she'd take Aaron to the lab herself and make them wait for the results.

Kelly waved at Emma from her desk while she talked on the phone. Fielding another call about why Rob was MIA and not doing any press for Breaking Rules, no doubt. Emma waved back and went into her office.

Emma went into her private bathroom and changed into a pair of clean yoga pants and a tee shirt. The shower would wait until she finished her busy work.

Seven phone calls, thirteen emails, and ten signatures later, Emma was ready to call it a night. Her bag was packed for LA and she didn't feel like going to a family dinner without Rob, so she was working late to keep herself occupied.

Her cellphone rang with Aaron's ringtone while she shut down her laptop for the night.

"Finally." She swiped across the screen to answer. "Please tell me you got the results."

"Yes, negative across the board," Aaron replied.

"Something is not adding up here. We switched to Quincy Labs just after Curtis Sharp became GM. I just know he has a hand in this. On top of that, I received a request for the Beesons manager to accompany them during their match on Sunday."

"Sharp?"

"You guessed it."

Emma groaned and rubbed the ache at her temple. "What are we going to do about this?"

"I happen to have a brilliant idea."

She knew she would probably regret asking the question, but she went ahead anyway. "What do you have in mind?"

After a tense but productive brainstorming session with Aaron, a shower was the next thing on the agenda.

The spray of warm water was a balm to Emma's sore muscles. She stood under the steady stream until the heat became too much.

She towel dried her hair before she dressed and returned to her office, where she picked up her cell phone to find she missed a call from Rob.

"Shit." She hadn't expected that he and Aaron would be done with their call so soon.

He picked up after two rings. "Hey. I just got the good news from Aaron." Relief resounded in his voice.

"Do you think this plan of his will work?" Emma admitted it wouldn't be something she would've suggested, but it might be their best bet to keep Sharp on his toes.

"I think keeping me away from the fans and press will make my appearance that much sweeter. If Sharp is behind this, he'll have a coronary once I make my entrance."

"We'll call Chance and work everything out. We can't tell anyone about this. Just me, you, Aaron, and Chance will know the plan." She could just imagine the look on Sharp's face. The man was going down. Nobody would mess with her man and get away with it.

"I understand. Where are you?" he asked.

"I'm at the office. I thought I'd just work through the night. I've got security here, so I'm not worried. Damn, I've got to call Phil and tell him to pick me up here in the morning."

"Wait. You're working all night?"

"Yeah. I didn't feel like going to the family dinner without you."

"Where are Al and Ben?"

"I sent them back to the hotel."

"I think being in your office is a bad idea. I know the building has great security, but I have an excellent alternative. Miss McLean, would you like to stay the night at my place?"

"Your place?" His place. That meant privacy. That meant intimacy. Which she was sure meant sex. A flicker of hope shot through her.

"Yes, my place. We have forty-eight hours of catching up to do. I have food and a comfortable bed and me."

"My three favorite things. I'll catch a cab and be there in twenty."

"Just enough time to clean up. See you soon."

She hung up and ran back into the bathroom. A quick check to see she had shaved all the right places and smelled good enough. All good to go.

31

Rob said a little prayer of thanks that his housekeeper, Louisa, had been in the day before. He found his apartment spotless and he had several meals ready to heat up. Louisa took such good care of him. Without her, he would starve on the days he was home.

He slipped a pan of lasagna in the oven and set the timer.

His conversation with Aaron was short, but he had to admit, his idea was brilliant. To keep Sharp in the dark, they would continue to keep Rob's whereabouts a secret. Rob would accompany Emma in disguise as her new bodyguard until Breaking Rules. Once safely in the arena, he would hide out with Chance until it was time for their match. Hopefully, Rob's reappearance would amp up the crowd's support and help secure them a victory against the

Beesons.

Once he had dinner squared away, he walked into the bedroom. His bed was made and the room was free of dirty clothes. He'd spent the last two days at the gym in his building or compulsively cleaning his apartment. At that moment, he thanked Aaron for the time off to make a good impression on Emma.

The buzzer from the security desk rang and he went to answer.

"Mr. Breyer, there is a Miss MacLean here to see you? Should we send her up?"

"Yes, Jamison. And please add Miss MacLean to my list of approved visitors."

"Of course, Mr. Breyer. Goodnight."

Rob laughed at the sly tone of Jamison's voice when he uttered goodnight. "Goodnight, Jamison."

One last check of the apartment told him he had an unopened box of condoms in his bedside table drawer. They hadn't had the protection talk, but he was sure the topic would come soon.

The knock on the door startled Rob even though he had expected the sound. With each step he took toward the door, his nerves calmed. By the time he'd opened the door, he was ready for whatever the night would bring. He didn't expect what he saw before him.

"Emma?"

"I swear I'm not moving in or anything." She looked at the suitcase beside her feet. "It's my bag for LA."

"No. It's fine. Come in." He picked up her suitcase and ushered her in. "I'll put it in the bedroom. Dinner is almost ready."

"You cook?" she asked.

"I reheat." He opened the bedroom door. He set the bag inside next to his own and closed the door.

"I knew you had to be too good to be true." Emma took a deep breath to pull in the aroma of the room, he assumed. "Italian?"

"Lasagna. This won't be like your grandmother's, but Louisa's will come in a close second."

"Louisa?" She took a few tentative steps toward him.

"She takes care of my apartment, does some laundry, and leaves me some meals." Rob reached for Emma and took her hand in his. "I don't know what state I would be in if I didn't have her."

Emma looked around at what he considered a comfortable and welcoming apartment. The place felt like the first real home he had as an adult. Rob would never forget the day he walked into his building, met Jamison and the real estate agent and saw his place for the first time. He had never experienced the feeling of belonging before, not even in his parent's house. The moment he spent with Emma in her new home envisioning their future there brought on the same elation.

"Not too cluttered, but it shows some character." She nodded to the framed vintage *Star Wars* movie posters.

"Good character?" He moved his hands to her waist.

"Oh yes." She ran her hands across his chest and around his neck. "I like this." She ran her fingers through the two-day growth on his cheeks.

"You do?" He rubbed his cheek against hers and sensed her shiver. "I might just keep it then."

They both leaned in at the same moment and gave into the ever-present pull between them.

Rob's lips brushed Emma's once then again before he

felt her tongue swipe his lower lip. Before he could fathom what had happened, he found himself hovering over her while she lay on the couch.

"I've missed you," she whispered between kisses.

If the damn over timer hadn't gone off, their relationship would have hit the next level.

"Time to eat," she said with a labored breath.

"Yes, seems so." He pushed himself up but was surprised when she grabbed his face with both hands.

"A girl needs her strength for the long night ahead of her." She moved up and kissed him again before she released him.

The statement sent a shock straight to his already hard cock and he felt it shift in his jeans.

"The quicker we eat, the sooner we get to dessert." He took her hand, pulled her up into his arms and gave her a quick kiss. His mouth watered at the thought of what delicacies awaited him.

"I might steal Louisa away from you. This lasagna is fantastic." Emma took another bite and moaned.

"I'm perfectly willing to share her with you." Rob laughed at her enthusiasm.

"Another thing in a long list I'll need to think about as a homeowner. I had someone come to my apartment once a week back in LA, but the new house is much bigger, I don't think once a week would work." Emma took a sip of her water and sat back in her chair. "How long has Louisa worked for you?"

"Since I moved to Boston three years ago. She works for Chance too so she knows how to deal with our lot." Wrestlers weren't usually the most organized people on the planet.

"I've got a bit of time to find someone. We don't close for two more weeks, but Nell and I wanted to get some painting done before we move in."

"I thought you loved the house as is?" From the way she and Nell had reacted when they went through the house, he was surprised she wanted to change a thing.

"A few small rooms. The downstairs bathroom, Nell's bathroom, and my nerd cave."

"Your nerd cave?" He shook his head, not understanding what she meant.

Her cheeks tinted a bit pink. "My dad called my office back in LA my nerd cave. I never thought of it that way, but the name fits."

"And what wonders are there to behold in this nerd cave?" He leaned across the table and took her hand.

"Um, normal office stuff. Desk, computer, lamp."

"And?" He ran his fingertip over the lifeline on her palm.

"Some collectibles, framed prints, books."

He felt the rapid pulse at her wrist. "Will I get to see this nerd cave?" He leaned down and kissed the inside of her wrist.

"I suppose."

"You suppose? You'd share the room with your father, but not me?" He trailed kisses up her forearm to her elbow.

"As long as you don't make fun of me."

He pulled on her arm by her elbow and brought her into his lap. She squealed at the sudden movement and grasped his shoulders. He wrapped his arms around her waist and nuzzled her neck.

"Never." He kissed from behind her ear and along her jawline. He nipped at her chin and continued his journey along the other side of her jaw.

"I, um, have a lot of comics and toys I keep in there."

"Toys?" He pulled back and looked directly into her eyes.

She tweaked his earlobe. "Not those kind of toys."

"Do you have those kind of toys?" His brow rose with the question. He hoped so. A few items he thought of would be put to use often if she would be agreeable.

"Those are in the bedroom, naughty boy."

"I'd like to show you how naughty, but I want to find out what kind of toys you keep in your nerd cave, too." He now had a different image of Lego mini-figures and Iron Man cardboard cutouts displayed throughout the room.

"My favorites are my Thor collectibles," she said with a moan when he licked and nipped at her collarbone.

"Thor, hun? You like the muscles, do ya?"

"Yes, I have to say . . ." She found the hem of his shirt, pulled it up, and ran the back of her fingers up and down his happy trail. "I do."

He flexed his abs at her touch. "I'm glad I have a nice set."

"Well, you're no Chris Hemsworth. Since he's married, I guess you'll do."

"I'll do?"

She nodded with a sweet twinkle in her eye.

"I guess I need to show you how well I'll do." He stood and hauled her over his shoulder.

"Rob!" She smacked his ass and laughed.

"Hold on, woman." He opened the bedroom door and walked in. "What do I do with you now?" So many possibilities came to mind as he caressed her thigh with his palm.

"I remember a promise." Emma lifted the back of his shirt and ran her hand across his back. "You said something about your tongue loving me in a way no one ever had before."

"Did I?" He bit into her jean-covered thigh to suppress the groan he was dying to let out.

"You did." She moved her fingertips down to his waistband and thrust her hand between to grab his bare ass.

The groan flew out without his permission. He moved his hand up the back of her thigh and stroked between her legs.

"And about worshiping me in your bed. Ugh," she whimpered when he pressed his fingers against a sensitive spot.

Rob threw her down on the bed. She bounced and let out a glorious laugh. He smiled so wide his cheeks stung with the stretch.

"I will worship you. All night if you let me." He slipped off her shoes.

"We can sleep on the plane," she suggested.

Rob reached for the hem of his shirt and pulled it off. He put his knee on the bed between her legs.

She held up her hand and halted his movement. "Just one thing."

"What?"

"I'd like to keep my top on. I . . . I'm not . . ."

"Shhh." He moved forward and covered her body with his. "I understand." He gave her a soft kiss on the lips. "Is it okay if I touch you here?" His fingertips hovered over her breast.

"I'd be upset if you didn't."

He caressed the side of her breast while his mouth explored hers again. His breath mingled with hers, spicy and sweet. The anticipation of the moments ahead of them fell heavy in the room with each touch.

Emma pulled on one of the belt loops of Rob's jeans.

"You want these off?" he asked and kissed the valley between her breast over her shirt.

"It's the only part of you I've never seen. I've felt him enough to know he'll be happy to meet me."

She would be getting a new nickname talking like that. The cock whisperer.

"Very happy." He moved from the end of the bed and stood. He popped the button on his jeans and stopped.

"No, keep going."

"Tit for tat." He pointed to her waist and raised his eyebrow. If she got a show, he sure as hell would get one too.

She popped the button on her jeans and he tried not to drool when she lowered her zipper. He noticed her skin pink up in her cheeks and down to her chest.

She slid her jeans over her hips to reveal her panties with a red and white circular pattern.

Is that a star in the middle?

"Don't laugh," she admonished.

"I'm not." He grabbed the waistband on her jeans and pulled them down her legs.

She wore a tiny pair of boy shorts with the *Captain America* shield on the front.

"Holy fuck! How did you know?" He didn't think

he'd said anything.

"Know what?"

"*Captain America* is my favorite Marvel superhero. I even have the complete original series of comics." He caressed the shield with his fingertips and moved lower to the wetness between her legs.

She moaned and arched her back. "Don't talk about the Captain right now."

He moved the material to the side and slid his fingers between her soaked lips.

She shivered while he stroked her then slid two fingers inside.

"Too much," she keened. "Take 'em off."

He didn't need to be told twice.

"Now you." Her voice sounded low and soft while she rubbed her thighs together.

The moment of truth. Women speculated about his girth. He'd seen pictures blown up to show his bulge in the grappling shorts he wore when he wrestled. In truth, he was average length but had a good bit of girth. His skin stretched tighter than he ever had before. He might have grown a few extra inches just for her.

Rob slid his jeans and boxer briefs off at the same time and kicked them away. Emma's eyes widened at the sight between his thighs. He glanced down and gripped himself to check any differences.

"Do that again."

He looked up to see Emma's hand between her thighs.

"Do what?" he croaked before clearing his throat.

"Stroke yourself."

One more look down and he saw a distinct

difference. He wondered how it was possible, but he felt bigger.

"I'd rather you do it."

Emma got to her knees on the bed before him. She grasped him with the hand she used to touch herself. The feel of her wet heat on him was almost too much. He grabbed her bare ass and pulled her closer.

"What's this?" He felt a small, square bandage on her ass cheek.

"My birth control patch."

He swallowed hard. "I've got condoms if you want to . . ."

She stroked him. "I don't."

No other words were needed. His mouth was on hers while he kneaded the flesh of her backside. She pulled him down on the bed with her and dug her fingers into his shoulders.

"So fucking beautiful." He licked and kissed his way down her neck and torso.

With a pause at her belly button, he shifted her shirt up a few inches. He circled her belly button with his tongue before licking from one hip to the other.

Her sweet aroma filled his lungs when he settled between her thighs and took his first taste.

He heard a faint groan when she moved herself away from him.

"None of that." He placed his forearm across her abs to hold her still. "I'm having my dessert."

Nip.

Lick.

Suck.

Repeat.

Her salty sweetness coated his tongue, but he needed more. He thrust his tongue inside her and was rewarded with a flood of her essence.

She tangled her fingers in his hair and held him close while she rode her orgasm out on his tongue.

"Rob," she panted.

He smiled against her and kissed the last waves of ecstasy away.

She pulled on his hair and brought his mouth to her own.

"You see how good you taste," he said between kisses.

"Ugh." She wrapped her legs around his waist and moved against him. "Please."

"My pleasure." He grasped his cock and slid it through her wetness before he pushed inside.

He stilled. If he moved, their night would be over in no time.

She squirmed beneath him and dug her heels into his back.

"Give me a second. I don't want to come until you do again."

She squeezed him between her thighs. "I promise we can do this as many times as we can tonight, please make me come again now."

He wouldn't deny her and began a slow rhythm. She moved her arms around his neck while he sped up.

The years of wanting and waiting were nothing at that moment. She was his. With each thrust and breath, he claimed her.

His thrusts became uneven as he felt her quiver around him.

"Fuck!" he groaned through clenched teeth. The power of his orgasm knocked the breath right out of him.

"Yes," her pelvis crashed against him and her whole body squeezed his.

After, Emma relaxed and released her hold on him. He slid out of her and moved to lie beside her.

"If there were a belt for this, you would so be getting it."

He laughed and pulled her into his arms. "Good?"

"Not ashamed to say. Best ever."

He smiled and pulled her up to face him. "And this is only the beginning."

32

Emma slept about two hours when her alarm went off at four am. She turned over to find her sexy man lightly snoring as he lay on his side.

My sexy man.

She had no idea what she had been so worried about. Rob was gentle and loving, even playful in moments. She had never felt sexier than she did when she was under him, meeting him thrust for thrust.

After she watched him sleep for a few moments, she kissed him awake.

"Hey," he said with a yawn. "What time is it?"

"A little after four. Phil will be here to pick us up around five." Phil didn't say a word of protest when she called him from the cab on her way to Rob's. The consummate professional, he had agreed to the sudden change of plans without complaint.

"Ok." Rob grabbed Emma's hand and kissed her palm. "Let's sleep for another half hour."

"Not me. You might not mind smelling like sex all the way to LA, but I need a shower."

"But I love my scent on you."

"I'm not sure if the crew on our flight would feel the same."

He rolled his eyes. "Well, if you insist. I'll jump in when you're done. Tonight, I'll make you smell sexy all over again."

She leaned over and gave him a kiss that told him she would not accept anything less.

Once in the shower, she let the warm water rejuvenate her muscles for a whole new reason. At this rate, she would never have to go to the gym ever again. Her workouts with Rob would be more than enough to keep her in shape for the rest of her life. She had no idea she could be so flexible in bed. A tiny shard of excitement filled her belly when she realized they had several days to devote to the exploration of each other's bodies once they landed in Atlanta.

Her smile never left her face as she dressed in her un-Emma-like travel clothes. Since she would arrive at the airport with Rob, they both needed to be in somewhat of a disguise. His new beard and different clothes would be enough for him, but she needed to dress more down than usual. The soft, worn jeans and her favorite *Soft Kitty* tee shirt would work as long as she wore a baseball cap and sunglasses too.

Rob sat up in bed when she came out of the bathroom fully dressed.

"Wow."

"What?" She laughed and placed her things from the shower back in her suitcase.

"I thought you were gorgeous the morning we had the photo shoot, but this . . ." He waved his hand up and down in the air. "You are my fantasy come true."

"You fantasized about me in tee shirts and jeans?" Emma thought guys fantasies were of women in lingerie or nothing at all.

"Those kind of shirts, yes."

She looked down at herself. Her gray tee shirt with the stripped kitty was cute, but she didn't think it was spank bank worthy. The top she wore the night before was tighter and her signature color of purple.

"I can't imagine why."

He got out of bed and walked to her in all his naked glory.

"Because." He placed his hands on her waist. His thumbs slid underneath her shirt and traced the skin there. "This shirt shows me the real Emma. The girl with comic books stashed in her nerd cave. She would rather stay home and watch episodes of *The Big Bang Theory* than go out to a club. This is you and I like this Emma."

She swallowed the rather large lump in her throat. No one but her family and close friends had ever appreciated the nerdy side of her. Derek did to an extent, but not like this. Not like Rob.

"I like being her. I'm glad I can be myself with you."

"Me too." He gave her a soft kiss and placed his forehead on her shoulder. "I've got to get in the shower now before I drag you back to bed and play with your other kitty."

She smacked his ass and pushed him toward the bathroom.

"Remember, no shaving."

"Got it."

Her lips twitched when he laughed and shut the door. With Rob, she hoped the way he talked to her would always leave her with a special kind of tingle only his voice created.

They managed to get to their flight without a hint of paparazzi, even with Al and Ben right behind them. Emma slept for most of the flight with Rob's arm around her.

She woke as soon as the plane began to descend and slipped into a hoodie she had in her bag.

"How are we going to play this once we land?" Rob asked and slipped his baseball cap on his head.

"I've got an interview with Garrett Green at the Nerdy Girl Nation offices. Then a board meeting there this afternoon. Tonight, I've got dinner with Troy Banks. I can meet you at the hotel around ten."

"Busy girl. I need to get this in while I can." He cradled her face in his hands and kissed her in a way that made her feel like flames were licking at her heels. "Text me when you get done with Troy."

"I will."

She tried to make light of their separation, but in truth, she didn't want to go.

Emma's regular driver from when she worked at Hunt was at the curb.

"Stavros? What are you doing here?" She hugged the man who had spent hours on end shuffling her from one meeting to another over the years.

"I'm at your disposal while you're in LA. Mr. Hunt's orders." He smiled and opened the door of the black limo.

"It figures he would do something like this. Good to see you."

"You as well, Miss MacLean."

Emma got into the limo, followed by Al and Ben. Her shadows began to film when her phone rang. She answered and pushed the speaker icon.

"Terrance."

"Emma. Glad you're finally back on the right coast."

She shook her head at what she assumed was a joke. "I haven't even been gone two months."

"I hope you won't be too busy to squeeze a few hours in to meet with me."

Emma would love to see Terrance again, but she wasn't sure why he needed to see her. "Maybe tomorrow. What's this about?"

"Some loose ends we need to tie up. Lunch?"

"I'll call you in the morning to give you a time." She hung up after their goodbye and sank back into her seat.

What the hell is he up to?

33

Emma's nerves were at an all-time high when she walked into the restaurant to meet Troy for dinner. Her day had gone remarkably well. Al and Ben got some fantastic footage of her and some of the kids at the Nerdy Girl Nation. She had forgotten how much she missed the place and promised herself she would make a trip out there more often.

This dinner with Troy was different from the usual. They had met before, but never just the two of them. He even told Al and Ben not to come and film their dinner.

"Emma." Troy greeted her with a kiss on the cheek. "I've got a table for us."

He placed his hand on the small of her back and led her to a table on a private terrace.

"This is nice, but I'm not sure what this is all about."

"Wine?" He lifted a bottle of red, but she put her hand over her glass to stop him.

"I'm still in training mode, so no alcohol."

"Okay." He poured a glass for himself and took a drink. "You want me to cut to the quick?"

"Not something you're used to, but I would appreciate an explanation."

"The network wants you. Your fans are begging for you to have your own series and we're listening."

"But I can't. I'm working for the IWA now." She imagined cameras would be around more than they already were. Her own show would definitely mean less privacy.

"I've talked with Aaron Russell and he is willing to work with me under the umbrella of the IWA production company. He thinks the show would be a fabulous idea for you and your fans."

"I love the fans. They are the ones helping the Nerdy Girl Nation thrive, but I don't think I can." Nell would never go for cameras in the house all the time. Putting on the mask full time? No, she couldn't. Her mask vanished the night before with Rob and she felt whole for the first time in years.

"You don't need to decide today. We wouldn't even start filming until after the New Year."

"I'll think about it." She would. She'd try to come up with at least ten different ways to say no.

"Terrific. Now, let's eat."

"You're own show?" Rob asked and slumped back on the couch in Emma's hotel room.

"Yep." She kicked off her heels and curled her legs underneath her. "We didn't get into specifics, but he'd already talked to Aaron. He apparently liked the idea."

"Of course he would. You have seen the numbers since you came on board, right?"

She nodded and scooted closer to him. Rob took the hint and put his arms around her.

"Your presence has injected a new life into the company. You've done more in a month than Curtis Sharp had in the last year."

Emma felt Rob's muscles tense when he said Sharp's name.

"I've only met him a handful of times and that was too many. Was he as bad off-screen as he was on?"

"Worse," Rob grumbled. "The guy thought he was God's gift to wrestling. He'd been around for so long, he believed nothing could touch him. I loved being pitted against him and even getting to throw a punch at him every once in a while."

"I saw the footage of WrestleCon where you knocked him out cold."

Rob laughed and seemed to relax a little. "Yeah, I accidentally on purpose hit him harder than I was supposed to."

"It was pretty hot."

"Oh yeah?"

"Yeah." She turned her head and kissed along his jaw now covered with a soft layer of facial hair.

"I'm worried," he said and groaned when she licked the shell of his ear.

"Worried?"

"Um, a . . . About Nick and Rick Beeson. They were kind of his little pets. Nick is an okay guy, but Rick is the brains of the two. I'm worried about them keeping Sharp to close."

"What do you think he's going to do when you come out on Sunday?"

"I think we need to be prepared for anything. Lazlo is the ref for our match and usually Aaron won't change things up when he's in the ring with us. He's been on Lazlo's bad side. Not a great place to be."

"You mean Lazlo has a good side?" Lazlo had worked her ass off while she trained. She wasn't sure the man had more than one dimension.

"He can. Lazlo is focused. His job is his life and he has made himself irreplaceable. If Aaron pisses him off, another outfit will pick him up in no time."

"We'll have to pray Sharp is smart enough to back off."

"With Curtis Sharp, always expect the worst."

The way Rob spoke of Sharp gave her chills. She'd make sure extra security was set up. Curtis Sharp would not get the best of Emma MacLean. Ever.

34

All Saturday morning, Emma gave one interview after another. The process seemed like a condensed version of a press junket for a movie. She sat in a chair while reporter after reporter came in to interview her. Al and Ben were sure to be bored out of their minds after the same questions were asked and answered twenty times.

Kelly came in and handed her a bottle of water. "One more, then you're done. Stavros is waiting with the car to take you to lunch with Mr. Hunt."

Emma grabbed Kelly's hand. "Bless you. I swear my ass has been asleep for the last hour."

"I'll show him in." Kelly went out and Emma took a moment to gather her wits.

"I'm sorry, Emma. The last interview is with Patrick Longwell."

"Patrick? I don't think so."

"He's substituting for another reporter. Aaron really wants an interview with this website."

She hated the thought of seeing Patrick, but Aaron's the boss. "That's all right. Show him in."

Emma took a few deep breaths to calm herself.

"Patrick Longwell from Contact Wrestling Forum," Kelly announced with a quiver in her voice.

"Thank you, Kelly." Emma hadn't seen Patrick since she threw his ass out of her apartment almost a year earlier, but none of his actions were Kelly's fault.

"You look good, Emma." Patrick smiled and showed his over whitened teeth.

"Can't say the same for you. Are those hair plugs?"

His hand went up to the top of his head. Emma figured a mention of the recession of his hairline would hit a nerve.

"Ask your questions, Patrick. I still have several things to get done today."

He cleared his throat and launched into all the same questions all the others asked. She tried to be as professional as possible but she came off with a little more snark than usual.

"If there's nothing else?" Emma questioned.

"Just a few more." Patrick motioned for his cameraman to stop filming. "How do I compare to Bobby Breyer?"

"What?" she spat.

"Size wise. I've always heard wrestlers have small dicks and you've seen what I'm packing."

"This interview is over." Emma stood and moved to take the mic pack off.

"Come on, Emma. You never complained. I want to know how the new boy toy measures up."

Emma paused to choose her next words carefully. "You want to know how you compare to other men?"

Patrick took a step forward, curled his lips into a grin, and nodded.

Emma thought about telling him the truth for a split second. She shook her head and realized she couldn't stoop to his level.

"We're done here." Emma walked out of the room followed by Kelly, Ben, and Al.

Terrance made sure everything was as perfect for his lunch with Emma. This would be the first time they'd spoken in person since her mother's funeral. So many things had happened in both their lives over the last few weeks, driving the friends further apart. With the end of filming *Hunt for Life*, there might be no ties at all. Losing her friendship was something he would not accept.

Emma entered the private dining room without her camera crew. She assumed his crew would be present but was shocked to see only Terrance seated at a table.

"It's been too long." Terrance stood and took Emma into his arms. He pulled back from her and noticed the slight redness around her eyes, something he had never seen before. "Are you well?"

Emma stepped out of his arms and waved him off. "A long day and I didn't get much sleep last night." She sat down in the chair he pulled out for her.

Terrance sat down in his own seat. Emma wore her poker face well, but those moments were when things were off. He almost hated the sight of her pleasant face in those moments because he *knew* her expression wasn't real.

"I've ordered your favorites. I hope they will suffice?"

Emma glanced over at the tray the waiter had brought out and her visage cracked a bit. Terrance smiled and relaxed.

"Wonderful. I can't eat everything, but I'll try a little of each." The genuine smile on Emma's lips made Terrance's heart melt. The issues bothering her seemed to slip away.

The waiter served their dishes then took his leave.

Emma moaned after her first bite of her favorite shrimp dish. "I forgot how good this was."

They made small talk throughout their meal and Terrance felt his old friend come back to him again. Their time together began to run short and he needed to make his reason for their lunch clear.

Terrance reached across the table and took Emma's hand in his like he had done so many times before.

"Emma?"

She put her other hand over his. "Talk to me, Terrance."

"You have been a joy to have at my side in my business and as my friend. Lydia and I have considered you another daughter."

Hurt fell across her face and she ducked her head.

"No." Terrance put his fingers beneath her chin and lifted her head up to meet his gaze. "We love Irene despite everything she has done, but that will never change how Lydia and I feel about you." Terrance squeezed her hand. "I found out why she wanted you gone." He laughed, but a pain seared his chest at the same time. "She wanted to take your place on the deal because she was pushing for more screen time."

"Screen time? Are you kidding me?"

"Evidently, she convinced Troy making you look bad would increase the ratings and get rid of her haters. They knew about your contract so they never thought it would be permanent. It was all to stir up drama and Irene wanted the London commission to buy some house in Maui."

Seventeen million dollars would come Emma's way with the success of the deal. The deal was worth over a billion, so the pay was relatively low. The work needed to secure the deal was priceless, so Emma deserved every cent.

"I have no idea where we went wrong. Irene was good at her job and was making plenty of money on her own."

"So, Troy was the reason she was such a bitch?" Emma whispered to herself, but Terrence heard her loud and clear.

"He contributed to her attitude, I'm sure. Once I came back from your mother's funeral, I began to investigate all your projects to see what needed to be done. Irene volunteered for the London deal right away. I was instantly suspicious. She never volunteered for anything, so I told her to give me a few days to decide. I met with your assistant and together we pieced together a trail. Irene had been swapping her name and signature with yours on several documents. She wanted the credit for the work. On paper, everything seemed like she had brokered the deal by herself. Thankfully, between my assistant and yours we had all of the originals with your signature." Terrence shook his head. His own daughter had spiraled out of control and he had no idea. "I flew out to London before I got back with Irene. I closed the deal without her. When Irene found out, she went ballistic. It took a while to sort everything out, but I eventually got the truth out of her. I just wish I figured it out sooner."

"I'm so sorry I didn't know what they were up to." Emma's decision about the series Troy offered the night before was no longer an issue. She would never work with him again after this.

"You have nothing to be sorry for. You did your job and did it well. Which brings me to this." He pulled an envelope out of the inner breast pocket of his jacket and handed it to her.

Emma opened the envelope and scanned the documents. Her breath caught and eyes widened. "No."

"Yes."

The documents detailed the transfer of the seventeen million dollar commission as well as a thirty-three million dollar bonus. The number was triple what the paperwork faxed to Harry stated.

"Fifty million dollars? This is way more than I expected." Her hand shook while she lowered the papers to the table.

"You earned every cent. For every missed birthday and holiday. For the twenty hour days and last-minute flights around the world. Emma, you are priceless to me. This is the least I can give you, plus an annual donation to the Nerdy Girl Nation."

"Terrance." Emma stood and pulled him up into her arms. "Thank you."

"You are very welcome."

"I haven't done anything with my accounts since I moved." She whipped a few tears from her cheeks and laughed.

"The number of the best financial advisor in Boston is in there. I've worked with him before and trust him implicitly."

"I'll give him a call next week." She laughed again and shook her head. "Fifty million dollars. Who'd have thought I'd ever be in this position?"

"Elaine and Mick always knew you could set the world on fire. I knew you could." They smiled at each other and Terrence placed both of his hands on her face. "Want to know another thing I'm sure of?"

"What?"

"You're going to look fantastic with a tag team champion belt around your waist."

She hugged him tight and laughed like he'd never heard before. Best sound ever.

Rob used the keycard Emma gave him to enter her hotel room late Saturday night. He heard the sound of running water in the bathroom and assumed Emma was in the shower. The thought occurred to him to join her, but he was sure she wasn't ready.

He heard the water turn off and decided to get comfortable. While he unbuttoned his shirt, he noticed papers on the nightstand with the Hunt logo on them. Curious, he sat down on the bed and picked up the papers.

"Kind of scary seeing so many zeros?" Emma asked when she stepped out of the bathroom in a blue top and blue plaid ladies boxers.

"Is this for real?" Emma was a wealthy woman, but adding another fifty million to her already hefty bank account intimidated him more than a little bit.

"Yes. Terrence explained everything over lunch." She sat next to him and picked up the papers with a sigh. "I don't know what I'm going to do with it all."

"You can buy a lot of Legos." He took the papers from her and placed them back on the nightstand.

"I can have my own personal Legoland," she laughed.

He pushed her down on the bed and hovered over her. "We can build our own castle and live the rest of our days as the king and queen of our own nation."

"The Nerdy Girl Nation?" she asked and slid her arms around his neck.

"Of course. We'd live off frozen meals Louisa would leave for us on the drawbridge and spend our days in bed watching *Doctor Who* marathons."

"Heaven." She lifted her head and met his lips with her own.

"You, my Queen, shall want for nothing." He would worship her until the day he died if she'd let him.

Rob stared into depths of her ice blue eyes. He told himself from the moment he reconnected with Emma he was in it for the long haul. At that moment, the meaning of their relationship hit him full force. He saw their relationship in the abstract sense, sharing his life with her someday. Their day finally arrived.

"And my King will always be satisfied." She moved her hands to grip his backside and wrapped her legs around his thighs.

He grunted and pressed his erection against her. "With you, I could never be anything else."

35

"This last month has been an interesting challenge." Emma stood tall in front of the IWA roster at their meeting a half an hour before the Breaking Rules event began. "I never expected to be in this position tonight, but I'm so grateful for such a terrific and talented group of people to work with and support. Let's go out and have the best pay-per-view event ever!"

The wrestlers and staff responded with thunderous applause.

Emma felt a wave of relief crash over her, the weight of the last month lifted off her shoulders. The card for the night was scheduled out to the minute. If the night wasn't as perfect as she planned, it wouldn't be for her lack of trying.

Cherry rushed to her side. "I've got a surprise for

you."

"Surprise?"

"Come on." Cherry pulled Emma away, but not before she took a glance over at Aaron.

What seemed like a mile away through the halls of the arena, Cherry and Emma arrived at the costume area.

"Millie, tell her," Cherry urged the IWA's costume designer.

"I came up with another design for the two of you, a backup just in case. Cherry thinks you should wear these instead." Millie turned to show her the outfit hanging on the nearest rack.

"Oh, wow." Emma moved over to feel the stretchy leather-like material between her fingertips.

The original costume matched Cherry's signature jean shorts and fitted tee shirt. A distinct zing rocked her back on her heels when she realized how much more she liked the new outfit.

The shirt was a combination of purple and black leather with a built-in bra. Black strips crisscrossed between the breast and shoulder blades in front and back. The shorts were the same material and seemed like they would hit her mid thigh. Knee high black boots with built in shin guards and knee pads completed the ensemble.

"What do you think?" Millie asked.

"I love it. Can I try it on real quick?" The outfit was almost identical to what she had envisioned herself wearing one day.

"I can do you one better." Millie pulled out a purple wrap dress with a flourish. "You can wear this over it. I swear you'll be comfortable. You can come backstage to take the dress off before your match and switch out your shoes for your boots and kneepads."

"And see, I match." Cherry slid the robe she wore off. Her outfit was like Emma's except the placement of the purple and the black was the opposite.

"I pray I look as good as you do in mine." Cherry was close to Emma's stature, but Emma had what she called a little extra junk in her trunk.

"You'll be stunning. You're not even wearing this yet and guys are already drooling." Cherry motioned her head toward the wall where Aaron stood with Chance.

Emma rolled her eyes at the sight of Chance's uplifted eyebrows and slacked jaw. She had one more night to keep herself in check. Al and Ben would be home in their beds and she would be off to Atlanta with Rob. She'd survive for a few more hours.

"Bobby, a minute please?" Aaron asked Rob when he entered the secluded dressing room with Chance.

"Sure."

Aaron and Chance sat on the couch across from Rob and got comfortable. "There are going to be a few changes tonight."

The way Aaron spoke made Rob feel uneasy. "And?"

"After your match, win or lose, you and Chance will be in the ring when Emma enters. Instead of a gracious defeat or being presented with the belts, you are going to grab Emma and kiss her."

"What? I don't think she'd be comfortable—"

"I discussed this with her. This is what we've been building up to for weeks. Emma will take it from there." Aaron winked at him.

Emma admitted to Rob, even before the attack,

public displays of affection were difficult for her.

Why didn't she tell me about this?

"Now, you won't need to sneak around anymore." A wide grin spread across Aaron's face. "I happened to see you slip into a different room late last night."

Rob had no response except to grin right back.

"Tonight will all work out for the best."

"You are one lucky man, my friend," Chance said then took a swig of water.

"Don't I know it?"

36

Emma spent the majority of the night at the announcers' table with the commentary team. Once a championship match was decided, she presented the winner with their championship belt.

A video montage and a segment with Aaron gave Emma enough time to get backstage to get ready for her match.

Emma met Millie and Cherry in the hallway. She loosened the ties to her dress and slipped it off while she flipped her heels from her feet. Millie took the dress. Cherry pushed Emma down on a chair and helped her into her boots.

"Nervous?" Cherry asked while she forced Emma's foot into the boot.

Lindsey Gray

"I feel like I'm going to throw up if I don't get out there soon." With the realization her match would actually happen, panic began to set in.

"You'll do fine. You're ready. You know. I know. Most of all, Lazlo knows."

Emma nodded. Cherry was right. All of their training sessions flipped through her mind like an old filmstrip. They *would* do it.

"You're right." Emma got her other boot on and secured the ties.

"Come here." Cherry pulled Emma up from the chair and put their foreheads together. "Tonight, Betty and Wendy are all those bitches who doubted us. We are here to show the world never to underestimate us. You ready?"

"Yes," Emma said with a note of confidence she didn't expect.

I can do this. I will do this.

"Cherry!" a stagehand called.

"I'll see you out there." Cherry brought Emma into a quick, tight hug and went to make her entrance.

Cameras were arranged in front and behind Emma to catch every possible movement.

"Here. This will help."

Emma turned to find Kelly with a phone in her hand.

She took the phone and brought it to her ear. "Hello?"

"How you doin', Princess?"

"Dad," she sighed. She felt the tears well but tipped her head back to halt the fall. "I'm waiting to go out."

"You're gonna be wonderful. Remember to use your momentum. Don't waste any opportunity."

"I know, Dad." She wiped her eyes with her

fingertips. "Lazlo has drilled it all into me. I'll do my best."

"I love you. Call me as soon as you can."

"I will. Give my love to everyone."

"Just a second." She heard the sound the phone made when switched over to speaker mode.

"Good luck, Emma!" The sound of the whole bar yelling at the same time filled her with the jolt of confidence she needed.

"Be safe. I love you."

"I will, Dad."

She heard her brother, Annie, and Nell yell out their love before she hung up and handed the phone back to Kelly.

"Thanks." Emma smiled, her nerves left behind her.

"So, what you gonna do now?" Kelly asked with a wicked twinkle in her eye.

"I think I have some ass to kick."

The familiar sounds of the electric guitar rang throughout the arena and there was no turning back.

Emma went out and stopped at the top of the ramp. The crowd erupted in a hail of cheers and hollers. She did a little spin to show off her new gear and they all seemed to approve. Her music continued while she basked in the energy ricocheting off the walls of the arena.

Instead of her usual casual walk down to the ring, she decided the time had come to show the world she meant business as a member of the Bombshell division. Emma ran down the ramp at full speed and slid under the bottom rope into the ring. She rolled and flipped herself up to stand next to Cherry. They held their hands up and played to the crowd for another minute before Emma's music faded out.

"Go time," Cherry said while she pulled Emma into a tight hug. "We got this." Cherry moved back to grasp Emma's chin and turned her head toward Wendy and Betty. "They got nothing on us. Those bitches are going down."

"Hell yeah!" Emma squeezed Cherry tight before she slid between the middle and top ropes to stand on the apron of the ring.

The bell rang.

The match started out as planned. Cherry attempted a pin within two minutes of the start. Betty took out her fury on Cherry after a kick to the face. Things went south after that. Betty put Cherry in a submission hold she wasn't supposed to until further on in the match. Cherry got out of the hold and tagged Emma in.

Betty tagged in Wendy and Emma realized their original plan wouldn't work.

Time to fight dirty.

"This is how it's gonna be?" Emma asked while the two of them stalked each other around the ring.

"I told you we wouldn't hold back because you're the boss." Wendy cracked her knuckles in an attempt at intimidation.

Emma laughed. The sound didn't go over well with Wendy, who lunged at Emma full force. Emma side-stepped and let Wendy bounce off the ropes. She wrapped her arm around Wendy's neck from behind and threw her down hard.

"Just because I'm the boss, doesn't mean I'm not gonna kick your ass." Emma gave her a kick to the ribs for good measure.

Wendy got back up and they went at it. Emma got

her bell rung when Wendy threw her down face first into the ring floor. When she had the strength to get up, Betty had taken Wendy's place.

Emma didn't let the urgency of the match dissipate and went at Betty with an unspoken rage.

Kick.

Jab.

Punch.

Slap.

Pull.

Push.

Bounce.

Jump.

One last dodge had Wendy eager to tag Betty's outstretched hand.

Emma changed Wendy's attitude toward her. She wondered if Betty might be impressed at Emma's performance so far.

Their back and forth was more than a little brutal and Betty got Emma into a strong submission hold. Emma was able to reach for the rope and the referee pulled Betty off.

Emma did a quick roll across the ring and tagged Cherry in.

She caught her breath while Cherry did her best to overtake Betty at every turn. Emma turned to the crowd and raised her arms to get them hyped up. She began to stomp her foot against the apron while the crowd did the same in their seats.

Betty made a mistake and threw Cherry into the corner instead of the ropes like intended.

Cherry tagged Emma in. "Take. Her. Out."

"Got it."

Emma went in to spear Betty in her midsection. She bounced her hefty opponent off the ropes and clotheslined her underneath the chin when she flew back toward her. Emma flipped Betty on her stomach in the middle of the ring and set her up for the very same submission hold she put Emma in moments before. Emma twisted Betty's legs around her own and sat down to force Betty to stretch in a way God never intended. With a secure hold under Betty's chin, Emma pulled to force Betty's head back. Betty's muscles quivered beneath her and Emma bounced on her body once to increase the pressure. Betty clawed at Emma's hands around her neck, but Emma kept her hold. A loud screech hurt Emma's ears before Betty's hand slapped the ring to tap out.

The bell sounded the end of the match, but Emma didn't release the hold until the referee pulled her off.

Cherry ran into the ring and jumped into Emma's arms. "You did it!"

The referee handed the championship belts to Emma and Cherry and raised their arms high while Emma's music blasted over the speakers.

Betty and Wendy slunk out of the ring and Cherry followed a few minutes later.

With the belt secured around her waist, Emma went over to the announce table to commentate for the men's tag team match.

The ringside doctor came over to ask Emma a couple of questions. Once he deemed she was fine, he handed her a bottle of water and congratulated her.

The commentators didn't get a chance to ask her any questions when the ring announcer began to introduce the next match.

Emma took a swig of water and waited to see her man fight for a belt of his own.

"Ladies and Gentlemen. Introducing the champions. From Las Vegas, Nevada at a combined weight of four hundred and sixty-seven pounds. Nick and Rick Beeeeeeeson!" The ring announcer tried his best to be enthusiastic, but everyone could tell he wasn't thrilled to be introducing the Beesons.

Nick and Rick appeared at the top of the ramp when their music blared. The crowd gave them a mixed reception, boos and cheers came in varied waves.

"Hold on. Turn off the music!" Rick waved his belt high above his head and the music stopped. "We wouldn't be where we are tonight without one man and we invite him to accompany us to the ring tonight. Mr. Curtis Sharp!" Rick screamed into the microphone.

Sharp walked in from the crowd, not from backstage and joined the Beesons. The three strutted to the ring like their shit didn't stink.

Chance turned to Rob where the two were waiting backstage. "He won't distract us. We've got this, boy. We've come too far to let this son of a bitch intimidate us."

Chance hoped his confidence would rub off on his partner. Sharp's presence was another challenge they would overcome.

"Introducing the challengers. First, from Atlanta, Georgia, weighing in at two hundred and forty-two pounds. Chance Rooooobiiiiicheauuuuuuuuuuuux."

Chance walked out to the top of the ramp to deafening applause. He took his time walking up to the ring, high-fiving fans and taking pictures. Once in the ring, he took the microphone offered to him.

"Some of you might have noticed my partner has been missing in action this last week." Chance turned his attention to Curtis Sharp. "There seemed to be some sort of a mix-up on whether my good buddy, Bobby, had broken the company drug policy."

Shock wove through the crowd and within a few seconds, anger burst through. The crowd began chanting at the top of their lungs, "Bullshit!" over and over again.

Sharp held up his hand. "We know your buddy isn't here and you can't fight by yourself. Just forfeit the match now so we can get on with our night." Sharp grinned and lowered his microphone.

Chance laughed and brought his microphone up to his mouth. "Every fan in this arena knows Bobby would never risk his nine years of sobriety right before a match like this. They all know the time he has devoted years to developing outreach programs and given speeches in schools across the country. His past is in the past. I for one believe in Bobby and his sobriety. Thankfully, so does Aaron Russell." The crowd roared their approval. After a few seconds, Chance waved his hand to get them to quiet down. "Another round of tests were done and wouldn't you know it, every single one came back negative." The grin dropped off Sharp's face. Chance turned to see the mile wide smile on Emma's face from where she sat at the commentators' table. "Mr. Announcer, I will let you introduce my partner now."

"Ladies and Gentlemen. From Baltimore, Maryland, weighing in at two hundred and twenty pounds. The Baltimore Bruiser. Boooobbbbby Breyeeeeeeerrrrrrr!"

Bobby's music blared louder than it ever had before and the crowd loved it. Chance noted some of the female reactions to Bobby's new appearance. The beard suited him, made him look a bit older but also a bit meaner. The ladies would love it.

Bobby entered the ring and his glare turned on Sharp.

"Save that fuel for the fire, brother. They fight dirty, we get dirtier."

Rob nodded to Chance and bounced from one foot to the other to amp himself up. Chance was up first, so Rob ducked through the ropes to guard their corner on the apron.

Rob and Chance were ready. They'd both beaten the Beesons in singles competition, so Rob wasn't worried as long as it was a fair fight. Nick stood in the ring while Rick guarded their corner and Sharp stood on the floor. Their corner was closer to the announcers' table, which made Rob wonder about what Emma would do.

The bell sounded to start the match. He didn't have much time to think about Emma when Chance took one step and kicked Nick in the face. Chance was on fire and his fire helped Rob focus on every move inside the ring.

Chance tagged him in and Rob got on the top rope. When Nick turned to face him, Rob jumped off with his hands clasped high above his head and clubbed him on top of the head.

Nick was dazed for a moment. Rob took advantage and went for the pin, but the ref only slapped down a two count before Nick got his shoulder up.

The crowd howled in disapproval and Nick rolled over to tag Rick in. Rob noticed Sharp had moved away from the Beesons corner and Emma was out of her seat.

Rick took advantage of Rob's misdirected focus and kicked him in the ribs. Rob fell back into the corner and Rick dealt him a series of punches to the head.

"Fuck no!" Rob thrust his forearms and clenched fists against Rick's face. Rob pounded at Rick's head with reckless abandon. His adrenaline spiked and the punishing blows didn't stop.

Rob heard the referee scream in his ear to stop or he would call off the match. It didn't stop him, but the sound of Emma's scream did.

Emma pushed Sharp away from the ring and he hit the front of the announcers' table. Chance came to the side of the ring closest to Rob and tagged himself back in.

"Take care of him. I've got this."

Rob nodded and let Chance take over in the ring.

Sharp and Emma were well into a verbal spar once he reached their side of the ring.

"Come on, little girl, let the big boys take care of business." Sharp snarled.

"There will be no cheating on my watch. I swear I'll drag your ass out of here myself if I have to." Emma stood firm with her hands on her hips and determination in her eyes.

"I'd like to see you try." Sharp scoffed then noticed Rob walk up behind Emma.

Rob glanced at the ring and saw Chance had everything under control. He turned his attention back to Sharp.

"Once Chance pins your boy, I will carry you out with her." Rob stood with his chest up against Emma's back.

"You don't scare me, Breyer." Sharp stepped forward and sandwiched Emma between him and Rob.

Emma's entire body went rigid and Rob realized they needed to do something to get Sharp to back off.

"I don't think . . ." Rob placed his hands on Emma's hips and moved her back a bit. She gave a small nod to show she understood. "It isn't me you should be worried about."

Rob stepped back while he lifted Emma up. Emma kicked her legs out and hit Sharp in the chest. Sharp stumbled back but didn't fall.

"Swing!" Emma yelled.

Rob picked her up once more while she jumped and threw her legs up to the side. He swung her and her legs made contact with Sharp's side. Sharp crashed into the announcers' table sideways.

Rob pulled Emma toward the opposite corner outside the ring.

"Are you okay?"

"I'm fine, but you're about five seconds away from losing this match. Get back in there."

Rob turned to see Rick attempting to pin a bloodied Chance.

How the hell did that happen?

Chance lifted his shoulder before the referee's hand hit the mat for the third time. Rob reached in, grabbed Chance, and pulled him out of the ring.

"My turn, brother." He handed Chance off to Emma and went in to finish Rick off.

The task was harder than he anticipated. Rob attempted to jump off the rope and clothesline Rick but was caught by Rick's arm. Dazed, Rob did his best to fight off Rick's blows.

Luck found him when Rob tried an old combination his father made famous. A jab to the throat with his elbow and a quick sweep of the leg to knock his feet out from under him made Rick hit the mat hard. Rob took both of Rick's legs and pinned them down to his shoulders for the three count.

The bell rang and Rob collapsed back on the floor of the ring.

Rob felt Chance pull him up to his feet and into his arms.

"We fucking did it!"

"How did this happen?" Rob motioned to the blood on Chance's face.

"I have no idea," Chance said with a smile.

"Gentlemen?"

They turned to find Emma with their new tag team championship belts.

"Congratulations." Emma handed each of them a belt and held both their arms up in victory.

As soon as she let go, Rob took Emma in his arms and secured his lips to hers. He never experienced the world fading away with a kiss until that moment. There was just him and Emma, two people who were well on their way to falling deeply for each other. They held each other tighter than he imagined possible but still weren't close enough. It should've been one of the best moments of his life, but he realized he'd made a grievous mistake when she froze mid-kiss.

Emma pushed him away and covered her mouth with her hand.

"Emma?" Rob was confused. Aaron said she—

"How could you?" she whispered behind her hand.

Aaron lied to him.

All the color had drained from her face and she started to back away from him. Rob reached for her, but she pushed his hand away and fled from the ring.

"What the hell?" Chance asked.

"I should've talked to her first." Rob thrust his hand through his sweat soaked hair in frustration.

"What are you gonna do?"

"Make something very clear to Aaron Russell. He can't fuck with us anymore." Rob stormed out of the ring with Chance at his heels.

37

O'Rourke's was packed to capacity for the viewing of Breaking Rules. Annie and Harry persuaded Teddy O'Rourke to throw the shindig in honor of Emma's first official match with the IWA.

Not the whole town, but several prominent members had showed to support Emma's debut. Mayor Rudy Babcock and his wife, the whole MacLean clan including Nell, and even Emma's ex, Derek McInerney and his cousin, Sully, were in attendance. Harry was lucky Teddy made sure the MacLean's had the best table in the place.

"She's quite dressed up for wrestling, isn't she? I wouldn't think she could do one of those power bomb things in those heels." Moira tsked and shook her head.

"It's not time yet, Nan," Harry laughed. "They'll get to her match here in a bit."

"Well, I want to see that Bobby fellow." Moira's eyes

lit up. "He looks just like my Michael, especially with his shirt off." She smiled and winked at Harry.

Harry shook his head before he took a drink and turned his attention back to the huge screen in front of them.

As the show progressed, Emma nervousness appeared to increase tenfold. He was about to pick up his phone to make a call when his father's cell phone rang.

"Kelly," his father said before he answered.

Mick talked to Kelly for a few minutes before Emma came on the line. Harry knew their father would be able to calm her down. Mick turned on the speaker and got the whole bar to wish Emma luck before they hung up.

The whole bar roared when Emma slid into the ring and flipped up on her feet. Derek's eyes were glued to the screen, but Harry saw how odd Sully seemed to be acting. The larger cousin had consumed at least two pitchers of beer and was on his third, but kept a stony expression on his face the entire time. The entrance of the devil incarnate, also known as Maria DeFazio McInerney, didn't seem to lighten his mood either.

Annie and Nell held each other tight while they watched Emma get thrown around the ring. They cringed and groaned when Black Betty attempted her first submission hold. Emma was able to get out of the hold and tag in Cherry. Harry heard his father release a long breath.

"Dad?" Harry asked with concern. Mick was pale and sweaty.

"I was there for every karate tournament. I know my girl can hold her own, but this is so much more than I ever expected. Some of these fellows get really hurt. I don't know if I could take . . . seeing her in a hospital bed again." Mick brought his handkerchief to his brow and patted away the perspiration.

Harry brought his arm around his father's shoulders. "She's been training for weeks. Years, if you count all that time with Bill Bell. You've talked to her. She's as comfortable as she can be doing this. We have to trust her on this."

"It's not her I don't trust." He reached for his beer but didn't pick the drink up. "I won't stop worrying until she calls after this is over." He chugged half of his beer and slammed it down to see Emma tagged back in.

Harry's gut churned. Visions of his battered sister in a hospital bed flashed in his mind. He took Annie's hand before the memories got the best of him. Emma would be fine. She had to be.

"She's got her!" Moira yelled at the top of her lungs.

Harry focused on the screen and found his sister using the same submission hold Betty had used on her earlier in the match. This time, Emma had Betty in the middle of the ring and there was no way out. A red-faced Betty finally tapped out and Emma, eventually, let go.

The bar erupted in cheers and hollers. The screen showed Emma and Cherry hug before the referee lifted their hands. They were given the Bombshell Tag Team Champion belts while Betty and Wendy sulked outside the ring. Cherry made her way to the back while Emma settled at the commentator's table for the next match, the Men's Tag Team Championship.

Harry noticed his father relax when he saw Emma smile and drink some water. Something was still off though. Harry's gaze landed on Sully McInerney again. His face was red and appeared as if the veins in his neck would burst with any more pressure. Derek seemed oblivious as he had an animated conversation with Teddy.

He was about to go over to their table when Annie grabbed his hand.

"Look!"

Rob's match had started and Chance had already kicked one of his opponents in the face. Harry got distracted by the fight and stayed in his seat.

Once the fight was over, Emma entered the ring with the belts for Chance and Rob. Before Harry followed what was happening, Rob kissed Emma, hard.

"Hell yeah!" Annie shouted.

"That's my girl!" Moira screamed.

Harry laughed at the sight of his sister ousted on live television. Guess they weren't keeping their relationship a secret anymore. He almost missed Emma pushing Rob off her.

"Oh, shit," he gasped. "Something is wrong."

Mick stood and to get closer to the screen, but Emma's tear stained cheeks were unmistakable while she ran back up the ramp.

"Dad, we can call her. If she doesn't answer, Kelly will." Harry reached into his pocket to grab his phone when he heard a crash from the table next to him.

Maria threw a pitcher and broken glass flew across the floor. The room went silent, even the television muted.

"Now you can all see what trash she is!" Maria yelled.

Harry felt every hair on his body stand on end as Annie stood from her chair.

Derek stood in between Maria and Annie, his hands out to stop the two from coming to blows.

"What the hell, Maria?" Derek asked. "This shit is really getting old."

"I don't care how perfect you all think she is. She just proved she's the same little slut she's always been." Maria turned to Derek. "You know she cheated on you in high school?"

Derek's hands dropped in apparent shock. "What? How do you . . ."

"I know for a fact that is not true. Emma was devoted to Derek." Annie crossed her arms and stood firm.

"That's right!" Nell added and stood by her sister.

"You all thought she was such an innocent, but you have no idea what she was doing behind your backs. Tell them, honey." Maria turned to a fuming Sully.

"I never wanted my cousin to know," Sully seethed at Maria. "Emma was all over me whenever Derek's back was turned. I'm a guy. I could only resist for so long."

"Fucking liar!" Derek lunged at Sully, but Harry caught him and held him back.

"She loved it. Every time we were at our fishing cabin, she'd moan my name." Sully looked proud while Maria continued to be completely disgusted.

"Enough!" Mick yelled from somewhere behind Harry.

"Come on, Mick. You can't believe that Derek was the only one. You think she really tutored kids almost every day after school? Nobody is that perfect. She was with me or maybe even some other guy more than once a week. Sure had Derek snowed."

Harry felt like a cannon ball had been shot straight into his chest. He knew none of the filth they were spewing was true. Emma wasn't like other sisters, they actually talked about stuff like that. First because she wanted to make sure he wouldn't hurt Annie. Then because she had questions she couldn't go to anyone else with. Whatever Sully thought happened between him and Emma was in his deluded mind.

"You fucking bastard!" Harry lunged, but Annie and Nell caught his arms in a vice-like grip.

"Oh, Harry. You sad she didn't give you a piece? I didn't know you were into the whole incest thing."

Harry ripped his arms from Annie and Nell's grasp to beat the shit out of Sully.

The few seconds it took him were a few too many. By the time he reached Sully, his father was already on top of Sully and had pounded his face into the floor.

Sully's arms swung and made a couple of good jabs to Mick's midsection, but blood flowed from Sully's mouth.

Teddy and Harry went to pull Mick off Sully while a few other men sat on top of Derek to keep him from joining in.

Less than a minute later, four police officers rushed in and grabbed Sully and Mick. A towel was thrown at Sully's face before he was brought to his feet.

"Did you do this, Mr. MacLean?" one officer asked.

"I sure as hell did and I'll beat the bastard again!" Mick shouted and spat at Sully's feet.

"I'm sorry, but you are under arrest for assault." The officer proceeded to cuff Mick and read him his rights.

"Arrest that bastard, too!" Harry hollered.

Mayor Babcock came up beside the officer who had Sully. "I witnessed the whole thing. Take McInerney in as well. He and his wife started the whole thing."

The officer nodded and slapped the cuffs on Sully while he read him his rights.

Harry grabbed his father's shoulder as one officer began to lead him out. "Are you okay?"

"I've been better. Call and check on your sister."

Harry nodded and turned into his wife's arms.

"I already called Kelly. She said Rob and Emma were talking behind closed doors, but she'll call as soon as she can."

Harry felt sick. He had to bend over and put his hands on his knees to keep himself from vomiting.

"Nell, can you take Nan home and sit with the kids?" Annie asked her sister.

"Of course." Nell turned to Moira and offered her a hand.

Moira took Nell's arm up but grabbed Harry's bicep before they started to walk. "I wish one of you could've given that man a swift kick to the nuts. I might do it myself if I ever see him again."

"I'll see what we can do." Harry leaned in and gave her a kiss on the cheek.

"Now, go get my boy out of jail."

"Will do." Harry's phone began to ring with Emma's ringtone. He took a deep breath and answered.

38

"Why did he kiss you?" Cherry screamed over the roar of the crowd when Emma ran backstage.

"It wasn't planned." Tears streamed down her cheeks as she hurried through the congested hallway.

Rob had kissed her. He kissed her on live television with over four million fans watching. Not a peck either. Her tonsils had experienced the workout of their life.

Her hand went to cover her mouth and she picked up speed, the cameras close behind.

"What the fuck was he thinking?" Cherry grasped Emma's hand and jogged along with her.

"I have no idea. This wasn't supposed to happen." If they won, she was there to present Rob and Chance with the Tag Team belts, not to be kissed within an inch of her life.

Emma and Cherry arrived at her private dressing area where the *Hunt for Life* cameras weren't allowed to follow. They rushed in and found Aaron on the couch.

"What the fuck!" Emma screamed.

"Would you've agreed if we would've told you beforehand?" Aaron asked and took a sip from a tumbler of amber liquid.

"Of course not!" She was furious. Not about the kiss itself, but for the fact she was completely blindsided. She needed to be prepared for something like that.

"Our mission is originality. We want everything to be real and in the moment." Aaron drained the rest of his drink and stood.

"Yes, but as Vice President of Creative, I am to be included in all possible outcomes. We never discussed a kiss." Emma walked over and got in Aaron's face. "If you ever do anything like that again, there will be serious consequences, Mr. Russell."

Aaron's resolve seemed to waiver a bit as his Adam's apple bobbed with a hard swallow. "I'll leave you to calm down for a bit. We need you in about an hour for some more press."

Before he reached the door, Emma spoke. "Send Rob in. We have a few things to discuss in private."

"Of course." Aaron nodded to both of them and left.

"What a night?" Cherry exclaimed with a laugh and brought Emma in for a much-needed hug.

"Is it possible for someone to be completely mortified and turned on at the same time?" Emma pulled back to see if her wise friend had an answer.

"Before tonight, I think I would've said no. But, I think that's the perfect description of what happened." She ran her hand across Emma's tear stained cheek. "You wanna change before Rob gets here? Cover up a bit?"

"Yes. Thank you, not just for tonight, but for everything you've done for me since we met."

"It's what friends do, sweetie. Now, change. Rob couldn't hold himself back in front of a sold out crowd. I worry what might happen with no one else around." Cherry smacked Emma's tush and left her alone in the dressing room.

Emma sat on the couch and took off the contraptions she was told were boots. They were comfortable, but a complete nightmare to get off. Once those were gone, she slid the leather-like shorts off. She attacked the top next. Once the top was off, she put on a calf-length, terry cloth robe.

Her back was to the door when the knock came. She called for him to come in, her back toward the door.

"I swear, Emma, Aaron told me you agreed. I had no idea," Rob rambled.

He stood a few feet behind her; the familiar warmth covered every inch of her skin.

"You kissed me."

"Yes," he whispered.

"You've never kissed me like . . . With so much . . ."

She felt his chest caress her back and his hand found purchase on her hip. "I don't know if I would've been able to stop if you hadn't pushed me away. I can't keep us a secret anymore. To be honest, the kiss wasn't about pleasing Aaron. Yes, he gave me the okay, but I wanted to kiss you. I've never wanted something so badly. Not even those belts. I kissed you and I'm not sorry. I want the world to know you are mine."

He moved his hand around from her hip to her stomach and pulled at the belt to her robe. As the robe parted his fingertips caressed right above the lace covering her sweet spot. The bit of lace was saturated with her sweat and arousal. She groaned when his hand dipped between her panties and his fingers began explore.

"Do you have any idea what it was like, fighting and clawing my way through my match when all I wanted to do was bury myself deep inside you?" He slipped his index finger inside of her and began a slow rhythm.

"I want you inside just as bad," she whimpered while she moved against his hand.

"I know there is so much we need to be doing right now, but I can't wait until later."

"Neither can I." She took his finger from inside her and turned to face him.

She pushed against his bare chest so there were a few feet of space between them. The robe opened when she reached for her panties. She slipped her fingers into the waistband, pushed them down her legs, and kicked them away.

"You don't have to." His fingertips caressed the valley between her bare breasts.

Emma knew Rob was the one. She wanted to bare all of herself to him. In her heart, she was positive he would accept every part of her.

"I want to." She parted the robe and slid it off her shoulders. The material hit the floor with little movement from her.

The scars her doctor had often described as barely there were on full display.

He caressed the top of her breast above her heart.

The feel of his fingertips on her bare skin was almost enough to make her come.

"This." He circled her puckered nipple with his thumb. "This is beautiful. These?" He traced a mark underneath her left breast. "These don't take anything away from you. They show how strong you are, how much you've overcome." He moved his hand up to tilt her chin up to look into his eyes. "I love every part of you, Emma."

She didn't want to cry again, but as each moment passed, her emotions were harder to control.

"I'm quite fond of all your parts, too." She brought her hand to where his grappling shorts sat on his hips. A few tugs and they fell to his ankles. The one part of him she needed to touch stood long and tall between his legs.

He began to step out of his shorts but she stopped him.

"No. Come here." She took two steps back and pressed herself up against the cool wall.

"Against the wall?" he asked and took a few small steps toward her.

"Yes." She reached to stroke him when he was close enough and elicited a low growl from him.

He took her hands in his, pinned them above her head and dove in for a searing kiss. One of his hands moved to hitch her leg around his hip before he positioned himself at her entrance. With another kiss even more savage than the one in the ring, he slammed into her in one quick thrust.

Every cell in her body was set aflame. Instinct took over and she brought her other leg around his hip.

He let go of her hands to hold her underneath her thighs, his lips never leaving hers. She wrapped her arms around his shoulders to get even more leverage as they moved against each other.

The years of mutual desire crashed in violent beauty as they came, one after the other.

Her legs shook when her feet touched the floor and he slid out of her.

His sporadic breaths continued while his forehead rested against hers.

"I'm completely ruined."

"What?" she laughed and released what little breath resided in her lungs.

"It will never get any better. You are stuck with me for life."

Her hands wandered down his backside and grabbed a hold. "Good thing we like each other so much."

Rob took a small step back to look at the two of them. Emma nude. And him with his boots on and shorts around his ankles!

"I never know what you'll do from one moment to the next."

"Guess you have a while to get used to it." She pulled him back in for another kiss.

"Forever," he murmured against her lips.

She pulled back. "Forever will have to wait a little longer. We need to get dressed."

"Ugh." He bent down to grab his shorts and kissed her nipple when he pulled them back up. "Once we reach our hotel room in Atlanta, we are not leaving for days."

Emma nodded in agreement and slipped her panties on. She put on a bra and got her wrap dress back on then slid her feet into her shoes. "We need to deal with Aaron. I told him off, but I think a united front before the cameras is a good idea."

"I knew I liked you for more than your smoking hot body." He pecked her lips and opened the door to find two camera crews filming Aaron and Kelly arguing.

"I will have your job!" Aaron yelled in Kelly's face.

"I work for Miss MacLean. I'd like to see how well she would take you firing her assistant after the stunt you pulled tonight!" Kelly gave just as good as she got.

"What's going on?" Emma shouted at the duo.

Kelly straightened up and turned to Emma. "Mr. Russell was insisting on interrupting you, but I made it clear you and Mr. Breyer were to be left alone."

"Thank you, Kelly." Rob smiled at the brave assistant.

"Yes, thank you. We did have a few things to talk about. Especially the fact that Mr. Russell decided that our private life was okay to publicize without my permission."

"Emma, all the fans could see—"

"No!" Emma shouted. "You saw a possibility to get a higher ratings share and you took it."

Rob chimed in. "You made a unilateral decision to make our personal life public with no regard to either of our feelings or what the fallout would be."

"Speaking of fallout." Kelly pulled out Emma's cell phone. "You need to call your brother." She shoved the phone into Emma's hand.

"Oh, God. They're freaking out, right?" Emma dialed her brother's number as quick as possible.

Troy walked up to the group and Emma turned to glare at him.

"I have no time for you right now," she spat.

Rob moved right in front of Troy, blocking him from Emma's sight. "Turn around and leave right now. I can't promise you'll leave here without a limp if you don't."

Troy turned tail and made his getaway before any harm could come to him.

Harry answered after several rings. "Emma?"

"Harry. Oh my God. How's Dad? I swear if I had any idea what was going to happen, I would've warned you all. Aaron pulled a fast one on me."

"No, Em. Calm down. Dad's . . . fine, I guess."

"You guess?" Something was wrong, very wrong.

"I know you and Rob had plans, but do you think you can put them off?"

"Harry, you're scaring me." Rob came to her side and took her hand.

"Well, I think you should come home because . . . Oh fuck. Um . . . Dad's been arrested."

39

Rob and Emma didn't get to the Marblehead Police Department until five in the morning. They were welcomed in the lobby by Annie and Harry.

Emma walked straight into her brother's arms. "What is going on? Why wouldn't you tell me over the phone?"

All Harry would say was their father was in jail, but not what for. She assumed something happened at O'Rourke's, but she had no idea what.

Emma pulled back; Harry's face was pale and his eyes bloodshot. She turned to her best friend and saw the same expression accompanied by tearstained cheeks.

"Please, don't tell me he killed someone." Emma reached for Rob and he wrapped his arm around her waist.

"I'm sure he wanted to. Hell, I wanted to." Harry ran his fingers through his hair and pulled at the ends in obvious frustration.

287

"What? Who in the world would you want dead?" She was so confused. Her father had never been in a fight in his life. What could've sent him over the edge?

"Sully," Harry stated with disgust and a dead look in his eyes.

Emma's creased brows and tilted head showed her confusion. "What does he have to do with any of this?"

Annie stepped forward and placed her hands in Emma's. "Maria started talking her usual trash except this time she pulled Sully into it. Sully said some things that none of us want to repeat. Just know, your father defended your honor."

Emma turned to Harry to see his eyes clenched shut in obvious anguish.

"I'm a lot stronger than you think." Emma turned back to focus on Annie and squeezed her hands. "You need to tell me what was said."

"Maria and her usual BS, except she started going off about how you cheated on Derek."

Emma took a sharp intake of breath.

Rob pressed himself against her back and placed his hands on her shoulders. "We didn't do anything back then. She wouldn't even let me kiss her."

"No." Annie shook her head and sniffled. "Not you. Sully claimed he'd been with Emma."

"Never." Emma shook her head in shock. "We never did anything. I could never have done that to Derek. I never even saw Sully like that."

"We know that," Harry seethed. "I don't know what Sully's game is, but when he accused me of—" Harry held onto his stomach like he was going to be sick. "Accused me of wanting to sleep with my sister, I lost it."

"Oh my God." Emma trembled for a second before her knees gave way. Rob and Annie held onto her and led her to a nearby chair to sit.

Annie knelt in front of Emma while Rob sat beside her, his arm around her shoulder.

"If Mick hadn't got ahold of Sully first, I'm sure Harry would be the one behind bars." Annie held onto Emma's knees to balance herself.

"Where's Sully?" Emma questioned.

"They arrested him too."

At that moment, Chief Simmons walked out into the lobby. "Miss MacLean?"

"Yes." Emma turned her gaze to the Chief.

"I have some questions for you. Would you mind following me to my office?"

"Um, sure." Emma stood and separated herself from Rob, Annie, and Harry.

"Follow me and hopefully your father will be ready to be released by the time we're done."

Emma followed Chief Simmons down the hallway.

"Emma!" Rob called.

Emma turned back to find his concerned face.

"I love you," he said and smiled like saying the words to her was the most natural thing in the world.

The moment was monumental in more ways than one. She had to give him the appropriate response but make it memorable.

"I know," she simply stated and turned to walk down the hall.

"Did she quote *Empire Strikes Back*?" she heard Harry ask Rob.

"She sure did," Rob responded.

Emma was sure her words put a smile on his face. After she got through the day, she planned on showing him how much she knew and how much she felt in return.

"We've had a break in your case," Chief Simmons said and gathered a few papers on his desk.

Emma sat stunned. Her case was not even remotely close to the forefront of her mind.

"This is one of the letters your attacker sent to you?" The Chief slid a sheet of paper encased in a plastic sleeve toward her.

She scanned the letter and remembered it clearly. It was sent two days after her breakup with Patrick. Several harsh words were written and accusations were made. She remembered running straight to the bathroom to vomit after reading it.

"Yes, it is."

"I'd like you to look at this handwriting sample and tell me what you see."

The Chief slid another plastic sleeve toward her with random words written on it. She moved her gaze back and forth between the two sheets. Every single random word was a word in her letter. Each word appeared similar if not exactly like their pair in her letter.

"They are very similar." Emma's throat tightened. "Who wrote these words?" Her voice squeaked and shook. Could it be possible her tormentor had finally been found?

"We made other arrests besides your father recently. A gentleman was asked to write out his statement. When my detective passed it on to me, I noted the similarities to the writing in your letters. I pulled in all the favors I could with Judge Kessler and got a warrant for this man's dental records."

Emma's stomach clenched and she wrapped her arms around her abdomen.

"They are a match, Emma. The district attorney is ready to press charges."

Emma closed her eyes and let out a sob of relief. "Who?" she whispered.

Chief Simmons cleared his throat and retrieved both plastic sleeves before he spoke. "Sully McInerney."

"Sully?" Emma's eyes opened wide. Shock shook her body to the core.

Sully. He'd been Derek's best friend as well as his cousin. Sully. The guy who was known as Big Teddy Bear. Sully. He was everybody's friend. Sully. The man who brought her flowers after the attack.

"He visited me in the hospital. That fucking bastard sat and played cards with me while I sat in pain from his beating!" Emma stood up and shoved her chair back in the process.

"I know just what will make you feel better." The Chief stood with a smile.

"What?" Emma looked at him like he just told her aliens existed and his wife would be giving birth to one any day now.

"How would you like to be behind the glass when we question him and make the arrest?"

She returned his smile. Her day just got a hell of a lot better.

Emma stood behind a two-way mirror with Chief Simmons. Sully sat handcuffed to a table on the other side, a visible fat lip and bruising around his puffy right eye. She smiled at the fact that her father dealt the blows to his lying mouth.

Detective Chris Durst walked into the interrogation room with a stack of folders in his hand.

"How much longer until my lawyer gets here, Durst?" Sully asked and licked his swollen lip.

"A few more questions." Durst sat across from Sully and pulled a plastic sleeve from a folder. He set the folders down and placed the plastic sleeve in front of Sully. "Is this the statement you wrote out about the incident at O'Rourke's?"

Sully nodded. "Yes. Look, I told the other detective everything. The old man came at me."

"After you insulted his son and daughter."

Sully shook his head.

"Would you look at this?" Durst passed over the plastic sleeve with the page of random words Chief Simmons showed Emma.

Sully scanned it. "Yeah. What of it?"

"This is your handwriting as well?"

"Yeah. I don't see the point of all this. My lawyer was supposed to be here over an hour ago. I'm sure my wife is worried about me."

Emma snorted. *Let the bitch worry.*

"This is about to get interesting." Chief Simmons grinned while the two watched a familiar form enter the interrogation room.

"Mr. Winterbourne." Durst greeted the man with a handshake and motioned to the chair at the head of the table. "Sully, you remember Silas Winterbourne?"

"Sure." Sully eyed Winterbourne with suspicion, which made Emma's smile even wider.

"The District Attorney is here to outline the charges we will be filing." Durst tried his best to hold back a smirk, but Emma could see the corners of his mouth verging upward.

"This was all a big misunderstanding. I'd had a lot to drink. I won't press any charges and Mick doesn't need to press any charges. I'll pay for any damages to O'Rourke's, so we can just forget the whole thing." Sully waited for a response, but both of the other men just stared at him for a moment.

Winterbourne broke the stare and placed a sheet of paper in front of Sully. "Your bail hearing is set for this afternoon after you meet with your attorney. I will let you know the state will be asking for you to be held without bail."

"What? This is all being blown way out of proportion." Sully seemed pissed if the color of his face and throbbing vein in his neck was anything to go by.

"Just read the charges." Winterbourne pointed to the sheet in front of Sully.

Sully scanned the sheet and his eyes seemed to bulge just a tiny bit more at the end of each line.

Sully pushed the paper across the table. "This is fucking bullshit! Attempted murder? Stalking? Please. I bet that old man is tougher than he looks. He got more hits on me than I did on him. What is he being charged with?"

"Oh, Mr. MacLean's charges were dropped. He's being processed out right now," Winterbourne stated with an air of authority.

"Then what is all this shit?" Sully lifted his hands as high as the cuffs would let him and pointed to the paper.

"Maybe I need to read this along with you."

Winterbourne stood and placed the paper in front of Sully again. He pointed his index finger on a line of the page. "Charges are being brought forth by the Commonwealth on behalf of Emma Jean MacLean."

Sully's face went from beet red to pale pink in a matter of seconds.

"I can't believe how good this feels!" Emma whispered and Chief Simmons put his arm around her shoulders.

"We have evidence linking you to the attempted murder of Miss MacLean twelve years ago and of stalking. I'm sure your lawyer will explain this all to you when he gets here." Winterbourne pushed the paper away with his finger and moved to stand behind his chair.

"Fucking cunt!" Sully roared and stood, pulling at his cuffs and flipping the table on its side in the process.

Sully continued to scream obscenities and slam the table against the floor. Several officers entered the room and demanded he calm down. As the rage continued and warnings were ignored, officers were forced to taser Sully into submission.

Sully lay on the floor, twitching from time to time, while Emma wept tears of relief in Chief Simmons' arms.

The Chief walked Emma out to the lobby where Rob, Harry, and Annie still waited. She didn't know whom she wanted to walk to first. The fates made the decision for her when her father entered the lobby accompanied by an officer.

"Dad!" Emma rushed into his arms and held tight.

"Princess," Mick sobbed into her shoulder and vibrated with each breath. "I'm fine."

"I know. Thank you, so much." Emma pulled back. "You didn't know it at the time, but you beat the crap out of the guy who has tormented me for years."

"What?" Mick stepped back, still holding onto Emma's arms.

Emma turned to look at the others and scanned each of their confused faces.

"Go on. Tell them," Chief Simmons urged.

"Sully McInerney is the man who attacked me and has been sending me threats all these years." Emma smiled and sighed in relief. "They matched his dental records and are going to officially charge him by the end of the week. He's going away for a very long time."

"Oh, Emma." Annie rushed into Emma's arms and held on tight.

"It's finally over." Emma gazed beyond Annie's shoulder and saw Harry and Rob with unshed tears in their eyes. "I finally won."

The five of them moved to the door and walked out to the steps of the Marblehead Police Department.

"Wait." Emma held Rob back.

He stood a step below her.

"I'm sorry about Atlanta."

Rob shook his head and laughed. "We can go down there anytime we want. This is where we need to be."

Emma gazed into his eyes and saw nothing but love and sincerity there. Everything she always wanted but never thought she could have stood before her. She wouldn't let him go. Not again.

"I love you," she whispered when she went in for a kiss. His brilliant smile kissed hers and a jolt hit her right in the chest.

Emma felt the steps beneath her feet fall away when Rob picked her up and twirled her around. He walked down the steps with her caged around him, arms and legs wrapped around him in a vice lock.

"She loves me!" Rob yelled at the top of his lungs and spun her around again.

"Yes, I do." She kissed him again while her family laughed and clapped beside them. "Let's go eat some breakfast, then I can show you how much."

Rob was the one to dive in for a back-bending kiss after he set her down on her own two feet.

Once he brought her upright, he smiled and let out another laugh. "You're the boss." He winked and turned her around to head toward Harry's car.

She would never get enough of this man. Playful, sexy, loving Rob Breyer was all hers.

40

A late July morning brought a new experience for Emma, her first family gathering at her new home.

Emma and Nell were all moved in and almost completely unpacked. The first Saturday in their new house was also the day they would host their first party. Emma, Nell, Annie, and Charlotte spent the better part of the morning making enough food to feed a small country

One thing that stood out to Emma was the fact her father and Rob were absent the entire morning. They were in the house somewhere, but she had not heard a peep from either of them in hours.

"Now we need to find a guy for Aunt Nell," Charlotte quipped while she frosted the last cupcake.

"What?" Emma asked. "Now you're a love guru *and* a pastry chef?"

"I'm an ambitious eleven-year-old. Runs in the family."

The little brat was right. But Emma wondered about Nell.

"What do you say, Nell? Any red-hot lovers on the horizon?" Emma threw her arm around her friend's shoulders and pulled her close.

"There's a guy I met at the library. We've been to lunch a few times, but I don't know if anything will come of it." Nell's cheeks were almost as red as her hair with embarrassment. She was almost as tight-lipped about her love life as Emma was.

"He's gotta be better than Stan." Annie nodded in agreement about Nell's ex-boyfriend. "Charlotte, you scope him out for us next time you're at the library." Emma snapped at her niece.

"This is going to be so fun."

"Oh, no," Nell spoke up. "You're not getting into my love life. I'm perfectly happy living vicariously through you. The walls aren't as thick as you think."

Emma was the one who turned red at Nell's comment. Nell evidently got a good earful the first night Rob stayed over.

"Let's not talk about this in front of Charlotte." Her niece had a huge crush on Rob but had pulled Emma aside and told her she approved of their relationship.

"What shouldn't we talk about?" Rob asked as he entered the kitchen with Mick.

"Nothing." Emma wrapped her arms around Rob's neck. "Where were you two hiding all morning?"

Rob grinned at Mick. "Excuse us for a while." Rob took Emma's hand and pulled her behind him.

"What's going on?" She asked and followed him upstairs.

"It's a surprise." Rob urged her down the hall and stopped in front of the door of her would-be home office.

"People are going to be here soon. I don't have time to start unpacking." Emma was upset she hadn't had the time to set up the room the way she wanted. She needed hours if not days to arrange everything the right way.

"Since your dad helped you pack up, he asked me to help him unpack for you." Rob opened the door and she took a cautious step over the threshold.

"Oh." Emma's chin dropped in awe at the perfection of her new nerd cave. Mick had paid attention and placed all her figures in the correct order on her shelves. Her comics were arranged on her old bookcase by series and date, just like they had been in LA. The framed prints were perfectly placed against the newly painted red walls. One thing throwing off the balance was the big lump of something covered by a sheet up against the wall.

"What's this?"

Rob wrapped his arms around her waist from behind and laid his chin on her shoulder. "I had to get you a housewarming present. Now, topping the Lego alarm clock was going to be hard, so I had to think this one out. It took us a while to get this together, an original piece your father and I made especially for this room."

"You did?"

"You wanna see?"

Emma nodded. Excitement rushed through her veins at the thought of Rob and her father spending time together to make something for her.

Rob pulled the sheet off with a flourish. "Tada!"

"Oh. My. God," she laughed. "It's perfect."

The couch was unlike anything she'd ever seen.

"We had a hard time finding the right color, so we ended up starting from scratch."

The overstuffed couch was a replica of the Tardis police box from *Doctor Who*. The L-shaped couch sat like the Tardis was on its side. It was even the right shade of blue.

"You two made this?"

"Yep. In Moira's garage." He kissed down her neck and across her shoulder.

Emma turned to face him and met his lips with delectable fury. "This is amazing." She continued her hurried kisses and fought his tongue for dominance.

Rob's hands found her round backside and pulled her hard against him, his erection at full attention.

Emma pulled back for a breath. "I've never had sex in the nerd cave before."

"Is that fact about to change?"

She didn't care if her entire family was in the house and many of their friends would be there in a matter of minutes. She wanted to make love to her hot as hell boyfriend on her new couch.

Emma pulled at the button on Rob's jeans. "Let's see how much bigger you are once you're inside."

Chance Robicheaux didn't have an opportunity to visit Emma's new house until the day of the housewarming party. He'd stayed over an extra week in Atlanta when his mama broke her ankle and had surgery to repair it. Emma and her roommate had moved that week and he missed the whole thing.

Chance parked his car in front of Emma's new digs and walked around the house to the back yard.

"Chance!"

He turned and saw Emma's brother, Harry, wave him over. "Hey, man." Chance shook Harry's hand.

"Emma and Rob disappeared, so let me show you around and introduce you to the brood."

Chance fell into the family atmosphere of the MacLean/De Lacy household with ease. He laughed with Harry, Mick, and Seamus over a recent Red Socks game, even though he was a die-hard Braves fan. Grandma Moira gave him her stamp of approval and a pinch on the tush. Even sweet baby Sam drooling all over him didn't change his feelings for the new clan.

After a half an hour, Emma and Rob were still nowhere to be seen. Chance opened the sliding glass door to enter the kitchen and was met with a bowl full of potato salad to the crotch.

"Oh, fuck. I'm so sorry." The bowl was deposited on the floor. In the next second, there was a woman wiping the salad residue from the front of his cargo shorts.

Chance didn't know whether to thank her for giving his cock a much-needed rubdown or back away in embarrassment. He didn't get the occasion to make a decision; the redhead's hand froze when he swelled and moved.

"I. Am. So. Sorry." She backed up with her hands in the air, her cheeks bright pink with mortification.

"I'm fine," he replied. *Hard as a rock, but mighty fine.*

She peeked up at him and every thought left his head. The brilliant green eyes, pink heart-shaped lips, and perfect curves were enough to stop any man walking through traffic. She was gorgeous.

"I don't think that is the appropriate response to this situation," she whispered and wrung the towel in her hands.

"I'm Chance. Well, if you want to get technical it's Charles Xavier Watson Robicheaux the third, but everyone calls me Chance." He held out his shaky hand to her.

"I know who you are." She slipped her hand into his. "I'm Nell De Lacy."

"Nell," he whispered as if the sweetest honey touched his tongue when he uttered the single syllable.

Nell let go of his hand and thrust the towel at him. "Again, I'm sorry."

It was time to turn on the Southern charm Chance was so famous for. He lifted her hand up to his lips. "No trouble at all, Miss De Lacy. Feel free to put your hands on me whenever you like." He kissed the back of her hand and winked at her.

Nell shivered at the action and slowly took her hand from his. "I'll think about it," she mumbled and turned away.

Chance grinned and wondered how much Nell De Lacy would affect his future.

"This is gonna be a wild ride."

Emma MacLean: Former VP of Operations for Hunt Consolidated. Current Executive VP of Talent and Creative and General Manager of Televised Events for the International Wrestling Association. Daughter of Mick. Sister to Harry. Granddaughter of Moira. Formerly involved with Derek McInerney. Currently involved with Rob Breyer.

Rob "Bobby" Breyer: Professional Wrestler with the International Wrestling Association. Son of Robert Senior and Lisa Breyer. Currently involved with Emma MacLean.

Harry MacLean: Lawyer. Older brother of Emma. Son of Mick. Husband of Annie. Father of Charlotte and Sam. Grandson of Moira.

Mick MacLean: Owner of boat charter business. Father of Harry and Emma. Son of Moira. Grandfather of Charlotte and Sam.

Annie MacLean: Homemaker. Wife of Harry. Mother of Charlotte and Sam. Twin sister of Nell De Lacy. Older sister of Seamus De Lacy.

Nell De Lacy: Librarian. Twin sister of Annie MacLean. Older sister of Seamus.

Chance Robicheaux: Professional Wrestler with the International Wrestling Association. Best friend and tag team partner of Bobby Breyer.

Robert Breyer Senior: Former Professional Wrestler with the International Wrestling Association. Husband of Lisa. Father of Rob.

Lisa Breyer: Former Talent Manager. Wife of Robert Senior. Mother of Rob.

Moira MacLean: Mother of Mick. Grandmother of Harry and Emma. Great Grandmother of Charlotte and Sam.

Charlotte MacLean: Daughter of Harry and Annie. Niece of Emma MacLean, Nell De Lacy, and Seamus De Lacy. Granddaughter of Mick. Great Granddaughter of Moira.

Sam MacLean: Son of Harry and Annie. Nephew of Emma MacLean, Nell De Lacy, and Seamus De Lacy. Grandson of Mick. Great Grandson of Moira.

Seamus De Lacy: Partner in Stanton Designs. Younger brother of Annie and Nell. Uncle of Charlotte and Sam. Best friend of Ellie Stanton.

Terrance Hunt: President and CEO of Hunt Consolidated. Husband of Lydia. Father of Irene. Former boss of Emma MacLean.

Lydia Hunt: Wife of Terrance. Mother of Irene.

Irene Hunt: Senior VP of Hunt Consolidated. Daughter of Terrance and Lydia.

Aaron Russell: President and Principal Owner of the International Wrestling Association. Boss of Emma, Rob, Chance, Cherry, and Kieran.

Troy Banks: Executive Producer of reality television show, *Hunt for Life*.

Derek McInerney: Marblehead High School Vice-Principal. Formerly involved with Emma MacLean.

Cherry Spencer: Professional Wrestler with the International Wrestling Association.

Gwen Stanton: Photographer for the International Wrestling Association. Older sister of Ellie.

Ellie Stanton: Partner in Stanton Designs. Younger sister of Gwen. Best friend of Seamus De Lacy.

Kieran Finley: Newly acquired Professional Wrestler for the International Wrestling Association.

Acknowledgments

To T.M. Franklin for designing the cover of my dreams. You made the fun, quirky couple that Rob and Emma are come to life.

To Lissa Bryan, Lisa Bilbry, Sydney Logan, Sherri Hayes, and again, T.M. Franklin for your support as authors and friends to help me jump into the word of self-publishing with as much grace as possible. I know I stumble at times, but it is nice to know I have all of you to help me get back on my feet.

To Janine Weathers and Jess Molly Brown for working your magic on this manuscript and pointing me in the right direction to make it what it is today.

To the professional wrestlers of the world. Thank you for putting your health and well-being on the line every time you step in the ring to entertain the masses. You have inspired this fan in ways you will never know. You are heroes in my mind.

To my husband, Steve. We share so many common interests. I'm so thrilled that being a die-hard wrestling fan is one of them. Thanks for sitting by my side while I yell at the television when my favorite wrestlers lose or cry when one of them gets hurt. I love you and thanks for not laughing too hard at my antics.

About the Author

Lindsey Gray typed her first complete novel at the age of twelve and dreamed of making her writing into a career. When her eighth grade class wrote a twenty year reunion story, casting her as a mystery novelist, she wasn't sure she could make it a reality. After years of writing off and on, she decided to make a go of it. In December of 2010 she finally made her dream come true with her first published novel, *Lies Inside*. Five years and thousands of written words later, Lindsey is releasing her seventh published work, *Nerdy Girl Nation*.

When Lindsey takes a break from writing, she spends time with her husband of thirteen years and their two children, reading all kinds of romance novels, and hosting her own weekly radio show, *Gray Matters*, on TMV Cafe Internet Radio.

Also by Lindsey Gray
Lies Inside
Redemption (The Redemption Series Book 1)
Revisited (The Redemption Series Book 2)
Fireworks
Not the Same Season
Holiday Cure for the Cursed